BETWEEN EARTH AND SEA

A SELKI TALE

THE SELKI SISTERS
BOOK ONE

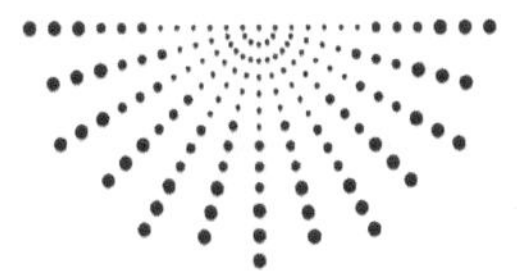

SHARON BRUBAKER

ACKNOWLEDGMENTS

Thanks abound! For Kathy MacDonald and Marcy Berbeza—you asked for it. Thank you to Meredith Boas of Grunge Muffin Designs

www.grungemuffindesigns.com

Many thanks to Alice, Barb, Bonnie, Laura, Marcia, Peggy, Sarah, Shauna, and MaryBeth, my beta readers, for their insight. Also, thanks to Alice, Barb, MaryBeth, Laura, and my family for the field trips to Brigantine. A special thanks to Heather Dale (www.heatherdale.com) for her inspirational, incredible story songs about Selkis and the goddess Sedna. Thank you to Rob for your ever-present support. You have my heart. Many thanks to Nicole Scarano for formatting.

A portion of the proceeds from this book will be donated to the Marine Mammal Stranding Center, 3625 Brigantine Blvd., Brigantine, NJ 08203

www.mmsc.org

1

IAN

Ian stumbled into the unusual, humid night air from the crowded, noisy pub. He couldn't remember ever having a November like this, where the temperatures had been holding above sixty-five degrees regularly. Was it global warming or late Indian summer? That was the leading topic of conversations that skittered around the pub that evening, some turning into mild arguments while he quaffed his beer. There was a rousing chorus of Bruce Springsteen's "Glory Days" by many of the patrons, adding to the chaotic atmosphere. After a few hearty belts of singing, Ian stumbled out the door and caught himself in the wake of the last chorus. The clatter of his steel-toed boots on the macadam of the parking lot was drowned out by the slew of inebriated patrons and loud canned music that whooshed out the door with him. He put his hands on his knees, took a deep breath, and quickly prayed he wouldn't vomit in the parking lot.

Too much beer. Too many shots. Usually, Ian didn't permit himself to drink to excess. He knew he had to get home but couldn't drive in this state. He stood up and lurched forward, looking over the parked cars for his truck. Deep breaths. There was no way he was driving the mile or so to his house. He needed to sober up. There was nothing open nearby for coffee. Brigantine was shut up tight, like the clams that washed up on the beach. The sharp razor clams and rounded little necks and mussels were picked clean by the multitudes of seabirds that haunted the shoreline daily. The houses in the neighborhood across the street were dark and silent. Their owners were evidently asleep and dreaming. He should be in bed asleep and dreaming, too. He chided himself about the late hour and the overload of alcohol in his system.

Ian and his co-workers had been celebrating the completion of a new mega-mansion on the Jersey shore. He was a carpenter who worked on new and old construction for any contract. His employment was largely thanks to wealthy people wanting gorgeous houses on the coast. With the destructive handiwork of Mother Nature, Ian seldom found himself out of work. This last mansion had been exceptionally challenging, with the owner nitpicking every detail. Whenever she stepped into the home in her seemingly painted-on skinny jeans and gaudy clanking jewelry, a shudder of dread went through the entire crew. Finally, the team had built things to her specifications, and they were all relieved the job was over. Tonight had been about rejoicing at their success by drinking. For some, a bit too much —at least for Ian. Now, he was paying for it. His head ached, and his stomach rolled. His rubbery legs didn't feel like his own.

Ian didn't want to sleep it off in his truck, but there weren't many options. A refreshing breeze came from the ocean as he stood dumbly pondering his inebriation. It pushed at his back, imploring him to turn toward the beach. He turned slowly, lifting his head as he did so, to drink in the salty air in small, deep sips. The breaths of fresh air made him feel slightly better. If he could find a quiet spot on the beach, he could sit and sober up before he attempted to drive home.

Ian negotiated the path to the beach, weaving slightly as he walked. He stumbled and fell into the soft, deep sand of the dunes behind the pub. In his addled brain, he marveled at the distinct difference between the raucous pub behind him and the peaceful beach ahead. He was surrounded by rasping green and brown beach grass that rolled and scraped in the wind. The dunes wove in and out of the edge of the broad stretch of sand that bordered the ocean in a scalloped design. The breakers rolled in with a rhythmic crash and whoosh as he walked toward the island's northern end. He kept walking. A round, full moon lit the sky, beckoning him to stroll further. A clear river of moonlight glittered with gold and silver confetti of light on the tide. It was just bright enough for him to see as his eyes adjusted to the darkness. The light of the moon winked off the empty beach house windows back beyond the dunes like soft beacon signals.

He staggered slightly as he made his way across the dunes. The combination of the alcohol sloshing in his gut and his feet sinking into the sand caused him to fall on his knees several times as he trekked along. But each time he fell, he pulled himself up and wearily walked on. He didn't know where he was going other than heading to the island's northern part. Ian squinted at the small street signs perched along the top of the beach, signaling the end of each street that headed toward the shore. He thought he saw the sign for 13th Street, but he wasn't sure. The restaurants and bars had given way to stately mansions more than a few paces back. He figured if he kept walking, his body would sweat out some of the liquor. His head was muzzy. He saw the lights of a few commercial fishing boats out on the sea through bleary eyes. He mused that he probably knew some of the ships and the captains; hell, his family were all fishermen. He was the sport that chose land over the sea. Ian was still the butt of many jokes among the men, and even some of the women, in his family for not following their traditional path of commercial fishing.

Ian was exhausted. Over the last few days, the crew had pulled long hours, and he hadn't bothered to eat much as they worked on finishing the rich bitch's house. His team always ribbed him about his penchant for perfection, but Ian treated each house he worked on as if it were his own. Now, the lack of sleep, lack of food, and drinking too much alcohol caught up with him. Weariness and sleepiness assailed him.

Still, he trudged around the curve of one dune and headed to the top of another. It was peaceful and quiet at the head of the dunes, where the sand was loose and deep. He knew it would be as soft as any bed. The main road, Ocean Avenue, seemed far away from where he was, and the shoreline homes gradually disappeared from his sight. Ian continued to climb the dunes with slow, careful steps. He fell again, but this time, he didn't feel the sand beneath him. Ian fell on something incredibly plush and soft. It was silvery in the moonlight.

When Ian touched it, memories washed over him. When he was small, he hid in his grandparent's closet to feel his great-grandmother's fur coat that dipped to the floor. His grandfather's bedroom had always been verboten. His first visit to the closet was during a hide-and-seek game with his cousins. Every closet and space beneath each bed in his grandparents' house was fair game—except for their bedroom. He had been dared to go into their room by his cousin Tommy. Tommy eventually ratted out Ian because of his excellent off-limits hiding place. His chutzpah in the choice of hiding place had earned him respect among his other cousins, but the velvety fur coat remained *his* secret. For years during his childhood, Ian would continue to go into the closet whenever he could to revisit the fur coat and snuggle into its folds. Often, he stroked the fur until he fell asleep. Later, he was pulled away from it by his parents. He sleepily protested being taken away from the fur and carried to bed.

Now, here he was, on a dark, deserted beach, and somehow, there was a soft, lovely fur coat beneath him once more. Ian didn't know how or why a fur coat came to be on the beach. He caressed it, running his fingers lightly through the pelt. It was soothing and lulled him toward sleep.

Then, somehow, through the roar of the waves and the wind's keening, Ian thought he heard something. It was just a lilt on the breeze, a whiff of a familiar tune. It sounded like the lullaby his grandmother used to sing about a seal. It had been a favorite of his when he was small. He could hear a bit of the tune on the wind again and widened his bleary eyes.

Craning his head over the edge of the dune, he thought he saw a young woman. A beautiful woman was dancing slowly in the sand below. She was singing and crooning the song from his childhood. The woman's voice was seductive as she resounded the Gaelic words.

"Hush, the waves are rolling in white with foam, white with foam. Father toils amid the din," she sang in a clear, sensuous alto.

Even more surprising than her singing was the fact that she was nude. Her long hair hung in lustrous rivulets down her back to the peaks of her ample bottom. The long curls framed her face and trailed down, caressing her firm, rounded breasts, her nipples hard in the cool ocean breeze. She looked soft. She wasn't heavy but had smooth, rounded curves of silvery, ivory flesh. He stroked the fur, nuzzling against it as he watched her. He stared in awe at the beauty of her movements. She was dancing. But it wasn't just dancing. She was undulating while she danced, mimicking the swirl of the waves and the breeze flowing past. As she continued to sing the next verse, Ian wondered how a lullaby could be so sensual. Her voice rose and fell with the accompaniment of the waves, and she weaved the song with the movements of her arms and steps.

Ian's arousal was apparent, and his jeans grew so tight that he bent over and grimaced. He moved uncomfortably, trying to ease the pressure. He desired the dancing woman on the beach, but at that point, he couldn't stand up comfortably to approach her and introduce himself. He wondered who she was and why she was dancing naked on a beach in Brigantine, New Jersey! That kind of thing didn't happen here. He wondered if she was high or inebriated like him. Perhaps she had drifted over from Atlantic City.

Ian was puzzled that she was singing in Gaelic, which sounded like an archaic form. Did he dare approach her? He wanted to approach her. He wanted to talk with her but thought she might run if she saw him rise from the dune with his obvious erection, stumbling and lurching like the Frankenstein monster in the old movies, trying to keep his balance. Ian's alcohol-addled mind drifted among the song, the fur, and the sound of the waves. The woman was very beautiful and very sexy. His tight pants were a testament to that. If he didn't approach her, he didn't know how he would ever find her again. His exhausted brain wasn't making any sense, and eventually, the alcohol and need for sleep overtook Ian, and he fell asleep on top of the soft, warm pelt.

2

KELSI

All Kelsi wanted was freedom. She swam swiftly along the bottom of the Atlantic, away from the bulls that wanted her. Kelsi wasn't ready to mate with any of them. Her sisters thought she was crazy. It was her time, after all, to mate with one or more bulls, haul out onto the beach, and become a seal mum.

But Kelsi wasn't ready. She wanted something more. She didn't know what, but something pulled her away from the group of seals. One of the bulls, Breách, was after her. She heard his cries while she swam. She shivered inside of her pelt from her whiskers to her tail. She didn't like him. His darkly speckled body was opposite her silvery gray speckles; she was light to his dark. He chased her through the water. Kelsi knew Breách wanted her by his persistence. Once the other bulls caught her scent, they would take their turn with her. There was something about this manic chase that sickened her. She didn't want the bulls. She didn't know why. Kelsi just wanted to be far, far away from them.

She turned quickly and sent her torpedo-like body coursing through the waves, away from the harem and away from the bulls. Belatedly, she hoped her sisters would understand. She hurtled through the water and headed south, skimming along the ocean's bottom, grabbing eels and small fish as she swam quickly to escape Breách. Kelsi's lithe, compact body shot quickly through the water, and she swam until she was exhausted. On her last foray to the surface to gulp some air, she saw she was close to some two-leggers from the buildings that crowded the shoreline. The air felt warmer, too warm. Her pelt felt heavy. She needed to haul out to rest, but it had to be somewhere safe.

Kelsi swam past a few entrances to small bays. She avoided their inky blackness. Some of the shorelines pricked her memory with familiarity when she came to the surface for air. Fishing boats were headed her way, and Kelsi quickly dove to the ocean bottom to flee from their rudders and prying eyes. There was a multitude of fish in their wake, and she filled her belly, snapping up fish after fish.

Kelsi tasted freedom now and somersaulted and swam upside down in delight. She swam for sheer joy because she was far away from Breách. She felt safe as she danced through the dark water. Not even a bull in sight. She was ecstatic and swam toward the surface for air and to look around, bobbing gently on gentle swells.

This beach looked quiet and safe enough. Kelsi swam to shore and slid onto the sand through the breakers. Her body was heavy and awkward on land compared to how she easily shot through the water. Using her flippers, Kelsi pulled her way along the hard, water-packed sand until she was away from the surf. After a few minutes of rest, she pulled her body tautly into a banana-shaped position and tugged herself from her skin once she caught her breath. Her pelt was cumbersome and thick. She eased the head up and off her shoulders, jerking her arms out as she did so and letting it fall to the ground. Her legs and feet were weighed down with the pelt. She took one leg out slowly and set her foot firmly on the ground while she extracted the other foot. She was free!

Kelsi stretched, standing tall with her feet planted in the sand. Oh, it felt glorious! The ocean breeze danced lightly over her skin. It felt deliciously refreshing and light, opposite to her warm, dense pelt. Kelsi paused, listening and looking around the beach, populated only by the silver beams of the full moon. The sparkle of the moonlight on the waves lent a mystical glow to the deeply dark night.

Further south, Kelsi saw distant lights, and her small, delicate ears picked up the noise of music and raucous two-leggers. Kelsi turned her head south, listening to the waves and the ocean breeze, which together made their own soothing rhythm. Her body swayed in time to the original music. She ran through the soft sand, eager to stretch and dance. She laid her pelt down in the grass of the nearby dunes and ran back to the hard-packed sand.

Her breathing was heavy. She wasn't used to having legs or to the difficulty of running in sand. Her feet sank heavily with each stride. The sand tickled between her toes. Once she had stilled, Kelsi closed her eyes and quieted her brain. She was just out of reach of the breakers and took long, deep breaths until she picked up the rhythms of the wind and the waves again. Her body began to sway, and her feet moved in time with them. She stepped over the sand in a complicated yet beautiful dance, with her arms waving gracefully in the breeze. She began to hum, and the hum turned into a song. It was an old lullaby passed through the millennia from Selki to Selki, and Kelsi liked its soft, mournful tune. She was thrilled to be free, but the realization that she was far from her family settled around her, and she felt a mixture of joy and sadness. Over and over, she sang the lullaby, letting her arms undulate and encircle herself with a hug.

Kelsi didn't see or feel the presence of the two-legger hidden by the massive dunes, but she heard something and froze momentarily in her dance. What was it? An animal? She moved even more slowly and carefully as she looked at the dunes.

Suddenly, Kelsi gasped as her nipples hardened and her back arched. She felt as though something was stroking her skin.

She stopped dancing and looked again, searching the dunes around, and it was then she saw the two-legger, and he was stroking her pelt! Each touch of his fingers sent ripples of pleasure racing through her body. What was happening? Kelsi had never felt these sensations before. She was caught between sublime pleasure and abject terror.

His touch lingered on her fur. She could see him staring at her, his gaze filled with desire. It was like, but unlike, the look Breách and some of the other bulls gave her. She could feel his desire, but his look was not about conquering. His look was one of wonder and appreciation. A slow, small smile came over her. Kelsi took up her dance in slow and graceful movements to give herself a moment to think. He did not approach her but instead seemed mesmerized by her pelt. But how was she to get her pelt back? She needed to return to seal form.

Abruptly, his stroking stopped. She could feel it. Slowly, Kelsi turned to look at the two-legger. He was on top of her pelt, and his body was still. She wondered if he was alive or dead. What was she to do?

Kelsi was horrified! She was somehow, in some way, attracted to this two-legger. Kelsi remembered what her grandmother, mother, aunt, and sister Selkis had said. They had drummed Selki lore and Selki interactions into Kelsi with many tales. Kelsi knew the old stories—the tales of men taking their pelts and enslaving them against their will. They mated with the Selkis, and the Selkis produced children for the two-legged men. Somehow, most Selkis got their pelts back and returned to the sea. At least, those were the tales that were told.

But Kelsi desired this two-legger more than any bull she had ever met. She wanted him. Kelsi wanted to mate with him. As she stared at him, her lust deepened.

And now he was asleep. She sighed in disgust and wondered what to do. She needed her pelt to return to the sea.

Kelsi crept over to him as silent as a breath upon the sand. He was truly, soundly asleep. He didn't move at her approach, not even a twitch. His breathing was slow, steady, and even. She crawled up next to him and took in his scent. She shuddered as the scent filled her with desire—an animal-like desire. She was determined to mate with this two-legger. She lusted him and knew she would not feel complete until she had been with him.

Kelsi was shocked at herself. She wondered briefly if this was how Breách felt, the overwhelming desire to mate that blotted out every other thought. As a Selki, she had been taught to be wary of men. If a man took her pelt, he could own her and have power over her. Ian did have her pelt, sort of. He was sleeping on it. She didn't feel fear of Ian. Kelsi craved Ian. It was a desire that tingled through her body. It was a blind desire that filled her mind. She moved to Ian with only one thought in her mind. She wanted him. She wanted him *now*.

Kelsi crept up and snuggled up next to Ian. She sniffed his hair and his skin. His scent drove her crazy. Lightly, she touched his sandy, red hair. It was so different from her fur. She carefully stroked his hair at the tips, marveling at its soft texture. And his cheeks! They were stubbly as if sand were glued to them. He twitched a little at the soft touch of her finger against his cheek. He murmured something in his sleep.

"Shh, muirnín," Kelsi whispered over and over to Ian. "Shh, beloved."

Kelsi began to kiss him with swift, tiny kisses. She found herself kissing and nipping at his face, neck, and down the happy trail to where his maleness swelled. Kelsi wanted to gorge herself on him. She took him in her mouth, and he groaned, finally waking up.

"Shh muirnín," she told him again.

He began to caress her, first her shoulder and then her breast. She gasped aloud in pleasure as he touched her nipples gently at first and then rubbed them lightly. They responded immediately to his lightest touch, becoming hard little pebbles on the swell of her breasts.

Without warning, he flipped her over and tugged his pants down to his ankles, revealing his two pale, freckled legs and an erect penis. He thrust into her like a bull seal. She gasped loudly, first in surprise and then in pleasure. She had no idea that these sensations existed. Kelsi reveled in how her body responded to Ian. This was what she wanted. Kelsi wanted him to fill her, and he did. She bucked with desire at his thrusts, almost growling in animal-like pleasure.

Ian slowed his thrusts and began a sensual assault. Kelsi mewed in pleasure as he began soft kisses and licks, tasting her body. She arched her back and stretched her toes before wrapping her legs around him. She wanted him to continue, and she writhed beneath him.

Their dance of passion was of rolling seas that climaxed into waves crashing on the shoreline. They cried out together in desire, passion, and joy as they climaxed.

Spent with their passion, Kelsi lay with Ian, curled up against him. Ian fell asleep again almost immediately. Kelsi found herself sleepily drowsing against him in absolute peace.

A few hours later, Kelsi awoke from her doze, surprised to find herself tight against Ian and his arm clasped protectively around her. The brilliant, full moon had traveled across the sky and was on its way to moonset. Ian had rolled almost completely off her pelt. Gently, she extricated herself from his arm. Quietly and carefully, Kelsi tugged the pelt from beneath Ian. He groaned, almost waking.

"Shh, muirnín," she told him again. "It's only Kelsi," she said in a whisper.

Blearily, in a sleepy whisper, Ian replied, "I am Ian."

"Ian," Kelsi whispered, "Muirnín, my beloved."

He quieted. His breathing turned soft and steady again. Ian had a small, satisfied smile on his face. Very gently, Kelsi touched his hair with a kiss transferred from her lips to her fingers to his hair.

Kelsi tiptoed away from the dune, carrying her pelt. When she reached the hard-packed sand and the water's edge, she stepped into her sealskin again. For the first time in her life, it surprised and distressed her. She wasn't sure she wanted to return to the seal realm. However, the sea and the animal life called Kelsi. She slid her feet slowly into the pelt and pulled it up and over her like a thick, tight body suit. Waddling clumsily over the sand, Kelsi clamored through the breakers until she could dive gracefully into the deeper water.

Several yards from shore, Kelsi bobbed in the water to watch Ian, still sleeping soundly on the dune.

3

IAN

A glimmer of sunlight teased Ian's closed eyelids. A chilly wind ruffled the dune grasses and tugged at his clothes. Something of a dream of a beautiful young woman in his arms, a beautifully sexy dream, teased his memory and blocked a smidgen of pain from his hangover. He opened his eyes and closed them quickly against the sunlight piercing his aching head. Slowly, slowly, slowly, he squinted his eyes open.

He was alone. He was on a dune. The morning sun crept over the line between sea and sky, sending piercing rays to his eyes and into his head. The wind that ruffled the dune grasses chilled him. Ian looked around again. No one was on the beach save for gulls picking at clams and small crabs.

Had it been a dream? He sat up, holding his head in his hands, pressing on his temples. His head ached incredibly. His mouth felt like it was filled with the sand surrounding him. He needed water. He needed coffee. He needed both badly.

As he sat, waking up slowly, he wondered if the woman last night was only a dream. Perhaps it had been the drinks and had someone slipped him a Mickey? Ian stared at the ocean. The Atlantic was a silent mass of rippling gray. He wasn't sure if he saw a bobbing head of a seal or perhaps a dolphin.

Seal. Ian sat up straighter, suddenly more awake. He vaguely remembered the lovely, soft, silvery, mottled fur beneath him. Now it was gone! Ian thought he remembered the fur being tugged from beneath him and a soothing voice reminding him that Kelsi was there. Who was Kelsi? The woman? The seal? He had drifted back into his dream and thought he saw the woman running toward the sea. She donned the seal pelt like a body suit and entered the water.

Ian rubbed his eyes. He had to be dreaming. The woman he had made love to was a seal? Ian couldn't get that concept wrapped around his brain. He shook his head, wondering about his sanity, and vowed never to drink to excess like he had the previous night. But it must have been real as his pants were down around his ankles. Goosebumps were popping up on his legs. He slapped off the sand stuck to his body, pulled up, and fastened his jeans and belt. Stumbling across the deep sand of the dune, he made his way down to the beach to the hard-packed sand. Ian returned to the bar parking lot where his truck stood, a solitary island in a sea of macadam waiting for him.

He drove home in a daze, pulling into the narrow driveway and slowly getting out of his truck. His home had been built in 1950, a celebration of turquoise stucco, and still had a lot of vintage charm. He had picked it up, 'as is,' for a song, thanks to a couple going through a nasty divorce settlement. It overlooked the bay on the northern end of Brigantine. The story on the damaged walls and ceiling in the small, two-bedroom home indicated that the divorcing couple had thrown many objects.

Ian made coffee in his galley kitchen and sank into his couch in the paneled living room overlooking the bay. He sat, staring out the large picture window at the water. The eastern light of sunrise gave the beach grass a golden quality and deepened the blue water of the bay. After one cup, he made another, and his brain woke up. He wanted to make sense of the previous night's events but could not.

Ian's cell rang. It was his foreman, Mike. He looked at the time and let out an expletive. He was very, very late for work.

"Where are you, man?" Mike's voice rang through the speaker of Ian's cell. "Are you coming to work today?"

Ian groaned in response.

"Drink a little too much last night, bud?" Mike teased in a booming voice.

"Quiet down," Ian growled.

"Okay, okay," Mike said, "You left the bar, and I thought you got lucky."

"Hmm," Ian replied, non-committal in his response. "Give me a few minutes. I'll be there."

"See you soon," Mike said cheerfully. "Bring some donuts."

"Later," Ian said.

Ian looked at the time. He was never late to work, but today... Ian jumped in the shower and soaked his head in the scalding, needle-like drops until he felt more awake. He dressed, went to get the requested donuts, and took them to the new job site, but not before he swallowed a couple of aspirin and another cup of coffee.

The guys at the new job site clapped him on the back. They followed him like lemmings to where he placed the donuts on the tailgate of Mike's truck.

"There you are! Finally!" Mike cried as he came out of the house, grinning. "Come look at the site." Mike led him into the house.

Armed with yet another cup of coffee and a couple of donuts each, Ian and Mike entered the latest McMansion they were working on. Ian sincerely hoped the owner was easier to get along with than the previous one. Mike pointed out areas where he wanted Ian to work, but Ian couldn't focus.

"Are you with me, Ian?" Mike asked, concerned. He had noticed Ian's distractibility.

"Yeah," Ian answered. "Still recuperating, I guess."

Mike just laughed. He continued the tour of the house.

Ian worked like an automaton for the rest of the day. His heart wasn't in the project, not yet. They were still putting up the studs for the walls. He could do that in his sleep. He kept thinking of Kelsi. Who was she? What was she? He kept remembering her small, lithe, but rounded body. Ian thought of her luxurious curls. He had knotted his hands in her hair -- like welcome shackles. And the taste of her... was unforgettable.

He was relieved when it was time to go home. On his way home, a weary Ian stopped for a cheesesteak and a six-pack of beer. He wanted to drown his sorrows, but not like last night. He needed something to quell his thoughts of Kelsi and his many unanswered questions. He sat in his living room and turned on the television, bypassing the news and talking heads on political discussions. He glanced at the upcoming weather and noted a continued warm trend and no rain. That was a relief. He surfed through the channels and settled into viewing a James Bond marathon.

Sunset came early on these late autumn evenings. Ian had caught the last glimmer of the color of the setting sun. It burned color into the marsh grasses and the bay water, casting them in a fire of color. His home, on the Northern spit of Brigantine Island, overlooked the bay and toward the wildlife refuge. It was a quiet and peaceful place. As the movie ended, Ian turned off the television and stared at the dark sky and water. He turned off the lights in the living room and sipped at another beer that was quickly becoming lukewarm. The luminescent glow from Atlantic City and his surrounding neighborhood was a small, warm light at the edge of the southern horizon. Ian watched, his eyes adjusting to the dark, seeing one or two stars wink brightly in the night sky. There had been a full moon overhead last night, but it was too early for the moon's rays to grace the bay that he looked upon tonight. The water was black and silent, rippling gently like smooth black onyx.

Ian thought again of the events of the previous night. There was no way he could explain the experience last night with Kelsi. Too much alcohol was the only reasonable explanation. Had it been a fantasy? Had it been real? Whatever it was, Ian wanted to find Kelsi again, but he didn't know how.

He slipped into the oblivion of memory, remembering her beautiful, petite body and the curvy smoothness of her skin. Last night, the light of the full moon made her skin look silvery in the moonlight. He remembered her firm, round breasts, and luscious mouth. Her skin was silky, and she had some unusual birthmarks, brownish patches that he had enjoyed kissing and licking. He couldn't get enough of the taste of her skin. It was incredibly salty but delicious. It was salty like brine but sweet, too. He still thought he could taste the sharp saltiness of her skin with a tang of underlying sweetness. That thought filled him with desire again.

But now, Ian had no way to find Kelsi. Since his breakup with Jessica, he had not been with a woman for a few months. Jessica was a high-maintenance woman he had met at one of the casinos in Atlantic City. After trying to keep up with her demands of what she considered a good lifestyle and going through his bank account, she moved on to bigger and better prospects. She had sneered at his profession as a carpenter and his family's longstanding career as commercial fishermen. Jessica was a gold digger looking for a wealthy businessman who wanted a trophy wife. Ultimately, he'd wished her good luck and riddance, ignoring her sarcastic comebacks. But Jessica had ruined his taste for women for a while. He had abstained even from flirting and any thought of hooking up with someone—until he met Kelsi last night.

Ian remembered how he felt when he'd laid eyes on Kelsi. Even with his alcohol-addled memory, Ian was awestruck at her grace and beauty. It was Kelsi who had come over and seduced him after he had passed out on top of her mottled coat of soft, silvery fur in the dune. Thinking and puzzling about the coat, he wondered what had happened. Was his dream and memory correct in thinking Kelsi had taken the coat and entered the Atlantic Ocean? Had her seduction been a part of a fantasy scenario before suicide? In his heart, he didn't think so.

Nevertheless, Ian turned the television back on to the local late-night news. There was no mention of finding a body washed up on the shore. Ian sighed with relief. The whole encounter was just so odd.

He cleaned his dinner debris and headed to bed. Tomorrow was another day. Maybe it would make more sense after a full night's sleep.

4

KELSI

"What have I done? What have I done?" Kelsi had shouted over and over inside her head. Her seal voice came out in short, frustrated barks. But no one was listening to her as she bobbed in the Atlantic.

After her encounter with Ian, Kelsi had bobbed offshore in the soft swells, still watching him sleep peacefully. Her heart wrenched in the memories of the night before.

She *knew* she was a Selki. It was in her blood and her bones. But Kelsi had *never* known the passion of a two-legger. Her feelings of passion and desire for Ian filled her. She was in awe. In the few hours they had been together, she felt more herself with Ian than with *anyone* she had encountered in her life. It was almost embarrassing how much she craved the man.

Kelsi remembered stories from Gran and Mum, warning her of two-legged men. They would steal your pelt and hide it, Mum and Gran had intoned, and then you'd be their slave. It was a curse of the Selkis. They told her stories of two-legged men wanting you to keep their house, raise their bairns, and find the fishermen fish in the sea. In the stories, the Selki was miserably unhappy. The stories kept Kelsi and her sisters wary of two-leggers. Kelsi had not approached a two-legger in her human form—until last night. It was always on a deserted beach when Kelsi and her sisters had hauled out to shed their pelts and dance in the moonlight.

Kelsi wondered about Ian. She wondered if he were one of the two leggers who would steal and hide her pelt. But Kelsi didn't think being at Ian's beck and call would be bad. Feelings for him stirred in her loins. She knew she would be blushing if she were in her human form. He made her feel so alive. Every nerve ending sang with pleasure when he touched her. How could this be a bad thing? She craved him the way she wanted certain fish in the sea.

She recalled how long she had watched him—until he had awakened near dawn. She had swum along as he walked back toward some buildings, climbed into a machine, and went down the road. Kelsi's sensitive ears had picked up on the roar of the engine. As he turned out of the parking lot and went north on the road, Kelsi swam north, craning her head to see if she could follow Ian and his machine. He turned off from the road, and she lost him. Disheartened, she dove deep and swam along the bottom.

Driven by an unknown force, Kelsi continued swimming north along the Atlantic's bottom. Ahead was the entrance to a bay that was to the west. Kelsi floated to the surface and looked around before swimming into the bay area. She had to swim through a long channel. Coming to the surface, she looked around again. The area to the west seemed uninhabited and safe enough to haul out. Kelsi realized how utterly exhausted she was. She swam slowly, keeping her head above the water and looking around. No buildings, no machines, no two-leggers. It looked safe enough. Kelsi hauled out onto the beach above the breakers and fell into an exhausted sleep that led to her dreaming of Ian. Her dreams were filled with memories and fantasies she longed for.

Something pulled Kelsi from her dreams. It was a nagging sound that echoed in her subconsciousness. Kelsi opened her eyes slowly. Further down the beach was a two-legger. It wasn't Ian. The two-legger had a barking animal on four legs—a dog. The two-legger was holding the dog taut on a leash several yards away. Kelsi's heart sank. She needed to get away from the dog. She craned her head toward the dog and then looked at the bay water, her fear palpable.

Further up the beach, to the North, were fishermen with their lines in the water. The dog was to the south. The water was her safety zone. Kelsi waddled back to the bay and dove into the water. She swam several feet before emerging. The dog and its owner were still on the beach. The dog was still barking at her. She hoped it wouldn't break free and come into the water after her. Kelsi knew she could outswim the dog instantly but didn't like the thought of being chased.

Kelsi dove down again and swam south along the waterway's thoroughfare. She was hungry and snatched at what she could eat along the bottom.

As she swam south, Kelsi noticed houses appearing east when she bobbed up to the surface. There was an open space to the west on her right. Kelsi scanned the shoreline: seagulls and a few other water birds. She didn't like eating birds, but she was starving.

Kelsi stealthily swam to the shore and grabbed the duck from behind. She tore into it and swallowed it despite the feathers. She was feeling desperate but was happy to have something in her belly.

She swam on, musing about Ian. She wondered where he lived. She knew two leggers lived in houses. Could he be close by? How would she know? How could she find him?

Kelsi thought of their night together. She still craved the man. She imagined feeling him inside of her again, with his lips traveling all over her body. She swam through the water slowly and sinuously, thinking about Ian. The water felt sensual, and she reveledin it, gliding over her body.

Oh, how she wanted Ian! How could she find him among all the other two eggers? She hauled out onto a muddy beach in a nest of marsh grasses to think and rest.

5

IAN

Ian's erotic dreams of Kelsi made sleeping rough. He awoke once to find himself wrapped and tangled in his sheets. After a particularly erotic dream, Kelsi came to him and offered herself to him, and he woke covered in his own mess.

"Oh, Christ!" Ian let out the expletive as he wiped his hands and body on dry portions of the sheets. He got up, stripped the bed, and put the soiled sheets in the washing machine before making a cup of coffee.

He sat with his steaming cup and stared out at the dark. The moon was setting over the marsh across the Thorofare. Birds and animals, not people, populated this beach. The simple, stark beauty appealed to Ian. The bay and marsh that had been on fire the previous evening at sunset were now mysterious with the setting moon. Silvery light played on the water, and the just-waning moon hung heavily in the sky. A stray cloud scudded along, temporarily muting the moonlight.

Ian shook his head at himself. He hadn't had a wet dream since his teens. What was this woman doing to him? She was definitely gone from his life. Why did these thoughts still persist?

Ian dressed and jumped into his truck. There was only one way to find closure in this situation. On his way, he picked up a large coffee at the convenience store.

The young man behind the counter was appropriately bleary-eyed from working through the night.

"You're up early, man," the cashier commented to Ian when he brought his breakfast sandwich and coffee to the counter to pay. "Early start today?" he asked him.

Ian nodded before answering, "Something like that," and returning to his truck.

Ian drove to the nightclub he had been to just two nights ago. The building was dark and silent in this early morning hour. The parking lot was deserted save for one car. Someone else must have taken a bender and not driven home the previous night. Ian parked his truck by the path to the beach.

He finished the sandwich and tossed the crumpled wrapper onto the passenger side floor. Ian took his coffee, stepped out of the truck, and headed down the beach to where he had fallen asleep a couple of nights ago. He wasn't sure what he would find, perhaps a trace from the evening with Kelsi.

The dunes held no answers. The wind had swept away any traces of where their bodies had lain. Ian sat in the spot where he had fallen asleep two nights ago. He stared at the ocean and sipped his coffee, pondering why he ventured to the beach. Kelsi wasn't here. The trip did not bring him peace but only brought more questions.

Ian sat until he was chilled and then walked toward the ocean, following the path he barely remembered that Kelsi had taken. He remembered how he desired her at first sight. When her mouth was on him, nipping and licking, it was as if it was a dream. Making love to a naked woman that came out of the sea didn't happen in real life. He had gazed into her eyes, and it was wondrous. Afterward, she left him, walking toward the waves with the pelt-like coat draped over her. He must have fallen back asleep, Ian reasoned. Kelsi probably rinsed off in the surf, donned her coat, and returned to the club's parking lot to get into her car while Ian passed out.

That had to be it. It now made sense in Ian's head. He drained his coffee and headed to work.

The day started well. As his mood lightened, Ian began putting framing together for the rooms in the house. He and his co-worker, Joe, stapled two-by-fours, framing the bedrooms on the second floor. They worked seamlessly, creating a loud, synchronous beat with their pneumatic hammering.

Joe was called away mid-morning to pick up his sick kid at school. Ian continued to work, but without Joe's constant banter, his mind again drifted to Kelsi when he walked down the hallway. There was a generator at the end of the hall, humming away, for the workers to use with their power tools. Its buzz reminded him of a hive of bees but with a deeper, more resonating tone. It was white noise to his daydream.

A dreamy smile played on his lips as he remembered Kelsi waking him with her gentle assault with her mouth and kisses. Her mouth and kisses left his body and senses, screaming in passion. He could almost feel her butterfly kisses on his face and neck as she trailed them down and down and...

Ian stepped on a traditional hammer someone had left on the floor. His foot slipped on the smooth, varnished wood of the handle. He skidded a few inches before sliding uncontrollably and becoming airborne. Ian put out his hand to stop his fall, and his forearm hit the generator's exhaust pipe, connecting his skin to the hot metal with a loud sizzle.

"Shit! Ow! Ow! Aargh! Damn it!" Ian screamed as he smelled the horrible scent of burning skin.

How stupid he was! He hadn't been looking where he was going. His co-workers had heard him scream. They came running at his first expletive. The men did not like the sight of the raw burn, and most of them backed off. Someone had called Mike out of the foreman's office, and he came running with a first aid kit. He stopped abruptly when he saw Ian's forearm's red, burned flesh, which was also beginning to bruise from the impact on the generator.

"Oh, Christ!" he said, shaking his head at Ian. "I guess we're off to the Emergency Room."

Ian was beginning to feel a little woozy from the shock and pain of his burned arm. Another co-worker, José, held him up by his elbow and led him to Mike's truck.

They had wrapped his forearm loosely with gauze from the first aid kit. The skin had bubbled up painfully and was a brilliant red. It felt like it was on fire. Every wisp of air caused pain. Ian gritted his teeth

"Try to hold your hand above your head. Take some deep breaths. Don't bump your hand on the door frame of Mike's truck," José advised.

He helped Ian climb into the cab. Mike was a little pale as he shoved the keys into the ignition.

"My truck," Ian said faintly.

"Don't worry, bro," José told him, patting him on the back. "We'll get it to your house. Give me your keys."

Awkwardly, Ian fished the keys out of his pocket, wincing at any movement of his left hand. He gritted his teeth and gave the keys to José. José helped him put on the seat belt, then shut the door to Mike's truck. Mike gunned the motor and peeled away from the building site.

Mike was quiet for a few minutes. They ran into school buses, depositing the students at home. They were held up, block after block. Mike swore softly under his breath.

"Come on! Come on!" he shouted at the school bus and its occupants. "I need to get off this island!"

Ian laid his head back on the headrest and closed his eyes. His arm was throbbing, and he felt he could feel each revolution of the wheels singing with pain through his arm.

Finally, Mike asked Ian, "So, what happened, Ian? You aren't usually accident-prone."

Ian opened his eyes. "Not sure," he answered Mike abashed. "I was distracted, I guess. I slipped on something. I think it was a hammer," he answered him

"What?" Mike asked. "That's not cool. No one should be leaving their tools lying around."

Ian told him. "It wasn't anyone's fault but my own. I must have been daydreaming."

"You?" Mike scoffed. "That's really unlike you, but you seemed off your game yesterday, too."

"Yeah," Ian answered, not elaborating.

"This isn't about some woman, is it? You're not back with that, Jessica, are you? That bitch took you for a ride and then some, didn't she?" Mike asked with concern in his voice.

Ian looked down and answered a little sheepishly, "No, not Jessica. Yes, a woman. But the whole thing is a bit weird."

"Okay, okay," Mike answered, "but with women, things can *always* be a little strange. So what?" he hesitated and then asked, concerned, "How weird?"

Ian was quiet for a few minutes, and Mike looked at him a couple of times. Ian was trying to form an explanation when Mike slammed on the brakes.

"Yow! Aargh!" Ian cried out in pain. He gritted his teeth and closed his eyes.

"Sorry," Mike said quickly, but he didn't take his eyes off the pedestrians.

They were heading to the emergency room in Atlantic City. It was near the casinos, which, even in hard times, had people milling around the streets. No one seemed to care that cars were trying to maneuver through the streets to get somewhere. People just stepped off the curb and walked in front of Mike's slow-moving truck. Mike swore regularly until they turned into the parking lot at the hospital.

"Okay," Mike said, "tell me later, but tell me! I'm sure we'll have some waiting time in the ER."

They walked into the ER and registered. They waited for the triage nurse to check him out. The nurse that took his vitals seemed calm as if she had always seen a severe burn on someone's forearm. They also wanted an X-ray to make sure his forearm wasn't broken. Mike and Ian returned to the waiting room and waited to be called back.

"All right," Mike said, "we have a couple of minutes. Spill."

So, Ian told Mike how he drank excessively and didn't want to drive home. Instead, he walked down the beach to sober up but fell asleep on a fur coat. He told him how he woke up to Kelsi seducing him and then leaving toward morning.

Mike's eyes bugged when Ian described Kelsi, how she walked away in the fur coat, and that he didn't remember anything after that.

"I can't explain it," Ian told Mike with frustration. "I don't know who she is, where to find her, nada, nada, nada," he said.

"That's tough," Mike said.

"And I can't stop thinking about her!" Ian told Mike. "No one has ever affected me like this!"

"Dude," Mike advised, "man, you know how to pick them! Think about it. She may have a screw loose. Remember your experience with Jessica? You've gotta be careful, man! There aren't too many women who run around naked in fur coats and go around seducing men. Hot, but weird! Let it go!"

Ian hung his head sheepishly. He felt like a fool. But did he?

The nurse called him back to a room in the Emergency Room. The rest of the afternoon, Ian wanted to forget. They gave him some shots for pain, nausea and antibiotics. It had seemed a lifetime before they came to take him to X-ray. The X-ray procedure with the technician gingerly moving his arm had Ian gritting his teeth. The pain meds were only partially working. Back in the ER cubicle, they waited for the results and to see the doctor again. Fortunately, Ian's arm wasn't broken. Ian and Mike could hear the codes and conversations of people in cubicles nearby: heart attack, overdose, car accident, and more. The nurse came to check on him and double and triple-checked the last date of his last tetanus shot. Mike kept impeccable records of his employees and made a phone call to find out the information, which he relayed to the ER staff. Another nurse came in with a tray of bandages. Ian almost passed out from the pain as they manipulated his arm. Mike started to sway as he watched the procedure. The doctor ordered Mike to sit down. Immediately. Mike sat on the floor. Heavily. They wrapped up Ian's arm. The procedure was over.

When they were finally released, Ian was exhausted. Mike stopped at the pharmacy for pain medications and an antibiotic. Ian dozed while Mike was in the store, barely remembering the remainder of the ride home.

When they pulled into Ian's driveway, Ian was relieved to see his truck there. Mike located Ian's keys after a text and a somewhat frantic phone call. Mike helped him inside and sat him on the couch.

"Dinner?" Mike asked wearily.

Despite Ian's wobbly state from the hospital medications, Mike's care was unwavering. He sighed as he rummaged through the cupboards and refrigerator, making a disgusted sound. Eventually, he called his wife and a local take-out place for delivery. He patiently waited for the food to arrive and for Ian to take a few mouthfuls, even though Ian couldn't eat much. Mike wrapped up the leftover food and ordered Ian to rest for a couple of days and to sleep. When he offered to assist Ian to bed, Ian declined, but Mike's concern was palpable.

"I'm all right," Ian reassured Mike. "Or, I will be. Thanks, man. Thanks for everything. I really appreciate it." His words carried a weight of gratitude that Mike could feel.

"No problem," Mike said. He laid a gentle hand on Ian's shoulder. "Take care of yourself."

As Ian nodded in response, Mike left to return home. Ian lay on his couch, his arm beginning to throb. He got up, retrieved his pain pills, and settled back on the couch, ready for a deep, pain-free sleep. Mike's parting words echoed in his mind, a comforting reminder of the care he had received.

6

KELSI

Kelsi dozed off and on, waking to look at where she was. This was a quiet and peaceful place. Beach and rustling marsh grasses surrounded her. There were many birds, but none near her. She sighed in relief as she stretched her head and rear flippers up into a banana shape. She held the position, enjoying the time in the sunshine. Her stomach growled again. She would need to find some food. She waddled to the water and dove in, skimming along the bottom, snatching small anchovies and silversides. It took a lot of those to try to fill her belly. She continued to swim and look for more fish. Kelsi spotted a couple of weakfish ahead. Kelsi put some speed on and snatched and swallowed the weakfish before heading up to the surface for more air.

Emerging from the water, Kelsi gazed at the houses along the shore. Many had piers extending into the water, and boats and personal watercraft were moored. The sight of these structures sparked Kelsi's curiosity. She couldn't help but wonder what it would be like to be inside one of them, shut away in the box-like structure.

But what was it about these particular structures that drew Kelsi in? She felt a strong attraction to these houses, a pull that she couldn't quite explain. There was something about them that captivated her...

Kelsi sniffed the air, her heart racing with excitement. Could it be? Was that the scent of Ian? She swam closer to the homes, her anticipation growing with each stroke. At a turquoise house, visibly less opulent than the surrounding homes, the scent of Ian was stronger than anywhere else. It had a small beach and no pier or bulkhead. Kelsi bobbed off the shore with her eyes trained on the windows. Even the faintest scent of Ian sent her pulses racing, building up the suspense.

Kelsi bobbed for hours, her sleek head just above the water. She tried not to doze. When the sun was beginning to drop slowly to the west, lighting up the marshland with a golden light, Kelsi began to see movement in the nearby houses. Ian's house was still dark. The house next to Ian's had light coming from the windows. Kelsi watched the movement behind the windows. A small face was pressed tightly against the glass doors that led out onto the deck. It was a small two-legger, a child, and she had her eyes glued to Kelsi, creating a profound sense of connection.

Kelsi wasn't sure what to do. Should she leave? She glanced at Ian's house again. It was still dark. Kelsi dove down and swam toward the marshes away from the houses, across the watery Thorofare. She hauled out and kept her eyes trained on Ian's house.

As twilight fell, a light came on at Ian's. A second and a third light came on, but he didn't emerge from the door leading to the grass and the beach. Kelsi's heart fell. She put her head down on her paws dejectedly. She would continue to watch.

As the twilight turned to darkness, the lights in the houses blinked out and were swallowed up in darkness. Ian's house went dark as well. Kelsi sighed and went to sleep.

Kelsi dove into the water when the morning light lit up the eastern horizon. She fished around for breakfast before taking up a vigil, bobbing up and down in the water just off the shoreline from Ian's house. She hoped, wished, and prayed he would come to the window or out into the yard. The young girl's small face peered out of the glass doors again until Kelsi heard another, insistent two-legger pulling her away from the window. A few minutes later, Kelsi heard a rumbling from the street, and the children's voices became loud and faded into the distance. Another person peered briefly from the same glass door where the child had been. Kelsi ignored her but kept her eye on Ian's house. She would wait forever if she needed to. Kelsi knew that. She *had* to see him. So, Kelsi waited, bobbing in the watery Thorofare that was thankfully free from boats and watercraft.

7

IAN

etween the stress of the accident, the pain, and the pain medications the emergency room doctor prescribed, Ian slept like the dead. It was mid-afternoon when he finally awoke. His forearm was throbbing, the pain echoing in his arm and his head. His mouth was as dry as a desert.

Ian groaned as he rolled out of bed. He gulped water from his hands in the bathroom and went to the kitchen to fill a tall glass and drink it down. The cold water did nothing for his headache, only making it sound like a beating bass drum. He pressed his forehead against the cold metal of the refrigerator. It helped only slightly, and the cold water on his empty stomach made it ache. He knew he had to eat something and take the pain medicine to rid himself of a damn headache and the throbbing pain in his arm. Ian made a cup of coffee and checked the refrigerator. Mike ordered a pizza the night before and pulled out the box. With one good hand, he awkwardly pulled a slice from the box.

Ian hungrily chewed his breakfast of cold pizza, barely tasting the first slice. He began to savor the salty flavors of bacon, black olives, and mushrooms while munching on the second slice, washing it down with hot coffee. His hunger satiated, Ian sipped at his coffee while standing at his counter in the kitchen. He looked around the kitchen to find the medications Mike had picked up at the pharmacy.

Ian glanced at the clock. He couldn't believe it was after three in the afternoon. Ian had slept for almost a day. The afternoon sun shone brightly through the living room window, blinding Ian momentarily as he headed for the stairs to the bedroom. He cleaned himself up, wearing a clean, long-sleeved shirt and sweatpants.

Ian went outside to get the mail. He could feel the pain medications beginning to work. They made him a little dizzy. He stood at the mailbox for a minute, steadying himself. A big, yellow school bus rumbled and stopped near the house. A flaxen-haired girl bounced out.

"Hey, Ian!" Brenna, his young neighbor, said excitedly. "How are you? Why are you home so early? Have you seen them? They're back!" Brenna prattled excitedly.

In his drugged state, Ian was slow to respond as he tried to sort out all the questions in his head.

Brenna continued. She had come closer and saw the bandage on his arm, "Oh, Ian!" she cried. "What happened to you? Are you all right?"

"I'll be okay," Ian responded. It was hard not to smile at Brenna's enthusiasm. She was a very cute young lady. "I accidentally burned my arm."

"Oooh!" Brenna cried. "That's yucky. Does it hurt?"

Ian nodded. "Yup, that's why I'm home."

"Hey! Have you seen them? They're back!" Brenna asked him.

"Who?" Ian returned. "Who is back? What are you talking about?"

His brain was a little fuzzy, and he was sorry if his response was sharper than usual. He had no idea what Brenna was talking about. Brenna didn't seem to notice if he was grumpy or not.

"The seals! The seals! The seals are back in Brigantine! I saw one yesterday! It was in the water near our house!" Brenna almost shouted. "I think it was okay. It was bobbing in the water. I know they haul out on the beach this time of year, but I've never seen one in the bay here. It was *so* cool!"

Ian was processing what Brenna had said. A seal? In the bay? The door to Brenna's house opened. Donna, her mom, stood there.

"Hi, Ian," she greeted before admonishing her daughter, "Brenna! Come inside and stop bothering Ian!"

"I'm not bothering Ian," she told her mother saucily. "I was telling him about the seal!"

Donna rolled her eyes a little bit. "Okay," she acquiesced and smiled at Ian. Donna noticed the bandage on Ian's arm. "Ian, what happened?" she asked with concern.

"He burned his arm," Brenna informed her mother. "Maybe you could help him with the bandage?"

Donna was a nurse at a local podiatrist's office. She nodded in answer to her daughter.

"Of course," she said. "Ian, let me know if you need anything. Are you going to be okay?"

"Yeah," Ian responded. "I'm just a little out of it on the pain meds at the moment."

"I understand. Let us know if you need anything, all right?" Donna told him. She turned her attention back to Brenna. "Now, young lady, homework, dinner, and then off to Girl Scouts. I also want to pick up some things at the grocery store."

"Okay," Brenna responded, a little deflated, and turned to go inside. At the door, she turned to Ian and said with a brilliant smile, "Don't forget to look for the seals!"

"I won't forget," Ian said a little more soberly than he had intended.

Ian, his curiosity piqued, went inside and sat on his couch, gazing at the water. Seals in the channel? This was a mystery. He knew seals beached themselves on the Atlantic side, but the idea of them coming through the Obes Thorofare outside his back door was a new one. It was possible, he thought, as it was a safe area for animals. His house was located across from the Absecon Wildlife Refuge, famous for birders, but he had no idea about seals or other creatures that might inhabit the refuge. The Marine Mammal Stranding Center was at the other end of the island, and he knew they released animals, but would they release a seal in the Thorofare? It seemed too close to the center.

Ian looked out at the water. The sun was beginning its descent over the marshlands of the Wildlife Refuge. It bathed everything in an orange-gold light. He squinted and concentrated on the water of the Thorofare. It rippled slightly in the coming evening's breeze. The tide was coming in, and he saw the current bringing in more water. But he didn't see a bobbing seal head.

Disappointment engulfed Ian as he realized he hadn't seen what he had been hoping for. He chided himself for his unrealistic expectations.

Was he really hoping to see a seal that might transform into Kelsi? The thought was absurd, yet it lingered in his mind. Shaking his head, he turned his attention to the pile of mail on the table. It was a mix of junk mail and bills, a mundane sight that contrasted sharply with his earlier hopes. He sorted the mail into two piles, deciding to deal with the bills later when his mind was clearer. The pain medication was starting to take effect, making him feel drowsy. He leaned back on the couch and let sleep overtake him.

8

KELSI

Kelsi bobbed in the water, watching Ian's house for hours and hours. She was getting weary, chilled, and hungry. The sun had passed its midpoint in the sky and was heading west on its daily path through the heavens above. Kelsi was a little sad that she had not seen anything of Ian in her vigil. She turned away from the houses and swam north through the channel. The tide was coming in, and fish were in the tide. Kelsi grabbed and snapped at the incoming fish. After filling her belly, Kelsi returned to her watery vigil outside Ian's house. Kelsi was weary of bobbing in the Thorofare. Did she dare haul out? She decided and hauled out onto the small beach at the edge of Ian's property.

It felt good to be on land. She felt heavy out of the water, lying on this small beach. A fluttering movement caught her eye. The child she had seen yesterday was gesturing wildly and hopping up and down and up and down until a faint, stern voice made her turn away from the window. Kelsi heard a door slam and the roar of a vehicle. She turned her attention to Ian's house. It was still dark and silent. Was this man ever home, she wondered? She put her head on her flippers and kept her eyes trained on Ian's house.

As the sun began to set in the west and the marshland grasses and the water were bathed in gold, Kelsi finally saw movement behind the dark window in Ian's house. A light was turned on somewhere in the house, and its reflection was a sliver of light and shadow. Ian was moving about somewhere inside. Kelsi's heart began to beat faster. Would he come to the window? Would he come to the door? Would he come down to the beach? In her heart, she wished it so. The shadows behind the huge window became larger. Her heart beat even faster. He was standing behind the window! He was looking out at her. His shadow grew bigger in the window frame as if he were trying to see her more clearly. His shadow pulled back again. Kelsi waited. She hoped beyond hope that he would emerge from the back door. She waited.

Darkness was beginning to gather. The light by the door flicked on. The glare of the light outside and from within made the form filling the doorway a tall, dark shadow. Ian just stood there, staring down at the beach.

Kelsi stared up at Ian. It was really him! She pulled herself up on her flippers to see him better. It was then that realization struck her. Ian was seeing her in her seal form and not her human form. Kelsi began to emerge slowly, pulling back the seal head like a hood, pulling her arms and legs out of her pelt like a tight pair of furry long johns. She stood naked in the golden twilight, the sunset framing her outline.

Looking up at Ian, her desire for him grew beyond belief, but suddenly, she was shy and diverted her eyes toward the ground. When she looked up at Ian again, she couldn't see his face but could feel his wonderment and desire across the yard and down to the sand. It was a moment, and only a moment, caught between time and space before she ran up to Ian and into his arms.

It was like coming home.

"Muirnín," she whispered in his ear. "Beloved."

9

IAN

Ian had awakened from his nap as twilight had begun to fall. A noise had woken him, or so he thought. He heard Donna roar out of the driveway in her car and assumed they were late for Brenna's Girl Scout meeting. The pain medicine made him so very thirsty. He stumbled out to the kitchen and drank one glass and then another of cold water. Feeling much better, he went back to the living room. He sat back on the couch with a third glass of water. He sipped at it, feeling more awake with each sip. Ian remembered Brenna's words about a seal in the Thorofare.

Ian looked out the window. There was nothing he could see in the water—no dark lump of a head bobbing in the tide. But then he noticed something on his beach. It was a longish mass in the twilight. Ian pressed his face to the glass and stared more. The lump shifted a bit, and he saw a roundish-shaped head. He saw flippers. There was a seal on his beach!

Ian went to the door to the deck and backyard. He stared down the yard to the little beach at the end of his property. The glare from the light and the setting sun had made it difficult to see. It looked like a seal on his beach, but he couldn't be sure. He kept staring.

He wondered what to do. He had read about not approaching a stray seal. There were signs on the beaches on the island about staying several hundred feet away due to seals' nasty bites. He would need to go inside and get the number to the Marine Mammal Stranding Center and report a beached seal. But, he thought, perhaps he should wait until morning.

In Ian's heart, he wished and hoped that Kelsi had some connection to the mammal on the beach. It was a crazy thought. He shook his head at himself and took a last look before he turned to go inside.

And then, the unthinkable happened. The seal moved. It raised its head and stared at him. And, as if in a dream, the head folded back, like the hood of a coat, and a person's head emerged. Kelsi was shaking her long, thick, curly dark hair out of her face before looking at him. She pulled her arms and legs out of the sealskin and stood still, naked in the last dregs of the golden light of twilight.

Ian's breath hitched at seeing Kelsi emerge. He wasn't sure if he was seeing things or not. Her beautiful, creamy body was bathed in the remaining golden light of the day. She looked like a dream with her ivory curves and long, curling hair. She reminded him of Venus coming out of the shell. His pulse raced.

And then she was in his arms. He kissed her over and over again, tasting her salty sweetness. She kept murmuring something in another language, and he kissed her each time she said *Muirnín*. Soon, they were holding each other and laughing with each other.

Kelsi saw his bandaged arm. "You're hurt!" she cried. "What happened?"

Ian was a little embarrassed, remembering how he thought of Kelsi and her naked body when he fell and burned his arm on the generator. He blushed.

"It's nothing," he told her. "I'll be fine. Come, come inside with me."

She nodded, taking his offered hand and walking toward the door. When they reached the doorway, Kelsi stopped. "Wait! My pelt!"

Kelsi ran back to the beach. Ian stared at her. She picked up the seal pelt, put it on her arm, and returned to him. Inside, she draped the pelt over the back of the couch. Kelsi turned to him, and he enfolded her in his arms. He held her and breathed in her scent. In a swoop, he picked up Kelsi and carried her upstairs to the bedroom.

Ian laid Kelsi gently on the bed and looked at her, mesmerized. God! She was beautiful. Her dark, soulful eyes took in his gaze. He wanted her, but he was almost afraid to touch her. She was so beautiful to him.

Kelsi reached for him with her hand. A simple, graceful gesture. He took her hand, and she pulled him gently to her. He touched her hair and kissed her again. And then again and again. Kelsi tugged at his clothes, and in a few moments, his clothes were strewn on the floor. They were skin-to-skin. Ian sighed. His erection swelled. Kelsi's eyes grew big. She smiled a small smile at him and slid her legs open a little. Ian didn't need more of an invitation.

Slowly, slowly, slowly, he explored every inch of her body. He licked the salty sweetness of her skin. It reminded him of salted caramel. Kelsi arched her back with his pleasurable assault. She stroked him and pulled gently at him. It was evident Kelsi wanted him inside of her. She was trembling beneath him as he touched her small pearl of pleasure. Kelsi mewled and writhed. She was so wet. His lips traveled south. He tasted her, lapped her salty juices, and she bucked beneath him.

"Please," he heard her beg in a ragged whisper. "Please."

Finally, he gave Kelsi her wish and entered her ever so slowly. She trembled more until he was fully inside of her. When Ian filled her completely, they both sighed simultaneously in contentment. He moved slowly. Kelsi climaxed again and again, but Ian did his best to hold off as long as he could. He wanted to savor each moment with Kelsi.

Their lovemaking took them into the night. Afterward, they slept peacefully, nestled together.

It was well into the night when Ian got up for a drink. He extricated himself carefully from Kelsi, marveling that she was in his bed sleeping softly. She murmured something as Ian stood there but didn't wake up. He looked at her gorgeous curves and rounded breasts softly topped with darkened pink.

Ian stood a few moments, lost in Kelsi's beauty before he tiptoed downstairs to the kitchen to get some water. He passed by the sealskin lying on the couch. He didn't want to think of Kelsi inside of it. Not yet. He could ask her questions in the morning. He got a glass of water and took it back upstairs with him.

Kelsi was still sleeping soundly. Ian crawled back into bed, spooning up against her. She nuzzled closer to him. He cupped a hand around her breast and fell asleep, content.

10

KELSI

Kelsi dreamed of their lovemaking. And her dreams were sweet. She was not used to these human emotions of joy, love, and laughter. Her emotions as a seal were more whole and simpler. These human emotions were complex as if they had layers and layers to them. She dreamed of coming into Ian's arms again, his wonderment of seeing her not only as a seal but emerging from her pelt to a human female. She reveled in the passion when he touched her intimately, and her skin tingled at the memory of his lips and his touch. Kelsi relived the moments of orgasm when she completely lost control and her body as it rippled and shook in the pleasures Ian was giving her.

When she awoke with the first slivers of dawn, Kelsi looked at Ian. She loved how his sandy golden red hair picked up the morning light. He was sound asleep, but as she moved a little away, his hand traveled to try to touch her.

She looked at his bandaged arm and wondered how he had injured it. She placed her hands above the bandage and felt the pain and burning from beneath the dressing. She murmured a few words and brushed away the air near his body in brief, sweeping strokes.

After tiptoeing from the bedroom, she wandered through the house. She found the bathroom and was awed at the fixtures. Kelsi turned and pushed some knobs and was delighted as water noisily spurted from faucets and showerheads. She didn't want to wake Ian and continued to tiptoe down the stairs. She saw her pelt lying on the couch. She wasn't sure what to do with it. At the moment, Kelsi didn't want to climb into it ever again. She just wanted to be with Ian.

Kelsi wondered what Ian thought about her pelt. Tomorrow. There would be time tomorrow to discuss it.

Kelsi's next stop was the kitchen. There was another faucet. She turned it on and lowered her mouth to the rushing water. It was fresh water and tasted delicious, with only a hint of salt. She drank greedily, not used to having fresh water.

Returning to the bedroom, Kelsi crawled back into bed with Ian. He liked to cup her breasts in his sleep, so she scooted into him, molding her body against his, and whispered his name. He moved to her and nuzzled her hair. Kelsi smiled, sighed, and dozed again.

11

IAN

The loud claxon on Ian's cell phone woke them both abruptly. Ian pawed at the nightstand beside the bed, searching blindly for the ringing, reverberating, offensive thing. Kelsi's eyes were wide with fear. He put a hand on her and told her it was all right while he looked at the caller ID. It was Mike. He answered.

"Hey there, Mike."

"How are you doing, buddy?" Mike asked Ian, his voice filled with concern.

Ian took stock of how he was feeling for a moment. "A little better today," he answered honestly. "Those pain meds really knock you for a loop! I've been sleeping almost 24/7."

"Well, take today and the weekend to rest," Mike advised, "and I'll see you bright and early on Monday morning if you can manage it."

"I'll keep that happy thought," Ian said drily.

Ian hung up the phone and glanced over at Kelsi. Her eyes were wide as saucers. The fear from the loud ringtone had gone, but she was still in awe of him conversing on the cell phone.

Ian laughed. "It's all right, Kelsi. That was Mike, my boss. He was checking on how I was feeling with this." Ian raised his injured arm in the air.

"What happened to you?" Kelsi asked him.

Ian looked sheepish. "I was thinking of you and not paying attention," he admitted, "and I slipped on a hammer and fell onto the exhaust pipe of a generator. A third-degree burn," he finished ruefully.

"And how is it feeling now?" Kelsi asked Ian.

Ian paused and thought, concentrating for a minute, "Much better," he admitted.

"Good," Kelsi murmured.

She turned toward Ian and kissed him softly and then more insistently. And their morning lovemaking was as sweet as the golden sun's gentle streams of light in the sunrise.

Hours later, Ian stirred. The pain in his arm had abated, but he had a headache from the lack of caffeine. He made his way to the kitchen to make coffee. Ian had a small tray to bring two cups back to the bedroom.

Kelsi woke sleepily, smiling when she saw Ian. He offered her a cup of coffee. She took it and jumped, spilling the hot liquid over herself and the bedclothes.

"What is this stuff?" she said, wrinkling her nose. "It's bitter!"

"It's coffee," Ian told her. "The nectar of the gods."

"I doubt that," Kelsi told Ian.

He climbed back into bed, carefully balancing his cup. Hers was on the bedside table, cooling. Kelsi had no idea about coffee. This is it, he thought, time to bring up that she is possibly a seal? He was questioning his sanity as he sipped his way through the top half of his coffee. Kelsi was looking at him inquisitively.

"What?" she asked him.

Ian didn't know how to answer her question. He looked at her, at her gorgeous face, her luxurious hair, and her beautiful body. How could she be a seal? How? And he blurted his question out loud, "What are you?" He didn't want to sound rude, but he didn't know another way to ask.

"I am a Selki," she answered. "I am a seal in the ocean and a human on land if I choose."

"But that's not possible," Ian insisted.

"Yes," Kelsi told him gently, "yes, it is." A little laugh escaped Kelsi; it sounded like music to Ian. "Selkis have been around since the time men have been on earth."

"You will have to educate me."

"I would be happy to." Kelsi's tone was more serious than she had intended.

Ian put his coffee on the bedside table and took Kelsi into his arms. "So, tell me the pros and cons of you being a Selki while you are in a relationship with me. Because it's surprising and amazing to me that you are the only one I want to be with."

Kelsi swallowed hard. "Being a Selki," she said, "I can turn into a seal when I step into my sealskin. Most Selkis' skins are taken by human males. The men hold the Selki hostage, forcing them to become their wives and bear children. The Selkis can also help them become successful fishermen. Most Selki brides are unhappy souls who always want to return to the sea."

"And you?" Ian asked her.

Kelsi closed her eyes for a moment. When she reopened them and looked at Ian, she realized he made her whole. Kelsi's voice was husky with desire as she answered, "I have never met anyone like you. I want to be with you. You are quite different from a seal bull, and I'm very glad of that."

"Different from a bull seal, eh?" Ian replied.

"Definitely," Kelsi answered, "and in an excellent way."

She snuggled into Ian's arms. He held her quietly. Both were caught up in their own thoughts. Their stomachs grumbled loudly as if conversing with each other. Both melted into giggles.

"Look," Ian said, "let's get cleaned up and get some food, okay?" he asked Kelsi.

She nodded.

He led her to the shower.

"The rain!" Kelsi burst out.

Ian laughed. "Yes, the rain. And it will help us clean up."

Ian turned on the water and let it run for a few minutes. He grabbed a clean towel and washcloth from the linen closet. Ian stepped into the bathtub and put out a hand for Kelsi to join him. She was a little shy at first but liked the spray of warm water coming down. She held her face and both hands up in wonder at the shower head. Ian took some shampoo and massaged her hair. He rinsed her hair and began soaping up her body. His soapy, slippery hands glided effortlessly over her body and into her curves from top to bottom. Kelsi started to respond to his touch.

Ian grew hard again as he touched her, getting aroused from her reaction. Kelsi began to return the favor of soaping up Ian's body, which only turned him on more. He couldn't help himself. Kelsi didn't seem to be able to help herself either. Their lovemaking was quick, slippery, and excellent.

Ian dried Kelsi off tenderly after their shower. He shook his head.

"No one, absolutely no one, has affected me as you have," he told Kelsi. "I cannot get enough of you."

Ian kissed Kelsi deeply. He forcibly pulled himself away.

"We both need some food. But, one problem, you have no clothes other than your sealskin. I don't think I can take you out for breakfast as a seal." He smiled as he spoke to Kelsi.

Ian rummaged through his drawers. He pulled out underwear for himself and a pair of boxers for Kelsi to wear. Ian found a comfortable pair of jeans for himself and a drawstring pair of sweatpants for Kelsi. They were relatively new, but Ian knew they would be much too big for Kelsi. He pulled out long-sleeved T-shirts for each and a couple of hoodies. What would he do about shoes for Kelsi? She was wrapped up in the sheet on the bed with the towel turbaned around her hair. She looked utterly delicious. His feet were on the smallish side. He hoped hers were of the largish size. Gently, he lifted the sheets and looked at her feet. She had incredibly long feet and toes. They were on the edge of looking odd. Perhaps she could wear a pair of his sneakers.

Ian helped Kelsi dress. The clothes were definitely too big, but they weren't too bad. He would need to take her shopping soon. He handed Kelsi a comb. She combed out her long, curly, thick hair over and over. He plugged in the blow dryer and helped her dry it. It was so very sensual to handle her hair. Ian had to keep control of himself.

Food, he kept thinking. *We need to get food and clothes for Kelsi.*

They finished dressing, and Ian led Kelsi to the truck. She was mesmerized as he opened the door, motioned for her to climb in, and assisted her with the seatbelt. Kelsi jumped when he turned on the truck and felt it rumble beneath her. Ian laughed. Kelsi giggled in delight.

Ian drove to the closest diner he knew, the Pirate's Swoop in North Brigantine. Kelsi was in awe of the scents and the noise of the restaurant. Once the hostess had seated them, Ian discussed the menu with Kelsi. The waitress came to get their drink orders. She gave Kelsi a rather odd look, taking in her outfit. Ian ordered coffee and smiled at the face Kelsi made when the waitress wanted to know if she wanted coffee.

"Just water, thank you," Kelsi told the waitress. She turned to Ian and said, "Look, I'm starving, but I've never eaten human food. She gestured to the ocean before continuing, "I should be out there, getting scallops, cod, and weakfish."

Ian patted her hand. "I'll think of some things you might like."

Ian watched the waitress return to the drink station. She chatted briefly with two other waitresses and shot Kelsi glances while she talked. The other two waitresses spoke and glanced at Kelsi as well. Ian wondered if they noticed Kelsi's odd clothes and commented about them. Ian wasn't exactly a regular to the restaurant, but he did frequent it many times. Kelsi was new to the restaurant. Perhaps the waitresses noticed she was a stranger. Maybe they were admiring her lovely hair and beautiful features.

The waitress returned with drinks, and Ian placed an order for several items, telling the waitress to bring two plates. Ian noticed Kelsi's gaze kept turning toward the ocean.

"You okay?" Ian asked her. "Would you rather be out there?" He gestured with his head toward the sea.

Kelsi looked out the window at the blue-gray Atlantic Ocean. It called to her. She imagined she could feel the sensation of the water flowing over her skin as she dove through the waves. She turned and looked at Ian.

Ian held his breath. She had a poker face that he couldn't read. She was quiet. He waited. She gazed at the rolling breakers and beyond, her dark eyes thoughtful.

Kelsi turned to look fully at Ian. He could drown in those dark fringed, dark eyes of hers.

"No, I would rather be with you," Kelsi murmured so quietly that Ian barely heard the phrase.

Ian sighed with relief. The waitress brought their breakfasts. Ian had ordered a variety of food: raspberry cheesecake French toast, bagels and lox and bacon, lobster, and tomato omelet with hash browns. The waitress also brought two plates. He portioned out a bit of everything for Kelsi. At first, Kelsi seemed nervous when the platters were placed on the table. He picked up the knife and fork and demonstrated how to use them. After several tentative attempts, Kelsi was a pro at using utensils. In fact, Ian was awed, amazed, and almost uncomfortable watching Kelsi eat human food.

It was true. They were both ravenous, but her total concentration on eating surprised him. She loved the lox but was a trifle surprised at the texture of the cream cheese and the bagel with the fish. Kelsi devoured the raspberry cheesecake French toast. Her complete devotion to the food amused Ian. She delighted in every bite.

Ian loved to watch her face. Her eyes were wide with delight at sampling the sweet and crunchy French toast. Her mouth made a delighted "O" while tasting the saltiness of the lox. A small dusting of confectioner's sugar graced her upper lip. Ian took his napkin and wiped at his own lips, thinking she might copy him. Kelsi didn't take notice. She was too caught up in her eating experience.

Ian couldn't help himself. He put a gentle hand on Kelsi's to prevent the next bite of food from reaching her lips. Kelsi looked up, surprised. Those beautiful, large brown eyes were rimmed with the longest lashes he had ever seen. He leaned over and kissed her gently, tasting the powdered sugar. Kelsi was so surprised that she didn't kiss him back. He stopped after that one soft kiss. Ian smiled at Kelsi before he picked up his own silverware and continued to eat slowly. She looked at him, still surprised, but she smiled. A few minutes later, Kelsi stopped eating abruptly.

"Are you all right?" Ian asked Kelsi.

"Oh, yes," she replied, "I'm done eating."

"Oh," he commented, feigning understanding. She had stopped eating so abruptly it surprised him. He probably thought that when seals ate fish in the ocean, they stopped hunting and eating when they were satisfied.

This breakfast was a series of firsts for Kelsi and for him. He slowly chewed the remainder of his food, pondering what other firsts would lay in store for them.

While he finished eating, Ian watched Kelsi stare out at the Atlantic. It was a pewter gray today, and large breakers hit the beach. Kelsi stared at the horizon, and Ian wondered what she saw out there. He observed how Kelsi leaned toward the window, nearly pressing her nose against the pane. Ian wondered what she was feeling, wondering if she wanted to be back in her sealskin, swimming far, far away. What if? What would he do?

12

KELSI

A two-legger's life was so very new and overwhelming for Kelsi. Fear shook her when Ian's phone rang, not knowing why the small device rang so loudly. The pain and surprise that overcame her when sipping Ian's "nectar of the gods"—coffee. The alien feel of the clothing's fabric against her skin.

The ride in Ian's machine—the *truck* he had called- felt like when she torpedoed herself in the sea as they hurtled along the roadway.

Everything was different from what her life had always been. After explaining to Ian that she was a Selki, she couldn't comprehend how they were ever meant to be, but all Kelsi knew was that she wanted to be near Ian. She imagined how horrified her mother or sisters would be if they saw her in bed with Ian, yet still, she wanted to be near him.

At the restaurant's parking lot, a high concrete wall hid the beach from the burgeoning ocean. Kelsi could feel the tide rising.

"Céol Mo Chridhe," Kelsi whispered.

Ian smiled. "What does that mean?"

"You are the music of my heart."

Kelsi softly moaned against Ian's mouth as he kissed her. She smiled as he jumped from his truck and came to open the door for her. The smile wrinkled a bit as the sea pulled her, but Kelsi concentrated on taking Ian's hand as he led her across the street.

They had entered a place that was filled with noises and many two-leggers. Humans, thought Kelsi, humans. One female led them to a table where Ian spoke about food. The woman glanced at Kelsi. She looked down, feeling small under the woman's eye. Kelsi blushed and wriggled in her seat uncomfortably. Ian was kind and put his hand over hers. She looked him in the eye. Oh! His eyes! How they mesmerized her. She felt like she was drowning in their depths. Drowning...but in a good way. Her heart fluttered under his loving gaze.

The food came, breaking the trance between them. The woman brought several platters that jostled together with clinks as the plates hit one another on the heavily laden tray. Kelsi jumped at the unfamiliar sound. The waitress loaded the table with the food. She placed empty plates in front of Ian and Keli. She looked helplessly at the food and the utensils. Ian gave her an encouraging smile. He showed her how to use the fork and the knife. Kelsi copied him. Kelsi glanced around at the other diners. She hoped she was eating properly. Her stomach growled loudly again. She took one bite and then another. Kelsi became engrossed in the tastes and textures of the foods new to her.

This food was unbelievable. Kelsi devoured bite after bite. In the ocean, she would grab and swallow her food whole. Tasting, chewing, and enjoying each bite was a new experience for her. She ate quickly, and she ate with gusto. Kelsi was startled when Ian put his hand on top of hers, preventing the next bite from going into her mouth. Kelsi looked up, eyes wide. Had she done something wrong?

Kelsi looked at Ian's chocolate brown eyes and felt mesmerized by his gaze. Her breath caught in her throat, and it seemed time had stopped for a moment.

Ian kissed her gently. Just one small kiss. After the kiss, he smiled and returned to his own food. Kelsi was surprised. Kelsi took a few more bites as she continued to sample the variety until she was completely satiated. She stopped eating.

Ian looked alarmed. "Are you all right?" he asked her.

Kelsi returned Ian's alarmed look with a look of surprise. "Why, yes," she told Ian, "I'm fine. I'm done eating."

She watched him as he finished his breakfast. Ian ate slowly. He seemed to savor his food. Is this how humans ate? Kelsi looked around at the other diners. Some were eating slowly. Some were eating quickly. Some didn't seem to care at all. Kelsi was shocked at some diners' cavalier atti-tude toward their food. The riches that were before them! They had no idea how difficult it was to catch food on occasion. No idea. She returned to watching Ian eat for a minute before staring out the window at the ocean

Kelsi felt she should be out in the ocean catching scallops, flounder, and weakfish. She could feel the pull of the sea. It was as if the ocean had tethers tied to her and tugged at her gently. Kelsi felt as though she could feel the sensation of the water flowing over her skin. She took a deep breath. Here it was. The truth. Kelsi swallowed hard. Where would she rather be? It was a choice of being free to swim in the sea or to be with Ian. But it wasn't a choice. It was with Ian that she needed to be. They finished, and Ian went to the counter, handing the one woman a small piece of plas-tic. They chatted, nodded at each other, while Kelsi stood quietly by, taking in the transaction. Ian and Kelsi turned to go. Just as the door was closing, Kelsi heard some rude laughter from the women behind the counter with sniggers escaping from behind their hands. At first, her cheeks blazed from embarrassment. Then she realized there was absolutely nothing to be embarrassed about. She straightened her shoulders and glided along beside Ian, holding his hand. She was with Ian, not them. Those ladies were behaving rudely, like seals she had once met from another herd.

Outside, the pull of the ocean was stronger. Ian walked her over to his truck, but before they got in, he asked her if she wanted to take a walk on the beach. She hesitated. This was another test for her.

"A short one," she answered him honestly.

Walking up the ramp to the top of the concrete wall that protected the dwellings from storms, they stepped through the deep, loose sand to where the sand was packed harder caused by the beating it had received from the pounding of the breakers in the last twelve hours. The tide was turning. The path of wet sand became wider and wider as they walked. Gulls wheeled overhead, grabbing lone pieces of shellfish that had washed up on the ocean's edge. Gulls and plovers danced as the foam chased them to and from the breakers, seeking their own breakfast. The ocean called to her. Those invisible, magnetic strands of energy of the tide pulled at Kelsi's innards. She paled under its pull and clung to Ian's hand.

Oh, Sedna, great goddess of the sea, help me, Kelsi thought.

"Are you all right?" he asked, concerned.

She nodded abruptly and pulled Ian's hand to return to the car without saying a word.

13

IAN

Ian was worried about Kelsi. She looked very, very pale under his gaze. She wanted to leave the beach, and he gently led her back to the truck. He was worried the human food didn't settle well with her.

When she was safely buckled in, and he was beside her, he questioned her again, "Are you all right?"

"I'll be fine," Kelsi whispered.

"Is it your tummy?" Ian asked. "Did the food settle all right?"

She turned and looked a little surprised. "Yes, my stomach is fine. It was the sea. It was pulling me." Kelsi closed her eyes and put a hand on her chest. "The pull is so very strong," she said faintly.

Ian wasn't sure he wanted the answer to this question, but he asked, "And who is Sedna? Is that a relative?"

Kelsi opened her eyes, turned, and looked at him abruptly. "What? What did you say?" she asked, with anxiety tinging her voice.

"Sedna," he repeated, "You said, 'Oh, Sedna!' on the beach the way I might say, 'Oh, Christ,' as a sort of expletive. I don't know who Sedna is. I thought you might be missing a friend or a relative," he continued rather weakly.

At this, Kelsi chortled, actually chortled in that musical laugh that Ian loved.

"Sedna is the mother of us all," Kelsi told him, "At least, the mother of all sea creatures, particularly seals, whales, and walruses."

Ian still looked puzzled.

"Okay, okay," Kelsi told him, "I will tell you the tale of Sedna. There are many stories of Sedna, but this is my favorite. Sedna was a young woman traveling with her father in their kayak in the cold and empty ocean, far North of here. Up came a monstrous storm, and the father wanted only to save himself. He knocked her from the kayak. Sedna clung to the kayak, only gripping it with her fingers. She did not want to die! Sedna clung, even though her father was whacking at her fingers with the paddle. The waves swirled around them, washing over them in great waves, leaving Sedna and her father sputtering.

"The chill wind came, and the clouds swirled as the sea swirled around them. Her fingers turned blue with cold, and the pain was unimaginable. Her father whacked at her cold, frozen fingers until they came off her hands, and Sedna sank to the bottom of the ocean. As she sank, her fingers turned into seals, walruses, and whales so that she wouldn't be alone. She is the mother of us all," Kelsi finished. "She is mother and sister to all seals. We owe her everything."

Ian listened to the story. He was stunned and fascinated. Another god was very foreign to his strict Catholic upbringing as a child. Although he wasn't a practicing Catholic, the thought of another god – a goddess, was inherently uncomfortable. He wasn't sure what to say or how to react to Kelsi.

"Okay," he said slowly. Ian went to turn on the ignition but paused to ask, "But what about the part where you said the sea was pulling you? What does that mean?"

Kelsi had taken a deep breath before she answered, "The sea wants me to come back. It pulls at every bit of me. I can feel the flowing of water over my skin. I can feel the tides rise and fall. It knows I am a creature of the sea and is pulling at me to return."

"You speak of the sea as if it is a being – a living and breathing entity."

"But it is!" Kelsi insisted. "Just like the entire planet is a living, breathing, life-filled being. Haven't you heard of the goddess Gaia? Gaia is this planet."

Ian hesitated and then nodded.

Kelsi stopped talking and looked at Ian. His face was now a shade paler, and her heart melted when she saw an expression of something like, but not like, fear in his eyes. He did not want her to return to the sea. He looked overwhelmed. Kelsi gently put a hand on his leg.

"I don't want to go back," she told Ian. "I want to stay with you. The sea will always pull me, but I have made my choice."

Ian leaned over and gave Kelsi a quick kiss. His relief was palpable. He turned the ignition in his truck and pulled away from the parking spot near the restaurant.

"If you're going to be a landlubber, then we have to get you some clothes," Ian told her. "The question is *where.*"

Ian made a U-turn, heading south on the island to the main road to go off the island. He was thoughtful. Ian knew of the outlets in Atlantic City before deciding to go to the nearby mall in May's Landing.

He glanced over at Kelsi. She was enthralled with the world flying by the car window. She seemed to drink in the sights. It was her first time, he realized, to be in a vehicle traveling any distance, or so he thought. Every experience was new to her.

They approached the exit for the mall. A sudden and overwhelming thought came to him. Kelsi would need *everything.* How and where would they begin? He remembered how uncomfortable she was, at first, at the diner. It had been her first time in a restaurant. It had been her first time eating like a human. She did well, but he began thinking of *all* the new experiences that today would bring. He looked at the brick-enclosed mall and the precise landscaping in tidy islands outside. What would the sales-people think of Kelsi?

As Ian parked just as panic struck him. What would the salespeople think of Kelsi? She had odd clothes, ill-fitting shoes, and no underwear! Neither Ian nor Kelsi had a clue to her sizes. This could be a nightmare. He wondered what to do. Ian glanced at Kelsi. Kelsi was looking at him expectantly with those huge, gorgeous brown eyes.

Ian started to speak. He wanted to speak, but the words he needed had not yet formed in his mind, and he could not look Kelsi in the eye. Her look of expectancy turned into a look of puzzlement.

"What is it, Ian?" Kelsi asked. "What's wrong?"

Ian hesitated a moment longer before he spoke. "I don't know how to voice this, Kelsi," he began, "but the humans selling the clothes won't understand you, um..." he hesitated again before saying, "your lack of understanding about female, human needs. They certainly won't believe you're a Selki."

"Really?" Kelsi asked him, her eyes wide in disbelief.

"I don't know how to explain your..." Ian broke off again, wanting to say ignorance, but that seemed harsh, "your lack of understanding," he said lamely.

Kelsi thought for a moment. Slowly, she answered Ian, "You can tell them I have been on a long journey, which I have!"

Ian chuckled, catching on, "And we can say you lost your luggage!" Ian turned and took her hand excitedly. "Hey! Maybe you can speak in that other language you were using? What did you say to me? I know I'll butcher the pronunciation, but it sounded like 'muirnín.'"

Kelsi liked Ian calling her his beloved in her language. His accent and pronunciation were different from anything she had ever heard.

"The Gaelic," she answered him.

"Is that the language you were speaking to me?" Ian asked.

"Yes," said Kelsi, blushing as she remembered some of the phrases she shouted at the height of her passion.

Ian answered Kelsi thoughtfully at first and then, with excitement building in his voice, said, "I think that would work! It might work if you could speak primarily Gaelic, and we tell them you lost your luggage!"

Ian's relief was palpable. Kelsi was relieved as well. Ian practically leaped from his truck and went around to open Kelsi's door. He took her hand with a smile and offered her a quick, hard kiss on the mouth before they walked to the mall entrance.

14

KELSI

Kelsi absolutely loved hurtling down the highway in Ian's truck. It reminded her of how she torpedoed through the sea. As they drove further away from the ocean, she felt the ocean pulling away as a wave pulls back from the shoreline. The feeling was almost bittersweet. But the excitement of being with Ian and this new adventure into the human world was intoxicating. The scenery flew past. Cars sped by them. Ian was an excellent driver, even when some cars seemed to bully or want to play games with Ian in his truck. Some of the seals in her pod did this as well. Most times, it was good fun. Occasionally, a rogue seal with a mean spirit deliberately swam dangerously around another seal, cutting off the seal that was hurtling through the sea. The bully seal created bubbles, so the other seal couldn't see or be safe. The vehicles that cut off Ian on the highway reminded Kelsi of the bully seal.

In a few minutes, their flight on the highway ended when Ian pulled into a parking lot of an incredibly large building. She was intimidated by its size, but it was Ian's behavior that truly gave her pause. He was concerned that the other people wouldn't understand who she was. A millisecond of hurt coursed through her, but Ian was right that she did not know human, female ways. She had come out of her sealskin several times in her life, but her forays as a human had been in remote places where she could dance and dance under the light of the moon with no other humans about. She danced and sang along with her mother, her sisters, her aunts, and her cousins. The circle of Selki women loved dancing under the soft, gleaming rays of the full moon. They never needed clothes. The clothes Ian talked about were foreign to Kelsi.

They entered the shopping mall. Kelsi was stunned and dazzled by the sights and sounds. After three steps, Kelsi came to a dead stop. She was astonished by the vista of light and sound before her. The sounds of the shoppers created a roar like sea waves washing up on a distant shore. The lights of the stores and signs were glaring, but the overall effect of the mall was like a subterranean cavern or deep water in the sea.

Ian tugged at Kelsi's hand, and slowly, she followed him. He walked to a standing map and pondered over it. Kelsi continued to look around, eyes wide, taking in everything. She watched the milling of shoppers as they strolled along. When someone jostled another shopper, Kelsi was reminded of the highway they had taken when they came to this place. The groups of shoppers also reminded Kelsi of schools of fish or a pod of dolphins.

"Come on," Ian told her.

He held her hand tightly and protectively in his. Ian led her past many stores. Kelsi liked many of the clothes displayed in the bright storefronts. She wanted to go up to the glass, press her face into it and get a closer look at some of the clothes, but Ian kept pulling her along.

Ian led her to the entrance of a huge store. It was a brightly lit cave of color, light, and smells. There was a human female who stood in front of a clear box of small pots and bottles of things. She approached them and squirted something in the air, asking if they wanted to try it. Ian shook his head vehemently. Kelsi didn't know why. She craned her head and looked back at the woman after they walked by. Kelsi wondered if there was something wrong with her face. It seemed to be covered in something. Her eyes were crusted in thick black and glittery stuff. Her lips looked odd, all puffy and covered in something slick.

"Slow down! Please, Ian!" Kelsi begged.

"Oh," Ian replied and stopped. "Sorry."

"Is that human all right?" Kelsi asked him.

"Who?" Ian wondered. "What are you talking about, Kelsi?"

"That woman," Kelsi explained, "the one who was spraying something foul."

"What about her?" Ian returned.

"Her face!" Kelsi exclaimed.

"What about it?" Ian asked, puzzled.

"It's crusted with something," Kelsi said, concern in her voice.

Ian looked at Kelsi. He glanced back at the woman at the perfume and cosmetics counter, now several feet away. Ian began to chuckle and then started to laugh. He laughed and laughed until he pulled his hand away from Kelsi's and held his stomach while he laughed.

Kelsi stared at Ian, surprised at this reaction. As Ian laughed louder and longer, her surprise turned to embarrassment, annoyance, and eventually indignation.

"Ian!" Kelsi chided. She put her hand on her hip and stamped her foot. "Ian!"

Ian's laughter slowed, and he reached out and pulled Kelsi to him, brushing a kiss in her hair.

"Oh, Kelsi!" He breathed into her hair with a chuckle or two, continuing to escape.

Kelsi pulled herself from him and scowled.

He sobered under her gaze. "She's wearing makeup," Ian explained. "Many human females think they are more beautiful wearing makeup."

Kelsi made a face that started Ian's laughter again. Kelsi scowled at him.

He sobered. "*Her* makeup is extraordinarily thick," Ian told Kelsi. "Most women do not wear it so heavily."

The scowl left her face when he hugged her to him again. He lightly rubbed her back, and then he pulled away and took her hand.

"Come on," Ian said, leading Kelsi past clothes, handbags, and other accessories to an area where small bits of fabric and lace hung on minuscule hangers. Kelsi thought they looked a little like the bathing suits she had seen on women on the beach. She noticed Ian looked a little uncomfortable. He looked around. When he saw an older woman, he pulled Kelsi toward her. Ian told her the story they had invented. Kelsi stayed silent and nodded along with Ian.

"Oh, you poor dear!" the woman exclaimed when Ian had finished the story. "I'll be happy to help you out. Let me run and get my measuring tape."

She returned to fetch her measuring tape a few moments later.

"Perhaps we should do this in the dressing room?" she suggested to Kelsi.

"Lead the way," Ian told her.

They followed the saleslady to the dressing room. Ian gave Kelsi a little push as the lady motioned for her to go inside a small, closet-like area. It had glaring lights and a huge mirror. It startled Kelsi to see her reflection. The saleslady motioned for her to hold up her arms. Kelsi complied but jumped back and bumped the dressing room wall when the woman went to put the measuring tape around her.

The saleslady sighed. "I have to measure here, here, here, and here," she said, pointing to her own body and demonstrating with the measuring tape to measure at her breasts, underneath her breasts, her waist, and her hips.

Kelsi gritted her teeth and put her arms up in the air. The woman measured Kelsi quickly and wrote the information on a small card. She motioned for Kelsi to follow her out of the dressing room. Ian was watching and waiting for them. He looked a little anxious.

"There, now," the saleslady said, "that's done. Let me show you a few things for you to choose from."

She explained the measurements on the card to Ian and led them into racks of bras and panties. The saleslady pulled out several possibilities to choose from. Kelsi had the gist of what the lingerie was for, but it seemed to her that humans wore too many clothes. As a seal, her pelt was all she needed. Ian definitely seemed drawn to certain pieces. She noticed his breath quickened at some of the smaller bits of fabric that had diaphanous cloth and lace. He looked at the lingerie, then at Kelsi, and then he didn't know what to do with his eyes. He actually blushed. Ian asked if her choices were all right, and Kelsi nodded. They were definitely beautiful. With an armful of lingerie, they made their way to the cash register, where the sales lady rang up the sale. As she folded the things in soft tissue paper before putting them into a handled bag, she told Ian and Kelsi to wash the lingerie on gentle and to hang them up to dry.

Ian thanked the saleslady and took the handle of the bag in one hand and Kelsi's hand in the other. He led her to the petite women's clothing department where a panorama of clothes lay before them. Kelsi was overwhelmed looking at the racks of clothing. There were so many to choose from. She gulped.

Concerned, Ian quickly said, "Kelsi, this is just one store. If you don't see anything you like, there's a bunch of stores in the mall we can check."

"I just," Kelsi began, "I just don't know where to start," she finished helplessly.

Ian paused. "I think you'll need a coat, shoes, jeans, and a couple of outfits today," he told Kelsi. "Then I should probably wait until my next paycheck to buy you more things. We still need to go to the grocery store to buy food."

Kelsi looked puzzled. "Paycheck?" she asked.

Ian sighed. There was so much Kelsi didn't know about.

He answered, "Yes, I work. I'm a carpenter. I build things. I get money, and that helps me buy food, have a home, have my truck, run my truck, and buy things. It's not a never-ending source of money. I need to work for the things I have."

Kelsi had a glimmer of understanding but was still very puzzled. "You'll need to tell me more about this later," she said. "It's entirely different, the life of a seal. You spend the majority of your life just trying to survive. To stay away from sharks and other predators. To find food to fill your belly, and a safe place to sleep."

Ian had laughed before he said, "It's the same in the human world, just a little different. I try to stay away from the sharks, too. They just look a bit different in the human world. I try to survive as well. That's why I work."

They were still standing in the petite women's section of the store. Kelsi was inadvertently stroking a sweater neatly folded on a table. It was as gray as the morning fog and felt as soft as the fur of a baby seal. Ian noticed her look of longing when she touched it.

"Do you like that?" he asked her.

Kelsi looked up, surprised. "Oh!" she exclaimed. "Yes, yes, I do. It's so soft."

"Then it's yours," Ian stated. He checked the size, asked Kelsi to turn around, and then held it up against her back. He put the sweater down and picked up another one, asking her to turn again. More satisfied with this choice, Ian laid it on his arm.

"Let's get this and a pair of jeans here, okay?" he asked Kelsi.

She nodded.

The woman had given Ian a size, and he pulled things from racks and held them up to Kelsi.

"Do you want to try these on?" he asked as he took a pair of jeans from the rack.

Kelsi was suddenly embarrassed. "I don't know how to fasten those things," she admitted, pointing to the buttons and zipper. "Can you help me?"

"Unfortunately, I can't go into the dressing room with you," Ian told her. "We'll have to practice with the fastenings," he paused and looked around. He spied a rack of denim leggings and pulled Kelsi over to the rack, "Here," he said. "The leggings don't have fastenings. You just pull them on over your legs."

Kelsi felt the fabric. It was heavier and stretched a little when she pulled at it. They were a dark blue, like the color of the ocean, where it was very, very deep. She liked them and nodded to Ian. She also loved the gray pair and the black. They reminded her of the color of seals. Ian nodded. They continued to look and chose a long-sleeved T-shirt, another sweater, and a sweater tunic. Ian led her to the coats. He explained that people wore these when it was cold outside and took them off in their warm houses and buildings. Kelsi was delighted to find a stormy blue coat with a hood. She put it on and then took it off with delight. She told Ian that, as a seal, when it was cold, you stayed warm by huddling with the other seals or swimming to a more temperate climate. Having something to put on and take off was astounding to Kelsi.

The fabrics' colors, textures, and smell were delightfully exotic to Kelsi. She wandered, starry-eyed, through the racks and tables filled with clothing. She touched and patted everything. She especially liked the soft knits but backed away from anything with fur on it. She wrinkled her nose at the fur-edged hoods and fake fur clothing pieces.

Ian found it amusing and commented, "You're like a kid in a candy store!"

Kelsi looked at him, puzzled. She didn't have any idea what he meant.

"I mean, you are so excited at seeing all these clothes," Ian explained, "it's an expression."

"Oh?" Kelsi responded, still not really understanding. "But, Ian! These clothes! Humans are so lucky they can change their skins with all of these different colors and textures. You can be warm or cool in these clothes. I never realized when I saw people on the beaches or in boats that they wore different skins, I mean, clothes," Kelsi corrected herself.

They walked by a display of autumn stretch velvet dresses. Kelsi picked up a deep, garnet red dress and hugged it to herself.

"It's so beautiful, Ian!" she crowed.

"Maybe we can pick it up on our next visit to the mall," Ian soothed. "Aren't you getting hungry?"

"Yes! Yes, I am hungry," Kelsi agreed.

Reluctantly, she put the dress back on the rack and stroked it wistfully before they turned and left the clothing department.

15

IAN

Ian was exhausted. Shopping for women's lingerie and clothes was clearly not his "thing," but he stuck with it for Kelsi's sake. He thought of his sister Meg and thought she would like Kelsi. Maybe she would take Kelsi out sometime soon. Introducing Kelsi to his family brought along a whole host of other issues he hadn't thought about.

Her feet and toes were incredibly long for all of Kelsi's petite size. No one in the mall had size eleven- or twelve-women's shoes. One of the salespeople in the shoe department suggested two different shoe chains that offered shoes in Kelsi's size. Ian loved Kelsi's hands and feet, but her fingers were incredibly long as well, as her toes. Could it be because as a seal, these were part of the flippers?

They lugged their purchases to the car. Kelsi looked exhausted, too.

"So, what would you like for lunch?" he asked Kelsi wearily.

She returned with a blank look. "I have no idea," she replied, "but the human food we ate this morning was delicious."

"Sorry," Ian apologized. "I keep forgetting that you don't know about this stuff. Let me think of something you might like." He closed his eyes briefly before smiling, saying, "I've got it!"

Ian hoped Kelsi would like Red Lobster. Afterward, they would tackle the conundrum of shoes. He drove out of the mall parking lot and pulled into the Red Lobster parking lot in just a couple of minutes. She looked surprised at the large lobster attached to its sign.

"It's a favorite human seafood restaurant," Ian exclaimed. "Not quite as fresh as you snapping it off the ocean floor, but I hope you like it," he told her with a smile.

Hand in hand, they walked into the aromas of a variety of seafood. Once they were seated, Ian asked Kelsi what her favorite seafood was.

"It really depends on the season," Kelsi told Ian. "I like perch, salmon, sole," she began, "mackerel, herring, crabs, and shrimp." She gave a little giggle. "When I was a pup, I *loved* shrimp. I just could not get enough shrimp for years and years. Scallops, too. I love scallops!"

"Well, that gives me some ideas," Ian pondered as he shooed the waitress off for a couple more minutes. "Do you want me to order?" he asked Kelsi.

Kelsi nodded.

As he did with breakfast, Ian ordered a variety of dishes. They feasted on pasta with lobster, shrimp scampi, and broiled, wild, caught salmon.

Once again, Kelsi was amazed at the tastes and textures of the human food. They couldn't eat it all, so Ian had them box up the remains for later consumption.

"Now for shoes," Ian said rather wearily when they stood up to go.

"You don't sound happy," Kelsi commented to Ian.

Ian stretched and paused a minute before answering. "I'm not a very good shopper," Ian admitted. "That's more for my sister Meg and my mom."

"We don't have to do any more shopping," Kelsi tried to insist.

"No," Ian said stoutly, "you definitely need shoes if you're staying on land."

"Okay," Kelsi agreed, her voice growing quiet. She felt overwhelmed.

Ian looked at Kelsi. Maybe he freaked her out by suggesting she needed shoes. Or was it more? He wondered what she was thinking.

He drove to a strip mall where a large shoe store stood. It was a large, cavernous store that was brightly lit and filled with thousands of pairs of shoes. It was a little daunting. Sales help was scarce, so Ian and Kelsi browsed. He watched her face, and he looked for her size when she looked interested. She was definitely overwhelmed.

They found a pair of black ballet flats, and he urged her to try on a pair of high heels. She teetered uncomfortably, but seeing the shape of her ankle and leg rising from the heels turned him on immediately. He urged her to consider these. Kelsi looked at him long and hard, and then she nodded. She smiled smugly at him when she took them off and handed him the box.

Ian noticed that Kelsi kept walking past a pair of knee-high leather boots. She would gaze at them, touch them gingerly, and then stroke them. He looked beneath the display to see if there was a pair in her size. There was. He pulled out the large box. Kelsi was surprised. Her smile lit her face with joy.

"Oh, Ian!" she gasped. "Really?"

He nodded.

"Thank you!" Kelsi squealed, giving him an impromptu hug. He returned the hug, smiling into her hair. They paid for their purchases.

Both of them were exhausted. Kelsi and Ian returned to the truck and sighed simultaneously.

"Home?" Kelsi asked hopefully.

"We really should be getting some food," he told her. "I guess we could send out for a pizza or scramble up some eggs."

"Anything," Kelsi said.

The late afternoon sun stretched toward the west when Ian pulled into his driveway. Brenna was outside drawing with chalk on her driveway. She jumped up as soon as she saw Ian and jumped up and down when he opened the truck's door.

"Ian! Ian!" Brenna exclaimed. "How are you? How's your arm? I'm so sad. The seal's gone away." Her questions and comments ran together in a rush.

Brenna stood, stock still, comments ended, and her mouth formed an "O" of surprise as Ian pulled many packages from the truck. Brenna's eyes grew wider and wider when Kelsi got out of the truck and came into view.

Ian cleared his throat and introduced Brenna to Kelsi and vice versa.

Stunned, it took a moment for Brenna to say, "Nice to meet you."

"Nice to meet you, too," Kelsi returned to the surprised Brenna.

Brenna's stillness only lasted a moment. Her curiosity got the better of her. Brenna started firing questions at Kelsi.

"Where are you from? Are you a friend of Ian's? How long are you staying? Did you know we had a seal at Ian's beach?" Brenna's questions tumbled out to Kelsi.

"Brenna," Ian said, holding up his hand. "Take it easy. Kelsi is a friend of mine. She comes from a remote, Northern part of Canada. Yes, I hope she is visiting and staying for a long while. Her luggage was lost on her trip, and she needed some things." He held up the bags in his hands.

"And, yes," Kelsi answered, her eyes twinkling, "I know about the seal. Where I'm from, they're everywhere." She glanced at Ian and smiled at him.

"Really?" Brenna said, awed. "I love seals. They are one of the *most beautiful* creatures I have ever seen. I've seen them on the beach and at the Marine Mammal Stranding Center, but we've never had one so close to our house. It was *so* cool! You'll need to tell me about the seals from where you used to live."

"We'll need to take a rain check on that," Ian told Brenna. "Kelsi and I are pretty tired from our shopping trip today."

Kelsi nodded in agreement.

"Oh, okay," Brenna said. She looked disappointed.

"Another time," Kelsi told her, "Soon."

Brenna brightened. "Nice meeting you," she said to Kelsi.

Kelsi flashed her a smile. "Same here."

Kelsi and Ian watched Brenna bounce into the house before Ian unlocked the door.

Ian was relieved when they got in the door with the packages. Encountering Brenna and answering her multitude of questions caused Ian angst and a little panic. If Kelsi stayed with him, there would be more and more questions. He would need to talk to Kelsi about this, but he wasn't sure she would understand. She didn't know about passports, Visas, or green cards. To her, the world was one big, happy oyster that everyone lived in. They would need to work on a story that was plausible and fast.

He took the bags and boxes up to the bedroom. He would need to make some room for Kelsi's things. He stared at the bedroom, trying to figure it all out. He didn't know what to do.

16

KELSI

Kelsi was overwhelmed and exhausted, but she wouldn't admit that to Ian. The human clothes had been lovely, but she had mixed feelings about wearing them. She had studied the groups of people while they strolled through the mall. They continually reminded her of pods of dolphins, seals, or schools of fish. She paid attention to what they were wearing and how they were acting.

The food had been tantalizing, the shopping overwhelming, and the shoes...the shoes were amazing. The sheer number of shoes and styles were intoxicating. Kelsi loved the comfortable black ballet flats, put up with the high heels that Ian loved, and was totally in love with the buttery-soft boots Ian treated her to.

Kelsi tried not to think of her seal self as they had shopped and maneuvered through the human world. It all seemed very dreamlike to her. Could it have been only yesterday that she was nosing for shellfish from the bottom of the ocean? Was it only two, no, three days ago, she was speeding away from Breách, not wanting to mate with him or any other seal? Now, here she was, acting like a human female. No, not acting, she insisted to herself. She *was* a human female.

When they arrived at Ian's house, a young, human pup was outside, a delightful child, even though she asked a lot of questions. Ian had seemed anxious to get inside, so they cut their conversation short with promises of talking another time. Kelsi followed Ian.

Ian took the packages upstairs to the bedroom, and Kelsi trailed behind. Ian seemed out of sorts, and she didn't know why.

"We'll have to find some room in my bureau for your new clothes," Ian said. He sighed when he stared at the multitude of bags.

"Ian," Kelsi asked gently, "is something bothering you?"

He shook his head, but Kelsi knew that he wasn't answering her question.

Instead, Ian almost snapped, "I don't know where to put your pelt!"

Kelsi jerked her head up at his tone. She swallowed hard. Was Ian unhappy with her? Why would he buy all these things for her if he were unhappy with her?

"I'd like it somewhere nearby and safe," Kelsi said. "Is that all right with you?"

"Yeah," Ian murmured, running his hand through his hair, "Yeah," he said again.

He glanced around the room and remembered he had an under-the-bed box. It was full of spare bedding and blankets for winter, so he took the linens and blankets out.

"Would this work?" he asked Kelsi.

"Oh! Yes!" she cried. "It would be wonderful to have it so close!"

Kelsi ran nimbly back down the stairs and returned with the silvery pelt in moments. She folded it gently and laid it in the box. Ian had difficulty looking at the empty openings where Kelsi's eyes would be, at the whiskers and the flippers. Looking at it felt as though he caught someone naked. He looked away as Kelsi finished tucking the pelt in the box, put on the lid, and slid it under the bed.

Ian busied himself and took the bedding into the second bedroom. He placed it on the closet shelf and returned to the bedroom. While he had been gone, Kelsi had stripped from Ian's borrowed clothes that she was wearing and had put on some of the lingerie. She was having difficulty with the bra fastening.

"Here, let me help you with that," Ian said.

He fastened the bra and gently turned her around. He sucked in his breath and felt himself grow hard.

Kelsi knew Ian liked these pieces of clothing. He had blushed in the store when they had chosen them. They were bits of satin and lace that held her breasts and pushed them up into curves. They had the effect on Ian that she had hoped for. She saw the desire in his eyes. She felt the need to mate with him.

Without knowing she was being coy, Kelsi backed up. She thought she saw something wrong with the high heel and put her foot on the bed to look closer. She heard Ian gasp as she bent over the shoe.

"Kelsi," Ian began with a huskiness in his tone.

And the doorbell rang.

17

IAN

"You look beautiful," he murmured. He noticed how the lace of the boy shorts hugged the curve of her bottom, as well as the delicate lace on the bra curved around her soft, swelling breasts. And when she put one foot up on the bed like a vamp from the 1940s, Ian went to her.

"I shouldn't take these off of you so soon," Ian told Kelsi as he pulled her to him, "but I'm not sure I can help myself."

He started toward her when the doorbell rang. It made Kelsi jump.

"Damn!" Ian spat out. "Who could that be?"

All of his focus had been on Kelsi standing there in all of her glory, in wisps of satin and lace lingerie. His stomach had turned to a ball of hot, liquid desire. He had wondered if Kelsi knew the effect she had on him, but her smug smile gave it away as he drew her closer. He wanted the lingerie off. Ian wanted it off right now. He wanted to take her that very second.

Groaning, he said, "I'll be right back. Don't move."

Ian went downstairs to find Donna and Brenna at the door. He let them in. Meaning well, Brenna had told her mom that Kelsi had lost her luggage. Donna, ever helpful, had come over to see if she needed anything.

Ian knew it was curiosity, too. He and Donna had a good, neighborly relationship. Once, after a neighborhood party, when they were both tipsy, they had shared a couple of kisses, but it hadn't gone further than that. Donna had been there to give him tea, or rather beer, and sympathy after Jessica, too. But they both knew that the spark wasn't there between the two of them. Ian briefly considered asking Donna to be a friend with benefits but had tossed the thought aside, not wanting to hurt either her or Brenna. He asked them to wait a moment and ran up to tell Kelsi to put on some clothes and come downstairs.

Brenna and Donna sat down. Kelsi came down wearing the deep teal sweater and black leggings. Kelsi looked shy when she stepped into the living room. Donna stood up to shake her hand, and Ian introduced them.

Kelsi perched on the edge of a chair.

"Ian and Brenna tell me you are from Northern Canada," Donna said.

"Yes," Kelsi answered. "It is a small island north of Newfoundland." She could easily and truthfully tell Donna where she lived. "My family comes and goes from the island. It's quite different from here," she gestured gracefully at the living room. "We do quite a bit of fishing."

"Ahh," Donna said, seeing the connection to Ian and his family, "I wondered how you two met."

"By the sea," Kelsi answered, merely stating the truth.

"How romantic," Donna returned.

Ian put his hand over Kelsi's and said, "Yes, yes, it was."

Kelsi glanced at him and smiled.

Ian smiled at Kelsi and nodded, approving of his story. Kelsi thought it easier to stick as close to the truth as possible without revealing she was a Selki.

"Momma," Brenna said excitedly. She had been holding in her excitement and her words burst out of her, "Kelsi knows all about seals!"

"Oh?" Donna questioned, and she turned to Kelsi. "Are you a scientist?"

Kelsi blushed. "No, I'm not a scientist, but I lived very closely with the seals. I have watched and lived with them all of my life."

"You should write a book," Donna suggested.

Kelsi gave Donna a blank stare, but Ian covered it with a nervous laugh.

"Good idea, if I can talk her into it," he told Donna, covering his nervousness with his comment

Brenna brightened and smiled at Kelsi. Ian could see that she was bursting with questions, and she bounced a little where she sat. Donna continued to ask more questions. Ian and Kelsi worked to answer and keep the story straight. When Kelsi made the trip South, she had lost her luggage, hence the shopping trip.

Kelsi piped up, "I had never been to a shopping mall before today," she told Donna. "It was unbelievable! And I loved the shoe store. Oh, my! It was incredible!"

"I'll have to take you to Atlantic City's outlets," Donna offered, "Sometime," she vaguely promised. Ian and Kelsi yawned simultaneously and then laughed.

Ian shook his head wearily. "I never knew shopping could be so exhausting."

Now Donna laughed and replied, "Now you know, don't you?"

Brenna watched Kelsi yawn again. "C'mon, Mom," Brenna said, tugging at her mom.

Donna nodded. "I understand. It was nice to meet you, Kelsi. How long will you be staying?"

Kelsi looked at Ian helplessly.

"Indefinitely," he told Donna as he held Kelsi's hand between his.

Donna looked back and forth between Ian and Kelsi. Finally, she teased Ian, "You *are* a sly one."

Ian smiled at Donna and nodded.

Donna and Brenna stood up to go. Impulsively, Brenna ran over and hugged Kelsi. Kelsi hugged back, and a glaze of tears covered her eyes. She blinked them away before Ian or Donna noticed.

When the door closed behind Donna and Brenna, Ian led Kelsi back to the couch. He held her tightly, and a whirlwind of emotions flashed through him. Thoughts of joy, doubt, and a touch of fear enveloped him. Ian thought of Kelsi seducing him on the beach. He thought of his lust and emotions for her. Now, she was here. Now, she was moving in. He wasn't sure he was ready for this. He wasn't sure if they were doing the right thing. Doubt grumbled in his stomach. Kelsi noticed.

"What's wrong, Ian?" she asked.

He pulled back from Kelsi. They sat. Ian took Kelsi's hands in his.

"I don't know," he started, "I don't know how to put this into words..."

Kelsi started to lean against him, but he put her at arm's length from him. He stared at her, seeking something in her eyes. He could see Kelsi questioning his thoughts and actions.

Finally, Ian said, "Kelsi, what are we doing? What happened on the beach and what has been happening for the past couple of days isn't..." Words failed him. "It's not exactly a normal relationship," Ian ended lamely. Now, he had difficulty looking into Kelsi's eyes.

"How can it be normal?" Kelsi returned.

Ian gaped at her.

"I mean, I am a Selki, and you are a human. Human beings and Selkis have mated through millennia, but it's not common. I know my original thought when I came close to you on the beach was only to get my pelt, but something happened to me when I came near you. I had an overwhelming urge to mate with you. I...I couldn't help myself."

Now Kelsi stared at her hands in her lap. They were both quiet for a minute or two. When she looked back up and into Ian's eyes, he saw the seriousness within them—and something like anger.

"I can assure you that choosing to mate with a human is *not* normal behavior for me," Kelsi told Ian with emphasis.

They stared at each other. Both were looking for answers in each other's eyes. As Kelsi looked deeply into Ian's eyes, her touch of anger changed. The emotions of love, doubt, lust, and a bit of fear volleyed between Kelsi's and Ian's eyes.

The pool of doubt that had settled deep in Ian's tummy turned into a pool of desire. Deepening his gaze to Kelsi, Ian was the first to break the silence, "I don't know what to call what we have, Kelsi, but I like it. I think I would like to let it grow and see what happens to it?" he asked with hope in his eyes.

Kelsi could barely nod in agreement before Ian took her in his arms and kissed her. Only a few minutes passed until they were bereft of clothes, and their limbs were entangled on the couch.

"Oh, God, Kelsi!" Ian breathed into her hair with a cry of passion.

They stared at one another. Their love and desire for one another overcome the fear and doubt. Ian took her in his arms again and kissed Kelsi deeply. They could not help themselves and pulled and tugged until their clothes fell away into small pools on the floor.

Kelsi pulled Ian to her. They were a knot of arms and legs on the couch. She pulled him into her, and Ian knew she wanted him as deeply inside of her as possible. Her desire and excitement grew as they moved from slow, sensual movements to a rhythmic wave that went deeper and longer. Wave after wave of pleasure caused her to cling harder to Ian.

"Oh, Sedna!" Kelsi cried out as her pleasure climaxed over and over.

"Oh, Kelsi," Ian breathed into her hair near her ear. "What you do to me! I never…" Ian broke off for a moment, and then he shouted her name as he climaxed.

They lay quiet then, still entangled together on the couch. Both breathed heavily. Kelsi reached up and pushed his hair back from his forehead in a tender gesture.

"I'm not sure what we're doing either," Kelsi whispered softly to Ian. "But I like how we're doing it."

Ian couldn't help himself. He started to chuckle at this. Ian kissed Kelsi all over her face and neck. Still chuckling, he took one of her nipples in his mouth, teasing it. Her nerve endings were at their peak, and she reacted almost violently to his light touch, her body bucking involuntarily.

"Mmm," he murmured, looking into her eyes. "Let's go to bed," he said suggestively. He took her hands and pulled Kelsi up and off the couch.

At that moment, Ian's phone rang.

"Shit!" The expletive came from his mouth as Ian fumbled through the puddles of clothes until he could find his phone.

It was his mother. He answered it, mostly listening and responding briefly to her conversation.

"See you tomorrow then," Ian ended.

Kelsi looked at him expectantly.

"My mom," he explained, "dinner tomorrow. It's a family thing of chowder and a movie."

Kelsi didn't understand.

"It will be okay," he told her. "My family and I get together for a meal and watch a movie together. It's been a tradition when the weather turns colder. It's a casual evening and nothing to worry about."

Ian looked down into Kelsi's beautiful, mottled brown eyes. They looked huge to him, almost as large as the character's eyes in anime. They were as innocent as a child's and always seemed to be filled with wonderment. He hoped he could help Kelsi keep that sense of wonder and the happiness mirrored in her eyes.

"Let's go upstairs," Ian suggested again, holding out his hand to Kelsi.

Kelsi took his hand and followed him upstairs. Ian put his arm around Kelsi in bed and pulled her toward him.

Finally, he said, "I'm sorry."

"For what?" Kelsi asked, surprised.

It took Ian a moment, but eventually, he answered, "For my doubts, I think."

"Ian!" Kelsi softly scolded him, "I have doubts, too! I think we're doing the best we can, feeling our way through this relationship. And it will be okay."

Ian leaned over to kiss her, and once again, his phone rang.

"Damn it!" he swore.

He looked at who was calling and answered.

"Hey there, Mike," Ian replied. "How are you?"

"Never mind how I am, man," Mike boomed through the phone, "how are you?"

"I'm all right, Mike," Ian told him as he extricated himself from Kelsi's naked limbs. Ian sighed and focused on the phone, raising himself on an elbow and touching his forehead.

After Ian put his phone on the nightstand, he put his arms around Kelsi. "No more phone calls," he promised.

"Tell me more about your phone," Kelsi said.

He pulled her tightly to him, and he tried to explain what a phone was and how it worked. Kelsi listened, wide-eyed with wonder. She interrupted Ian a few times.

"And what about the people at the mall?" Kelsi asked Ian.

"What about them?" he asked, amused.

"They didn't sound like you. The other people spoke your language, but it sounded different," Kelsi tried to explain.

Ian was thoughtful for a minute, thinking of their time at the mall. He remembered how many of the store clerks were from other countries. They spoke English, but some had spoken with difficulty and had thick accents.

Finally, Ian answered, "Those people are sort of like you, Kelsi. They came from another country in the world and are learning English. They were all speaking English but with accents and intonations that came from their native language. Sort of like your accent," he told Kelsi.

"I have an accent?" Kelsi asked Ian.

"Yeah, you do," Ian answered, "and I find it adorable."

Kelsi smiled at Ian rather shyly.

"Don't the animals in the ocean communicate with one another?" Ian asked. "Do they all speak one language?"

"Yes," Kelsi answered, "they communicate after a fashion. They don't all speak the same language. There are many forms of communication between ocean animals. It's a little more complicated with some movements of the body or talking with their minds, like with whales and dolphins. They do communicate. Yes."

They talked late into the night. Later, when Ian woke up, he didn't know who fell asleep first. He gently pulled himself from Kelsi, got a drink of water, and turned out the lights. When he returned to bed, he found Kelsi had moved into the warm spot where his body had been. She looked so young and innocent, lying asleep in bed. Kelsi had incredibly long eyelashes that curled against her cheeks. She almost looked like a doll to Ian. Her nose actually twitched, and he thought of the old television sitcom Bewitched, where the witch, Samantha, twitched her nose. He moved in beside her carefully, and Kelsi murmured and smiled in her sleep. Ian felt very protective of her. He slid in as closely as possible, trying not to wake her. He put his arm around her, and she nuzzled into him with a sigh. Ian felt complete as he fell asleep.

18

KELSI

elsi slept soundly with Ian beside her. She felt safe near him. Kelsi loved nuzzling up to him and smelling his musky maleness with a hint of salt. Ian seemed a little embarrassed when she snuggled so close to his armpit. He seemed embarrassed by his scent. He didn't appear to realize that the scents of animals called them to one another. His scent was one of the things that attracted her to him. Their respective scents spoke on a cellular level.

Kelsi extricated herself from Ian at dawn. She quietly made her way to the kitchen to get some water. She loved how the water came out of the faucets. It fascinated her. She went back upstairs to the bathroom. Ian called the rain a shower, but they had stepped into a large tub for the water to drain away. Kelsi fiddled with the hardware and found that the tub would start filling with water. It was like a small pool. She filled it and lay in it. It was a lovely little pool for her. She stretched out the length of it, relishing in the warm water.

Ian had used some good-smelling stuff on their skin yesterday. Soap, he called it. It covered their scents, almost. Kelsi liked how it smelled. She reached for the soap and rubbed it on her body. Kelsi found great pleasure in having her hands run over her limbs. Her flippers didn't permit her to touch her body, not in this way.

Kelsi lathered the sweet-smelling soap over her body. She especially liked the tiny bubbles shimmering in the morning light streaming through the bathroom window. When she felt very clean, Kelsi stepped from the tub. She not only felt spotless but also sparkling, like the bright sunlight glinting off the waves.

Kelsi took a comb from the drawer and tiptoed into the bedroom. She didn't dry off with a towel like Ian. Kelsi didn't mind the dampness. After all, she was part seal.

Kelsi didn't want to wake Ian. If he woke, he would want to mate again. She certainly wouldn't mind, but she wanted a few quiet moments for herself right now. The air had turned colder since yesterday. Kelsi didn't have her pelt, and goosebumps raised up on her damp flesh. She tiptoed to Ian's bureau, pulled out a T-shirt, and put it on. It was soft and much longer on Kelsi than on Ian. It was almost like a short dress on her petite frame.

Ian slept peacefully with his arm thrown over his head. He wore a small smile. Kelsi hoped he was having happy dreams, so she went downstairs.

Kelsi stood before the large picture window that looked out over the Thorofare. The sun rising in the East was reflected in a gentle, golden light on the water and the gold and brown grasses.

Kelsi combed her long hair, carefully and gently separating knots and tangles. As she combed, she hummed a lilting tune. She didn't hear Ian coming down the stairs. Kelsi was lost in thought until Ian came and cupped her bottom in his hand. Kelsi jumped just as Ian swooped in for a kiss in the crease of her neck. Ian drew back quickly when Kelsi's shoulder smacked him in the nose with a thwack.

She swung around. "Oh, Ian! I'm so sorry!"

"It's okay," Ian answered, rubbing his sore nose. "My fault for sneaking up on you."

Kelsi put her hands on his shoulders and kissed his nose gently. Ian leaned down and kissed her on the mouth.

When he pulled away, Ian commented, "You're up early."

Kelsi nodded. "A habit," she said, "and I had a lovely cleanup in your little pool."

Ian looked puzzled.

"Where the rain comes in," Kelsi explained. His look was still blank. "I'm sorry, you called it a shower."

Realization dawned in Ian's eyes. "Oh!" he exclaimed. "You mean you took a bath!"

Kelsi nodded. "I loved the little bubbles," she said with a smile.

"Well, we'll need to pick up some bubble bath for you. If you liked the tiny bubbles, you'd love bubble bath!"

He nodded at the Thorofare. "You were lost in thought. Were you thinking of all of the fish and crabs swimming out there for breakfast?" he teased.

Kelsi didn't understand his teasing, and she took his words seriously. "I wasn't thinking about food. I was thinking of my mother and my sisters. We're all Selkis in my family. We've all been out of our pelts and danced on the beach in the moonlight, but I don't think my sisters or mother have been with a human. A man. And, as far as I know, no one has spent any significant time on land. I am the first."

Kelsi looked a little embarrassed at first but plowed on with her explanation. "You see, Ian, my sisters and I were constantly warned about humans and how we had to stay away from them. My grandmother, aunts, and mother would warn us and nag us daily about humans. I had an aunt once that fell in love with a human. He was a fisherman. Apparently, she used to watch him on his boat, day after day. He knew about Selkis. He knew they could help his fishing business. One night, while dancing on the beach, she was captured and put to work helping him with his catch. My grandmother said he chained her to the boat and prodded her with metal things to make her tell him where there were good fishing grounds She did, but she was unhappy. You could hear it in her song, my grandmother said. It broke my grandmother's and my mother's hearts. And one day, she never came back out on the boat. We don't know what happened to her. If my mother and sisters knew I was with a human, I don't know what they would do. If they were near you, they would probably bite you before I had a chance to explain about, about..." She was at a loss for words.

"About our relationship?" Ian asked.

"Yes," Kelsi agreed, "about our relationship. You're not going to tie me up to a boat to bring in a larger catch, are you?"

Ian looked at her and said slyly, "I might want to tie you up and make love to you until you scream Sedna's name over and over again."

"Oh!" Kelsi replied, blushing, "That doesn't sound so bad, as long as you can release me to put my arms around you. I love feeling your body against mine."

"Guaranteed," Ian assured.

They were both quiet for a moment, lost in their imaginations.

When Kelsi's eyes crept toward the stairs that led to the bedroom, Ian laughed.

19

IAN

"You're wicked, you know that?" Ian insisted. "We didn't make it to the grocery store yesterday. We really need to do that today. I don't have much food in the house," he told Kelsi, a little embarrassed about the bareness of his pantry. "Let's get dressed, get some breakfast, and go to the grocery store."

As Ian dressed, he thought about Kelsi's story. He was stunned that people would abuse Selkis and make them their slaves. It was another sad realization of man's inhumanity toward man.

If Ian had thought the shopping mall to be an exciting experience with Kelsi, it was only a blip in experiences for him and Kelsi compared to the grocery store. Kelsi was fascinated by the drive-thru for breakfast. He ordered for her again, choosing a sandwich and hash browns. Kelsi particularly liked the hash browns. Ian had heard the fast-food restaurant used a type of fish oil to fry their French fries and other items. He suspected this was why she liked it. Ian told Kelsi they were having a car picnic. She returned a blank, unknowing look to him. He explained what a real picnic was and promised to take her on one on the beach or at a park when the weather was warmer.

The November air had a harsh, winter edge. When they stepped from the car, a piercing, little gust whisked open Ian's coat. He shivered and pulled his jacket tightly about him before he helped Kelsi from the car. She was wearing her new blue coat but had it open.

"You should button up," Ian told her.

Again, she looked at him blankly, and he explained that she should close her coat so she wouldn't feel the cold.

"I'm all right, Ian," she told him.

Ian realized that she wouldn't know how to button or zipper and promised himself that he would teach her that day.

Ian pulled a grocery cart from the queue.

"Come on," Ian told Kelsi gently. "Let me show you how most humans get food."

They maneuvered through the fresh fruits and vegetables. Ian put bananas and a small bag of potatoes in the cart and later added a bag of salad. They wandered the aisles, where Ian filled the cart with pasta, sauce, peanut butter, jelly, and a few cans of soup and bread. He added cream cheese, yogurt, lox, bagels, and milk in the dairy section. Then, they came to the meat section. Here, Ian stopped. Kelsi looked at him with a question in her eyes.

Ian admitted, "I'm not a very good cook, Kelsi. I know, as a seal, you ate food raw. Humans can't do that. We need to cook our food, or we'll get very sick. I'll pick up some things I think I can cook. I hope that's okay."

Kelsi put a hand on Ian's arm before saying, "I'm sure it will be all right." She paused and brightened. "Maybe I could learn how to cook? Maybe you could teach me?"

Ian chuckled. "I'll try," he said. "My mother, though, is an excellent cook. She could teach you. We're going there later today. We can ask her," he added hopefully.

"All right," she said faintly.

Ian picked up an array of ground beef, pork chops, and chicken. They then went to the seafood department, where the fish and shellfish were displayed on piles of ice.

Kelsi stopped and stared at the fish in the case.

"Ian! Look at that!" Kelsi exclaimed.

Ian looked at the seafood case nonchalantly. He gave a small shrug that Kelsi did not see. Kelsi had rushed over to the case, her eyes wide and her nose practically pressed against the glass. The display held whole fish, eyes glassy in death, and salmon, shark, cod, and tuna filets. There were shucked oysters and scallops and whole clams.

"Ian! Look! The scallops are out of their shell! Look at the oysters! Why is that fish just lying there? Why is it dead? Look! There's fish outside of their skin! Look!" Kelsi pointed and talked excitely to Ian.

"What looks good to you?" Ian asked Kelsi.

Kelsi's mouth watered at the suggestion. "Everything," she said. "It's all good. I'm just amazed that it's just lying there!"

Kelsi's attention was distracted by the lobster tank at the other end of the seafood section. "Oooh! Look at that!" She ran over and looked at the lobsters. To Ian, looking at the fish, Kelsi looked like a kid gazing at piles of candy.

"So, what's your favorite?" Ian asked Kelsi.

She looked at him, eyes wide before she answered, "That's a hard question to answer. Probably, the salmon and flounder," she told Ian, "and any of the shellfish."

Ian got the attendant's attention and had them wrap up some flounder and salmon.

"Next time, shellfish. Okay?" Ian asked Kelsi.

She nodded. Ian stopped by the fresh flower bins and picked up a large bouquet.

"What are those?" Kelsi asked. "They're just beautiful!"

"Flowers," Ian told her. "I thought it would be nice to take my mom a bunch when we go over for dinner tonight. Here, smell them."

Kelsi gently sniffed. A broad smile lit up her face. "Oh!" she exclaimed ecstatically. "I could swim in these. They smell wonderful!"

They picked up a few more things before they checked out. Kelsi trailed by Ian's side, her eyes taking in everything.

Back in the truck with the bags behind the seats, Kelsi told Ian, "That was incredible!"

He chuckled. "Glad you enjoyed it."

When they returned home, Ian and Kelsi unloaded the car. Ian showed Kelsi where he stored the groceries and explained how the refrigerator and freezer kept things cold so they wouldn't spoil. For lunch, he made tuna salad sandwiches for Kelsi, showing her the steps of opening the cans, draining, adding the condiments, and working the toaster. Kelsi loved the sandwiches and the salty, crunchy potato chips Ian served with them.

They spent the afternoon talking. Ian explained that he would need to return to work on Monday. He had concerns about what Kelsi would do with herself all day. Ian realized quickly that she couldn't read. He showed her how to use the television remote and how to access PBS for some of the children's programs that focused on reading and phonics.

"I know these are for children," Ian told Kelsi, "but if you want to be human, you definitely need to learn how to read. In fact," he turned to her as an idea excited him, "we could go to the public library. They should have some classes or something to help you out. We can stop by on the way to my parent's house. Let's go!"

Ian bundled Kelsi in her coat, and they got in the truck. It was only a few blocks to the library. Ian parked, and they walked up the stately steps to the double glass doors. Ian opened the door for Kelsi and ushered her inside. The library was bright and light, and the spacious room was filled with shelves and shelves of books, tables, chairs, and computers. The library was bustling in a quiet sort of way. Ian breathed in the comforting smell of books. Kelsi seemed nonplussed.

Ian whispered in Kelsi's ear, "Once you learn to read, you'll love it here."

Kelsi looked doubtful but followed Ian to where a woman was sitting at a desk.

Ian spoke quietly to the librarian, explaining that his friend could speak English but not read it. She was going to be in the area for an indeterminate amount of time and asked if the librarian could help. The librarian nodded briskly and typed on her computer. She led Ian and Kelsi to the shelves. The librarian pulled out a couple of books.

"Are you planning to help her learn to read?" the librarian asked Ian.

"I...I guess so," Ian stammered.

"There *are* classes for ESL students in Atlantic City," the librarian told Ian and Kelsi.

"That would be great!" Ian exclaimed, "I would love that information."

"But you'll need to help her at home as well," the librarian told Ian.

She handed Ian the stack of books, printed out class information, and asked if he had a library card. Ian whipped out his keys and showed the librarian his library card, who smiled.

"There's a lot online as well. Scottish Gaelic, eh?" she said rhetorically to Ian and Kelsi. "Interesting."

Kelsi smiled and said, "Beannachd leat."

Ian smiled and said, "Goodbye."

Kelsi and Ian headed to the circulation desk to check out the books. Back in the truck, Ian took a moment to read the titles: Yes, I Can Read, You Can Teach Someone to Read, and Teach Anyone to Read, the No-Nonsense Guide. These three books had advice, lessons, skills, and strategies for reading. Ian rubbed his forehead. This was another surprising turn in his life in the last few days.

"Are you all right?" Kelsi asked.

"I'm okay," Ian replied. Overwhelmed wasn't the word he wanted to use for how he felt, but he wasn't sure what to say to Kelsi. Finally, he said, "It's just a surprise, some of these things," he admitted. "I doubt that I'll be any good teaching you to read."

"Sure you will!" Kelsi said stoutly. "Do I *have* to learn to read?"

Ian laughed ruefully before saying, "You have to learn to read if you want to be successful as a human."

"Brenna talked about going to school. Do you think she could help?" Kelsi asked.

Ian turned to Kelsi with surprise and broke into a smile. "That's a very good idea! She would probably love it. We'll probably get home too late tonight, so let's ask her tomorrow."

"Okay, onward to Mom and Dad's," Ian said to Kelsi as he started the truck. He was relieved to have an idea that might help Kelsi and him.

KELSI

It had been an incredible day thus far, Kelsi thought as she sat in Ian's truck. She had found the grocery store a remarkable place. The bright lights, the movement of people, and the numerous items for sale stunned Kelsi. She was amazed by the array before her – the large, bright signs, the fruits and vegetables that were arranged artfully, and towers of boxes and jars of various food. How humans found, prepared, and ate their food fascinated her. As a seal, it was all about survival. Finding food and shelter was paramount each day. Watching for predators was constant. The grocery store was quite different from her skimming along the ocean's bottom and snatching fish and shellfish. Their shellfish, or most of it, was out of the shell! She ruminated that humans didn't have sharp teeth to break the shells. Getting their food seemed much easier to her. It was interesting.

And reading! Those marks in the books made absolutely no sense to Kelsi. She wondered if they ever would make sense, but she trusted Ian and Brenna. If anyone could help, they could, she thought.

As they headed to Ian's parent's house, Kelsi thought of her seal family. Her mum, her sisters, and her aunt. She didn't know which bull was her dad. The biggest and strongest bulls were the ones who dominated mating. Kelsi had a small brother, but he was killed in a seal hunt. Two-leggers, no, humans, she corrected herself, evil humans, who clubbed baby seals to death for their pelts and the males for their penises. It was horrible, but it happened each year. Kelsi wondered what Ian's family was like. She wondered how human families were different from seal families.

She remained quiet and thoughtful during the ride until Ian asked, "Are you nervous about meeting my family?"

"Yes, yes I am," she replied, taking a deep breath. She held it for a few moments before releasing it and letting it go with a long sigh.

Ian reached over and patted her leg. "Don't worry. They'll love you!"

Ian's truck slowed as they left the highway and drove into a development. There were lovely, two-story homes nestled among tall trees. Ian pulled into the driveway of a two-story, blue-sided house with a crisp, white, wraparound porch. There was a statue of a lighthouse in the corner of the yard with stones piled to look like a rocky shore. There were a couple of cars in the driveway. Ian pulled in behind a little red car.

Ian helped Kelsi out of the truck. She held the bouquet tightly; her hands were clammy. She looked up at Ian. He gave her a swift, one-armed, very tight hug and kissed her.

"Come on," he urged.

They walked into the house into a small foyer, and Ian called out, "Hello."

"In here," Kelsi heard a voice respond. "We're in the kitchen."

"Of course," Ian told Kelsi quietly, but he was smiling.

Kelsi looked around as Ian led her down a hallway. They walked past the staircase in the foyer. The colors in the house mirrored the outside as it was a medley of blues and whites. It was peaceful and lovely, Kelsi realized. The rooms on either side of the hall looked comfortable. The kitchen was at the end of the hallway, emanating a warm light and murmured sounds.

"Hey, Bro!" Kelsi heard a cheerful voice say as Ian entered the kitchen. A kitchen towel flew across the room. Kelsi was slightly behind Ian, and the towel sailed over Ian's head, heading for Kelsi's face. She couldn't catch it as one hand held the flowers, and the other tightly clutched Ian's hand. Ian grabbed the towel with his other hand and managed to knock it to the ground before it hit Kelsi's face.

"Whoa!" Ian said. "Meg, what are you doing?"

The woman's face went from a mischievous grin to horror when she saw Ian had someone with him, and the towel was about to land on Kelsi.

Kelsi watched as the woman with shoulder-length, very dark brown, wavy hair and bright blue eyes dropped her mouth open.

"Oh, oh! I'm so sorry!" Meg said. She looked up at Ian, guilt on her face.

A woman with her back turned to them and craned her neck around. This must be Ian's mother, Kelsi thought. She had snappy, red hair and lots of freckles, like Ian. Her eyes were a brilliant blue like the brown-haired woman's.

"What's going on, kids?" she said before she turned. "Oh!" she said in surprise when she saw Kelsi. "Who's this?" she asked.

"Mom, this is Kelsi," Ian introduced, "a friend of mine."

His mother's eyebrows raised ever so slightly.

"Kelsi, this is my mom, Beth Dunaway, and you have met my sister, Meg," he ended acerbically.

"Hi," Kelsi said faintly. She remembered the flowers in her hands and held them out to Beth. "Here, these are for you."

"Thank you so much, Kelsi. These are beautiful! I love flowers!" Beth replied. She took the flowers from Kelsi and turned to Meg. "Meg, be a doll and get a vase for me?"

Meg went to a closet and opened the door. Kelsi could see there were white wire shelves filled with boxes and cans of food. On the top shelf were large dishes, large pots and pans, and a couple of clear glass vases. Meg took one of these down and took it to her mother.

"Kelsi, why don't you have a seat," Beth directed. "Ian, take Kelsi's coat and hang it up."

"I promise I won't throw anything else at you or bite you," Meg said and motioned for Kelsi to sit on a tall stool next to where she was sitting.

A seal would bite, Kelsi thought grimly as she sat a little uncomfortably on the tall stool. Ian had taken her coat and left the room, heading back down the hallway toward the foyer. He was out of sight.

"Sorry again for that weird introduction," Meg apologized before she said with a grin, "I love to harass my baby brother."

"Baby brother?" Kelsi asked.

"Yes, Ian is the baby of the family. I'm just a couple of years older," Meg told Kelsi.

"So, Kelsi," Beth asked, "do you live nearby?"

Ian entered the kitchen as his mother asked the question. "Kelsi has moved in with me. She just came down from Canada," Ian explained, using the same story he and Kelsi had used.

"Oh?" Meg asked. "What part of Canada?"

"Northern," Kelsi answered. "I lived on a remote island."

"North of Newfoundland and Labrador," Ian interrupted.

"Wow!" Meg said. "That is remote. What did you do there?"

"I didn't really have a job," Kelsi admitted. "I lived there with my family, sisters, and mother. I mostly interacted with the seals."

"That's really cool!" Meg said enthusiastically. "I see them occasionally from the boat. I fish with Dad and Pops. I joined the family scallop trawling business while this one," and she gestured to Ian, "went off to do his own thing with wood."

"And we're having some of your work tonight, Meg," Beth said and turned to explain to Kelsi. "When the weather turns colder, we like to have a family night of eating scallop chowder and cornbread and watching an old movie."

"Mmm," Kelsi replied. "Scallops are one of my favorite foods."

"Then you're in the right place," Beth told her.

"Where are Dad and Pops?" Ian asked.

"They went out to get some beer and wine," his mother told him. "They should be back any moment."

As she ended her comment, the door from the garage opened. A tall man with dark hair like Meg's and eyes like Ian's came in with a case of beer and a large paper bag on top. He was followed by a man just a couple of inches shorter, more rotund, with the same dark brown eyes, snowy white hair, and a beard. The tall man set the load down heavily on the kitchen island. He nodded to Ian and looked inquiringly at Kelsi.

"Dad," Meg told him, "this is Kelsi, a friend of Ian's. A very good friend, I think," she said with a twinkle in her eye.

Ian shot her a look, and Kelsi blushed profusely.

Ian's dad held out his hand. "I'm John Dunaway," he introduced, shaking her hand firmly, "and this is Ian's grandfather, Ron Dunaway."

Ron Dunaway didn't look friendly, and he didn't offer his hand. He gave a sharp look to Kelsi and nodded. Ron Dunaway glanced at Kelsi, then at Ian, and back to Kelsi. After he had nodded to Kelsi, his gaze returned to Ian. He shook his head. His glare made Kelsi uncomfortable.

She had proffered her hand but pulled it back under his sharp, intense gaze.

Beth broke the sudden, awkward moment of silence. "Boys, why don't you get drinks and the movie set up? We'll work on dinner," she ordered.

John put some of the beer in the refrigerator and took a cold bottle out for himself, his dad, and Ian. He handed another cold beer to Meg. The men went into the other room.

"Kelsi, what would you like to drink?" Meg asked.

"Water would be great, thank you," Kelsi said.

"Meg, be a dear and open the wine, please," Beth asked her daughter. "My hands are a mess."

Meg was using scissors to cut bacon into small chunks. The savory, salty smell rose from the pot.

"Mmmm, bacon," Kelsi said. "It smells wonderful."

Beth gave a little chuckle. "Yes, it's one of the main ingredients in this chowder," she told Kelsi. "Next, we'll chop some onions and peel potatoes. You two can help me with that. Meg, can you get out paring knives and a cutting board?"

"You'll need to show me how," Kelsi said shyly.

"You never chopped onions or peeled potatoes?" Meg asked, surprised.

"We primarily ate fish and shellfish," Kelsi told her truthfully, "There weren't any grocery stores where I lived."

"Wow!" Meg exclaimed. "Weird."

"What's weird?" Ian asked as he came in for additional beers for the guys.

"Kelsi said there weren't grocery stores where she lived," Meg informed him.

Ian nodded and put his hand on Kelsi's back. "That's what I understand. We went to the grocery store this morning, and Kelsi was astounded."

"I'm going to show her how to peel potatoes and chop onions," Meg said.

"I'm almost ready for the onions," Beth said.

"Okay, okay," Meg complained, "keep your hair on."

"What?" Kelsi asked, wondering what she meant by the hair comment.

"It's just an expression," Ian whispered in Kelsi's ear.

Kelsi still looked a little confused. Meg put a tall, cold glass of ice water in front of her, along with a knife and a cutting board. She showed Kelsi how to peel the onion, cut it in half, and mince it into small rectangles. Kelsi practiced but soon teared up from the onion fumes.

"Breathe through your mouth," Beth told her. "Meg!" her mother admonished. "How could you forget to say that?"

Meg looked guilty. "Sorry."

Beth had been scooping out the small, browned bits of bacon. She poured most of the hot, sizzling bacon fat into a can with a spoon inside of it. Then Beth came to gather the bits of onion and put them in the large pot. She also pulled out a large skillet and put it on the stove. She went to the refrigerator and took out butter and a large bowl of scallops. Kelsi picked up on their scent, and her mouth watered. She watched as Beth melted the butter and browned the scallops.

Beth next went to the pantry to pull out small bottles. When she opened them, Kelsi could smell clams. Clam juice! Who knew? Her mouth watered again, and she watched Beth pour the bottles of clam juice into the large pot and some white wine.

"There," she said, "we'll let everything simmer a few minutes until the potatoes cook through, and then add the scallops and the cream, and we're done."

Beth refilled her wine glass. There was a moment or two of silence, and Kelsi wondered what Beth and Meg were thinking.

"You have a lovely house," Kelsi said. "It's so big!"

"Thank you, Kelsi. It's comfortable," Beth replied.

"You have a lighthouse on your lawn," Kelsi queried, "but no water nearby. Why?"

Beth and Meg laughed a little at this.

"Wow," Meg commented, "you *really* must have lived remotely!"

Kelsi turned to look at her and answered earnestly, "I did."

Beth answered Kelsi's question thoughtfully. "I put a lighthouse on the lawn as a symbol for my family to always find their way home."

"Oh! That's a really nice thought," Kelsi replied.

"Thank you. I think so, too." Kelsi's comment clearly touched Beth and she became a little emotional. She turned to hide her emotions and said, "I think the potatoes are done. Meg, let the boys know dinner will be in about five minutes."

Meg left the kitchen and went into the other room to deliver the message. Kelsi could hear her laugh. She reminded Kelsi of a dolphin, always wanting to play and have fun.

"Can I help you with anything?" Kelsi offered.

"Yes, you can get the bowls and plates from the cupboard. We'll need six each," Beth told Kelsi, motioning to the appropriate cabinet with her hand. "Spoons are in the drawer in the island where you're sitting."

Kelsi opened the cabinet door and pulled out plates and bowls. She found the drawer with the spoons. Meg returned with Ian in tow. Beth put the scallops in the liquid mixture on the stove and added cream and some of the bacon bits. She stirred everything together. A heavenly, rich smell emanated from the large pot. When everything was stirred, she ladled the chowder into bowls and topped the chowder with the crispy bits of bacon.

"I'll take a bowl to Pops," Meg offered. "He's setting up the DVD player."

Ian picked up a bowl and motioned for Kelsi to do so as well. "Follow me," he told her.

Ian led her to a wood-paneled room with a fireplace, a comfortable couch, a love seat, and an upholstered rocking chair. The television was mounted above the fireplace. A coffee table with cornbread, butter, and jam was on a tray. Extra napkins were alongside. Ian sat on the loveseat and patted the seat beside him. Kelsi joined him. Meg sat cross-legged on the floor, resting her back against the couch. The movie was queued up and ready to play. Beth and John sat on the sofa, and John cut and passed the cornbread to everyone.

Beth sighed. "This is nice," she said as she settled in. "We haven't done this for a long, long time."

"Yeah, not since last November, Mom," Meg reminded her.

"You're right," Beth agreed.

Pops started the movie. The music swelled in the room. Kelsi savored a spoonful of chowder. It was delicious and flavorful. She closed her eyes and almost moaned. When she opened them, Ian was looking at her with amusement.

"Good?" he asked.

She nodded. "Fantastic. I've never had anything like it. I would love to learn how to make this."

"Did you hear that, Mom?" Ian said. "Kelsi has fallen in love with your chowder. Can you teach her how to make it?"

"Of course!" Beth answered, tearing her eyes away from the screen for a moment. "Here's Cary Grant." She sighed.

"*To Catch a Thief* is one of Mom's favorite movies," Ian said sotto voce to Kelsi.

They ate their chowder and watched the movie in near silence. Kelsi was entertained but also a little confused by some of the characters' social interactions on the screen. The people in the movie weren't wearing the same kind of clothes as the people she saw at the mall and the grocery store. It was interesting. She really liked the scallop chowder and the contrast between the smooth chowder and the sweetness and texture of the cornbread. Midway through the movie, Ian got up to refill everyone's bowls. When the movie ended, Pops stood up to go.

"Excellent meal, Beth," he said in a gruff but loving voice. He briefly put his hand on Meg's head, and she smiled at him.

"See you Monday, Pops," she told him.

Pops nodded in Ian and Kelsi's direction. "Ian, walk to my car with me," Pops requested.

"Sure, Pops," Ian said, taking his bowl and Kelsi's to the kitchen.

"So, what do you do, Kelsi?" John asked, making conversation. "Do you have a job here?"

Kelsi looked surprised by the question and floundered for a minute, trying to think of an appropriate answer. If only Ian were in the room with her! She was beginning to realize that humans had jobs that they worked so they could buy things at the mall and the grocery store. She didn't completely understand it but had the gist of it.

"I don't have a job," Kelsi told them. "I need to learn to read English first." She was a little embarrassed by this and looked down at her long fingers that she was twisting together on her lap.

"Oh?" Beth asked, "What is your primary language?"

"Gaelic," Kelsi answered, "Scottish Gaelic."

"Oh! It's a shame Pops just left!" Meg cried. "His mother, my great-grandmother, spoke Gaelic! He knows a few phrases, but I don't think he remembers much."

"How interesting," said Beth, "and how are you planning on learning to read English?"

"Ian picked up some books at the library today," Kelsi informed them. "There's a class nearby, and some television shows might help."

"Oh," Beth and Meg said simultaneously.

"That sounds like a good plan," John answered.

Kelsi wondered where Ian was. "Could I use your bathroom, please?" she asked.

"Certainly," Beth replied, "There's a powder room at the end of the kitchen."

Kelsi excused herself and went in search of the powder room. Ian's family was friendly, and she liked them a lot, although she wondered why his grandfather didn't like her.

When she approached the bathroom, she heard voices.

"What do you think you're getting into, boy?" Pops hissed at Ian.

"Pops, I don't know what you're talking about," Ian said, sounding confused.

"You're letting your Johnson play in the wrong places," his grandfather said sternly.

"But, Pops!"

"You're only going to get yourself into trouble, son. I don't want to see your heart get broken."

Kelsi heard his grandfather turn and mutter goodbye. Ian came inside from the garage, so Kelsi scooted quietly into the bathroom. She wondered what Ian's grandfather didn't like about her. He couldn't know that she was a Selki, could he?

21

IAN

After Pops saw his way out of the house, Ian stood at the door, dumbfounded. Pops rarely had an opinion on girls he had brought home. He usually teased him about being a young buck and needing to sow his oats. Still, this time, he lectured Ian about keeping his Johnson in his pants and not getting his heart broken. Ian was confused. He wondered if Pops was starting to get a bit of dementia. Perhaps he thought Kelsi was Jessica, not remembering that he had broken up with Jessica months ago. But Jessica and Kelsi didn't look anything alike. Jessica was the epitome of what people coined a "Jersey girl" with big hair, lots of makeup, killer nails, and high heels. Kelsi, Ian paused to think a minute. Kelsi was just Kelsi. She was absolutely beautiful to him. He knew he was smitten, but he couldn't help it. He definitely didn't understand the reaction to Kelsi from Pops.

When the powder room door opened, Kelsi appeared, and Ian smiled. Boy, was he glad to see her! He grinned at her. She smiled back a little wanly.

"Are you okay?" he asked.

"I'll be fine," she answered, snuggling up to him.

Ian put his arms around Kelsi. She felt so good in his arms and smelled so good to him. Perhaps Kelsi was right. Perhaps scent had something to do with attraction. He held her more tightly, and she clung to him as well. Meg came into the kitchen.

"Hey, you two!" she interrupted. "Do you two want to head to St. Barts? I hear they have a band tonight. I think it's a Celtic band and maybe some karaoke," Meg added hopefully.

Ian shrugged. "I'm game." He turned to Kelsi. "You? Are you up to going to an American bar, Kelsi?"

"I guess so," she answered slowly, not knowing what they were talking about.

"Uh, oh," Meg said, "You better watch out for my little brother. He's going to corrupt you."

Kelsi grinned up at Ian. "You would do that for me? Corrupt me?" she asked him, a sly twinkle in her eye.

"You bet, baby," Ian answered, kissing her with a promise to be fulfilled later.

"Now, now," Meg admonished teasingly. "Not in front of the children. Let's wash up for Mom, and then we can go," she suggested. "Ian, I'll wash, and you can load the dishwasher. Kelsi, can you get the rest of the dirty dishes?"

Kelsi nodded and went into the family room to retrieve the bowls, plates, and cutlery.

While Kelsi was in the family room, Meg turned to Ian. "Quick," she hissed, "where did you meet her?"

"By the sea," Ian told Meg.

Her eyes popped at her brother's poetic description.

"Well, don't throw this one back. I like her!"

"I have absolutely no intention of doing that," Ian assured Meg.

"Good," she said, swatting her brother with the kitchen towel as Kelsi returned with the plates and bowls.

It only took a few minutes to clean up, and then they said their good-byes to his parents.

"It was delightful to meet you," Beth said, quickly hugging Kelsi. "I hope you won't be a stranger."

"I'll second that," John told Kelsi.

Ian grinned at his parents.

"Stop it!" Meg teased her brother. "You look stupid!"

"Be careful," his parents chorused in their usual goodbye advice.

Kelsi and Ian climbed into the truck. Meg climbed into her little red sports car. Ian liked to tease her that it was "arrest me red," which wasn't so far from the truth. Meg was a little heavy-footed on the gas pedal and was pretty good at sweet-talking the cops out of many tickets. They drove back to Brigantine. Ian pulled into the strip mall near the grocery store. St. Barts was a well-known local bar and restaurant. They featured good food and entertainment. Tonight, there was a Celtic band. Ian could hear the strains of an Irish tin whistle, and the beat of the Bodhran. Kelsi cocked her head at the music. They found a seat in the corner of the restaurant that gave them a good view of the band, far enough away to save some of their hearing.

"What do you like to drink?" Meg almost shouted at Kelsi.

Kelsi shrugged. "I don't know."

"You mean you've never had an alcoholic drink before?" Meg asked.

"They weren't available on the island. Sometimes, I would find bottles washed up along the shoreline, but they were empty."

"Hmm, Ian, what kind of drink do you think Kelsi would like? Maybe something sweet?"

"I would think she would prefer something salty," Ian replied.

"A dirty martini or a Bloody Mary?" Meg mused.

"A Bloody Caesar has clam juice in it," Ian told Meg and Kelsi.

"That sounds good," Kelsi said.

When the waitress came, Meg greeted, "Hi, Colleen. Lively night tonight."

Colleen gave a little frown and nodded. "Good music, though," Colleen said, nodding at the band.

Ian and Meg ordered a Black and Tan. When it was Kelsi's turn, the waitress asked for identification.

"She doesn't have any," Ian told the waitress. "Her luggage was lost when she came from Canada."

The waitress frowned. "I don't know. I could get into serious trouble."

"Come on, Colleen," Meg asked coaxingly. "Kelsi is definitely over twenty-one."

"Well, only since I know you and Ian," Colleen grumbled. "What'll you have?" she asked Kelsi.

"A...a Bloody Caesar with extra clam juice," Kelsi told her.

"And some extra olives," Meg requested.

Colleen nodded and went to get their drinks.

"You'll love olives, Kelsi. They're really salty," Meg told her excitedly.

The band started playing again. They belted out "Whiskey in the Jar." Meg was tapping her foot in time with the music. They followed with "The Rising of the Moon."

Colleen brought the drinks, and Ian and Meg watched Kelsi as she tried the Bloody Caesar. She delightedly nodded and started drinking quickly, taking long sips through the straw.

"Easy there," Ian told her. "This has alcohol in it. You can't drink it so fast."

Kelsi stopped taking the long draught through the straw and looked at Ian and Meg. She gave a little giggle.

"Oh, boy," Meg said. "We may have turned her into a monster."

"No, no," Kelsi insisted, starting to get a little tipsy. Breách is the monster."

"Who's Breách?" Meg asked.

"Never mind," Kelsi told her. "Another time."

The band had started another song, "The Rocky Road to Dublin."

Kelsi was tapping her feet and clapping along, enjoying the beat. Her head swayed, and her hair swung.

The band took a short break, and things quieted to a dull roar in the bar.

"I would love another round," Meg told Ian, "but I think we should get some munchies. Nachos, maybe?"

Ian nodded, and Meg looked around for Colleen. They put in their order when she made her way to their table.

"What brought you to New Jersey, Kelsi?" Meg asked.

Kelsi blushed at this. Ian had opened his mouth to explain, but Kelsi replied, "I was being forced to be with a man I didn't want to be with. I just couldn't stand it. I left. Somehow, I made it here, and then I met Ian."

Her story was simple, but it shocked both Ian and Meg. Ian had not heard this before, and his eyes were wide with surprise.

"That's barbaric!" Meg said. "You poor thing!" She put her hand over Kelsi's. "Don't worry, Ian will take care of you, won't you, Ian?" she said rhetorically with almost a threat in her eyes. "If he doesn't, I will." Meg became very fierce about causes.

The band came back onto the small stage. The leader spoke into the microphone, "We're going to start off a little slower here, folks. This is a story song. It's about a Selki. You may ask what a Selki is. In this story, the Selki is a seal in the sea and a man on the land. He cannot stay for more than one night. This story comes from Heather Dale, a fabulous storyteller and musician.

Ian and Kelsi looked at each other and drew closer together. The story song told of a Selki man in love with a fisherman's daughter. He would give his life to become her husband, even if he were to die the next day.

Ian gripped Kelsi's hand tightly as the band leader sang of the Selki's love for the fisherman's daughter. Afterward, they moved into another slower, beautiful song, "Will you go, Lassie, Go."

Kelsi started to hum along with this song. She was halfway through her second drink, and Ian could see that her inhibitions were down. Kelsi quickly picked up the lyrics, and her voice was clear and pure and rang true. She closed her eyes and inadvertently sang louder with the music. Heads started to turn in her direction at the sound of her voice.

Ian and Meg were astounded. Ian shrugged at Meg's questioning look and held up his hands.

"Sounds like we have a competitor in here," the band leader said when the song was finished. He motioned for Kelsi to come up. She became shy and shook her head, but the bar was full of semi-drunken patrons. They started clapping and stomping their feet for Kelsi to go up on stage. Someone plucked at her sleeve, and Kelsi looked at Ian pleadingly.

"Go on if you want to," Ian assured her.

She looked at him pleadingly, but the sea of hands pulled her along up to the stage.

Standing beside the tall, thin, angular band leader, Kelsi looked very small.

"What's your name?" he asked.

"Kelsi, Kelsi Muir," she told him in a whisper.

But Kelsi was near a microphone, and her whisper came out low and sultry. Some of the bar patrons clapped.

"So, you like to sing, Kelsi?" he asked.

She nodded.

"Any favorite songs?" the band leader asked again.

Kelsi shook her head. "No, I mostly make up my own," she told him.

"Hmm..." the band leader hesitated. Finally, he said, "Would you sing one of your songs for us?"

"I...I guess so," Kelsi stammered.

In her beautiful, clear voice, Kelsi began to sing quietly. The band leader held the microphone for her. She closed her eyes and sang of the wind and the sea, of waves crashing on the shore. Her voice went high, and her voice went low, clear, and bell-like. Everyone was silent, listening to each word, mesmerized by her voice.

When she stopped, thunderous applause broke out. When the band leader quieted everyone down, he told Kelsi, "If you ever want a job singing with a band, come see me." He smiled warmly at her.

Kelsi stumbled back to her seat. Whispers about her voice followed her like quiet waves on the shore.

"We're going to step it up again," the band leader said, and they launched into "Steppin' out Mary" and "Marie's Wedding."

"You are amazing, Kelsi!" Meg took her hand and pulled her back to her seat. "If you ever want a job, you could sing professionally!"

"I don't think so," Kelsi protested.

They settled in, listening to the band. Fortunately, the bar patrons turned their attention to the band, Kelsi, forgotten for the moment.

All of a sudden, Ian wanted Kelsi all to himself.

He whispered in her ear, "Are you ready to go home?"

Something in his voice sent Kelsi electrical jolts. She looked at Ian and saw the glint of desire in his eyes.

Kelsi nodded. "I would like that."

"Meg," Ian shouted over the music, "we're going to head home."

Meg looked up at them and nodded. "Me too, I think," she agreed.

Ian got the check, and they gave Colleen the payment for the food and drink, plus a hefty tip.

Colleen leaned toward Kelsi and said, "Look, honey, if you ever want to get your own gig singing here, just let me know. I think I could work it."

Kelsi smiled and shook her head.

"Think about it," Colleen insisted.

Kelsi shook her head again. They left the crowded bar and went out into the crisp November night.

"That was fun," Kelsi told Meg and hugged her impulsively.

"We'll do it again soon," Meg assured her.

Meg embraced her brother. "Talk soon," she said, giving him a knowing look.

"Okay," Ian agreed.

Ian's only desire at the moment was to take Kelsi home and get her into bed as soon as possible. He helped her into the truck and drove swiftly to his home, only a few miles away. Kelsi leaned on him. She was yawning. He didn't want her to go to sleep. He ran his hand up and down and up and down her leg. Waking up slightly and feeling frisky, she stroked him while he drove. He groaned as he swelled against the fly of his jeans. Pulling into the driveway, Ian jumped out of his truck.

The scene was nearly cinematic when the pair tumbled into the house —the main characters tearing at each other's clothes. Now, it was happening to him! What this woman did to him. Kelsi tugged at his hand to pull him up the stairs. Her sweater was off, and her bra loosed. Her breasts bounced beautifully to Ian. He wanted to grab them.

This time, Kelsi pushed Ian onto the bed. She climbed on top of him, swaying her hips back and forth and in a figure eight like a belly dancer in a dance above his penis. Kelsi leaned over to kiss Ian, and he groaned at the sensation of almost being inside of her. She lifted her hips teasingly out of reach of his penis as she arched her back. He took her breasts in his hands. This time, she groaned in pleasure. Finally, little by little, Kelsi permitted Ian to go a little deeper and a little deeper. Finally, when he was fully inside of her, she stopped and sat. Kelsi closed her eyes. Ian felt himself swell inside of Kelsi. He wanted to move inside of her, but he watched her face.

Ian ran his hands slowly up and down her body, playing with her nipples. Kelsi leaned back and started to hum a low, lovely tune that changed into a ribbon of a song. It was magical. Ian was as mesmerized as the patrons were earlier in the bar. Then Kelsi started to move on top of him; her inhibitions gone. She moved slowly at first, teasing Ian excruciatingly. Her nipples became hard as small pebbles, her back arched, and she started to ride Ian hard as wave after wave of orgasm overtook her. She finally let out a small scream and collapsed on top of him.

Ian held her, stroking her hair. "Are you all right?" he asked.

Kelsi opened her eyes, luminous in the light, and from her passion, "Oh, yes, Ian," she panted, "I am quite fine." She snuggled onto his chest, and Ian continued to hold her.

"That's good. That's very, very good," Ian answered in a sultry tone.

He gathered Kelsi in his arms and held her tightly, feeling as though the whole world was his oyster and that he was the luckiest man alive.

2 2

KELSI

Kelsi couldn't help herself. She was wide awake now. It had been an incredible evening with Ian's family and her experience at St. Barts. She had never sung outside of the herd, usually alone or with her family. The crowd's applause and the band leader's kind words were an unexpected but pleasant surprise.

And then there was Ian. The look in his eyes reached to her very core. There was something primal about mating with Ian. They stood inside the door, tearing off each other's clothes. Half undressed, Kelsi took Ian's hand and led him up the stairs. She climbed on top of him, teasing him with her body. Finally, Kelsi lowered herself onto Ian's shaft, bit by bit, driving them both crazy. Kelsi began to move her hips in a figure eight as belly dancers do but kept herself anchored on his shaft. The squeezing and releasing of her muscles as she danced on top of him started to wrack her body with tremors of orgasm after orgasm. Ian stroked her body and her breasts, the nerves so alive that she cried out in pleasure that was almost pain. Ian watched, pleasuring her as he could but enjoying the dance and pleasuring herself. Kelsi was like a volcano with tremors of orgasm building until she erupted and screamed in its force until she collapsed on top of Ian. She could not move but clung to him, heaving with the effort to catch her breath.

Ian stroked her hair. "Are you all right?" he asked her.

All right? All right? Kelsi felt like screaming the words to him. Every tiny nerve in her body sang to the point she could not move. Kelsi felt luminous, lit from inside, and light pouring from every pore in her body. She raised her head and looked deeply into Ian's eyes. She wished he could feel what she was feeling. She hoped he could glean some of it from her body.

"Oh, yes, Ian," Kelsi panted. She could barely speak. "I'm just fine."

Kelsi curled up with Ian and fell into a deep sleep.

Kelsi woke up just after midnight. She could barely move; her limbs felt like brittle sea stars that might break if she moved. Slowly, slowly, slowly, she moved her one foot, sliding her leg that was looped over Ian. Carefully, she pulled herself from Ian and felt her body creaking when she slid from the bed and stood up.

Kelsi stretched and stretched her limbs. It was a time she wished she could swim. She didn't want to lie in the little pool of the bathtub. Kelsi wanted to stretch and twirl and swim in the deep water of the sea. She glanced at the box tucked under the bed and considered getting her pelt and putting it on. She glanced out the window. It was also low tide, and the Thorofare was a muddy track of water. Getting to the Atlantic wouldn't be any fun and would take forever. Kelsi sighed. The little pool in the bathtub would have to do.

Kelsi filled the tub and added the bubble bath she and Ian had picked up at the grocery store. The bubbles welled up as she filled the tub. Kelsi turned off the water when the tub was full and lowered her sore body into the hot water with a hiss. She soaked until her aches and pains were minimal, climbed out of the tub, and this time, dried off, for Ian's sake, before crawling back into bed. Kelsi was exhausted. She snuggled up to Ian and fell into a deep, dreamless sleep.

Hours later, something woke Kelsi. It was the sound of the shower and Ian whistling while he cleaned up. She stayed in bed, pulling the covers up to her chin. Kelsi continued to doze until Ian came out and softly kissed her forehead.

"Good morning, sleepyhead," he said.

He crawled into bed beside her.

"I have no energy today," Kelsi told him. "I don't know why."

Ian chuckled before he answered, "I think it's because you used so much energy yesterday. Let's just take it easy this morning."

Kelsi was relieved Ian didn't have the glint of desire in his eyes this morning. She was exhausted. He put his arm around her, and she molded to him. They lay quietly for quite a long while. Kelsi continued to doze off and on. A cloudy sky sent filtered light through the window when she fully awoke. It looked like it was going to storm. Kelsi was glad she was inside.

"Welcome back to the world," Ian greeted Kelsi. He kissed her on top of her head. "What if we just stay in and hang out today?" Ian said. "I have to go back to work tomorrow. I should show you a few things."

"It's turning colder," Kelsi commented.

"Yeah," Ian confirmed. "Winter's coming. It's the wind that's so biting here. It sweeps across the island." Turning to Kelsi, he asked, "How do you keep warm in the winter as a seal?"

"We head to warmer waters, like here," Kelsi told Ian. "We have our pelts and our blubber. We find a sheltered area to hunker down. We keep together to get extra body warmth. Sometimes, it's very, very cold. We survive, or most of us do."

"I know we get some seals here during winter," Ian said. "If a seal is hurt or sick, we have the Marine Mammal Stranding Center in town. They take care of sea life up and down the New Jersey coast. We're lucky to have them so close." After a moment of peaceful silence, Ian added, "Let's get up. If it's not too cold, we can take a walk."

They dressed. Ian gave Kelsi a bulky sweatshirt to wear. He helped her roll up the sleeves. Like Ian's T-shirts, the sweatshirt draped to mid-thigh. It was toasty warm and cozy.

"We need to get you some sneakers on my next payday," Ian commented. "Let's eat some breakfast before we head out."

Ian popped a couple of breakfast sandwiches in the microwave. After the microwave beeped, he handed one to Kelsi.

"Hot!" she cried, burning her fingers as she picked it up and dropped it quickly back on the plate.

Ian took her hand, blew on her burnt fingers, and then kissed each one. After the sandwiches cooled for a minute, they ate.

Because Kelsi was still tired, rather than walking half a mile to the beach, Ian drove the truck. He stopped at a small store with a twinkle in his eye.

"I'm just going to pop in here for another cup of coffee and a little surprise," Ian told her. "Stay here a minute."

Ian emerged from the convenience store carrying two hot cups and smiling. Kelsi opened the truck door for him.

"I think you'll like this," Ian told Kelsi in a somewhat singsong voice.

"It's not more coffee, is it?" Kelsi asked, wrinkling her nose.

"No, coffee for me and hot chocolate for you," Ian told her.

"Hot chocolate?" Kelsi asked. "What's that?"

"Here," Ian said, and he handed her the cup. "Be careful. It's hot."

Kelsi took the cup carefully. The creamy, chocolatey sweetness reached her nose long before Kelsi had a sip. She breathed in the heavenly fragrance. It was quite different from the bitter scent of Ian's coffee.

"Sip it," Ian advised.

Kelsi took a sip gingerly. Her eyes grew wide with delight. "This is yummy!" she told Ian.

He smiled. "I thought we would like to drink something hot since it's chilly out." Ian put the truck into gear and headed toward Ocean Avenue.

Something was calling Kelsi as she approached the sea. Kelsi thought, in fact, that it was the tide. She could feel the pull and ebb of the tide, in and out, in and out, in her blood and in her tissues. The ocean, to Kelsi, was like a huge, breathing being, wildly alive. From the tiniest micro-organisms to the largest whale, the ocean sang with life and joy. Oh! It was good to be back!

He parked at the pub, which was closed now. The parking lot had only a couple of cars. Kelsi couldn't wait for Ian to open the door. She sprang out of the truck, hot chocolate in hand. Kelsi stood, poised with excitement, and breathed deeply as she gazed out at the smoky, gray Atlantic Ocean with the lacy edging of the breakers coming into shore. Ian came round the truck. They headed North on the beach toward the wildlife area. Ian kept his head down, sipping his coffee as they headed into the wind. Kelsi kept looking out at the ocean. She could feel the tide in her body. It pulled, and it tugged at her. Automatically, she scanned the water for predators. She didn't have to worry about sharks while on land. Kelsi felt as though somebody had spoken to her. At first, she thought it was the ocean singing to her blood. But suddenly, Kelsi saw some heads bobbing in the water. They were seals! She stopped and stared. Ian hadn't realized she had stopped. As she called him, her voice was lost in the wind. Kelsi looked at his back as he disappeared down the beach. She looked at the seals. There were two, no three, seal heads bobbing in the distance. Did she know them? She couldn't tell. She walked closer to the water and squinted hard. Did she know these seals? There was something about them that was familiar. Kelsi put her hand up to her eyes. They *did* look familiar. She walked closer to the water. Suddenly, a breaker broke over her boots. Kelsi jumped back in surprise as the cold water soaked into her boots.

"Kelsi! Kelsi!" she heard Ian's voice call to her. She turned, and he was running toward her.

"Everything okay?" Ian asked, anxiety clearly in his voice.

"My boots! I'm so sorry, Ian!" Kelsi started to cry.

Ian took her in his arms. "It's okay, Kelsi. It will be all right," he said soothingly.

He looked into her eyes. Her eyes had a wild glint that he hadn't seen before. "What had happened?"

Kelsi pointed with a shaky finger. "Seals. There are seals out there," she stammered. "I think I know them."

Ian looked out at the Atlantic Ocean. He didn't see anything.

"Kelsi, there's nothing there," Ian told her.

Kelsi looked out over the waves. The seals were indeed gone. This caused her to cry harder.

"Oh, Kelsi!" Ian said, holding her tight.

He gently led her away from the water and back to the truck. Ian tucked Kelsi in and pulled the seatbelt around for her. By the time he got to his seat, she was shivering.

Ian turned on the truck and put the heat on high. Kelsi wasn't sobbing, but she was quiet.

"Let's get you home and warm up," Ian said tenderly.

Kelsi craned her neck to look at the Atlantic when he said *home*. She could see that he was worried about her actions, but she couldn't explain her feelings.

They were both quiet on the ride home.

As soon as they entered the house, Ian sat Kelsi on the couch and pulled off her boots and socks. He told her to go up and take a hot bath or shower to warm up. Kelsi went up the stairs.

Kelsi filled the tub with hot water and took another bubble bath. She sank into the water until only her nose, eyes, and forehead peeked out of the bubbles. Seeing the seals in the water made her wonder if her decision to become human was correct. She knew the seals in the ocean were familiar. Something told her it was her mum and her sisters, but she couldn't be sure. In such a short time, life as a human had taken away most of her communicative sense as a seal. She wasn't able to talk with them when she was a human. As much as she loved and desired Ian, Kelsi missed her family. Kelsi sat in the water until it had cooled. Before returning downstairs, she dried off and wore a pair of sweatpants and Ian's long sweatshirt.

Two glasses on the coffee table held a deep, dark red liquid. Ian had just cooked a fresh pizza he had purchased yesterday and was taking it out of the oven when Kelsi came down the stairs.

"I need to let the pizza rest for a couple of minutes before I cut it," Ian told her. "Let's sit for a minute and talk."

He handed her a glass of wine. "I hope you like this. It's a blend, but it's delicious and fruity. Even though I'm a beer drinker, it's one of my favorites," Ian went on about the wine.

Ian seemed nervous to Kelsi. She picked up the wine glass. He held it up to her and touched his to hers. She didn't understand. But she let him clink her glass lightly, and they both sipped before he went to cut the pizza. This wine *was* good! Kelsi took a sip and then a long drink. It tasted like the fruit juices Ian had introduced her to at breakfast, but it had a kick to it, like the drink she had the night before. She drained the glass. Ian came back with the pizza, and his eyes widened.

"Glad you liked it, Kelsi," he said, "but you usually sip it."

Kelsi blushed at her mistake. Ian put the plates on the table and went to the kitchen to get the wine bottle. He filled her glass again. Ian picked up his pizza and blew on it before he took a bite. Kelsi still wasn't saying anything. Ian chewed on his pizza and eyed Kelsi, slowly taking small bites and chewing carefully. She sipped at her wine and, still rather quickly, drained the second glass.

Her thoughts were a mass of confusion. She nibbled a bit on the pizza. Ian filled the glass a third time.

"Kelsi?" Ian asked tentatively.

Kelsi couldn't answer Ian's query at first. Her thoughts jumbled, her head feeling the impact of the wine. She looked up at Ian and then looked down at her plate again. Ian noticed that Kelsi's eyes were filled with worry and confusion.

"Ian," Kelsi cried, "I think that was my family out there!" She gestured wildly to the East. "But I'm not sure! I couldn't communicate with them because I'm human!" Kelsi stopped and began to sob. "I don't know what to do!" she said, anguish in her voice.

Ian took Kelsi in his arms. "It will be all right," he assured her.

Kelsi, all of a sudden, pushed back. "How can you say that?"

Ian looked downcast. "I don't know," he admitted. "I really don't know. It's what I hope for you and for us. Do you want to go back? Do you want to go back to the sea?"

Kelsi didn't answer. Ian continued, "Your pelt is under the bed. Help yourself."

Kelsi shuddered. "I couldn't go now. I couldn't go at night. The sharks are there. They love to sneak up on you!"

"What do you want to do, Kelsi?" Ian asked quietly.

"I want to be with you, but I'm worried something is wrong," Kelsi said.

"Do you think they were just looking for you to ensure you were all right?" Ian asked.

"Maybe," she said slowly. "That has to be it. I just wish I had a way of talking with them."

"Let me think about it," Ian said. "We'll figure something out."

Kelsi wasn't sure. She was worried. The faces of her seal family filled her vision each time she closed her eyes: Mama, Maura, and Rhona, their dear faces, bright, black eyes, and long whiskers, stared at her from beneath her eyelids. They looked at her questioningly in her imagination about why she was with a human. Surely, they could see and feel her happiness. She hoped so. Kelsi hugged herself tightly in her grief and homesickness.

23

IAN

Ian was worried about Kelsi. He knew she was exhausted from the last few days, but there was a different, almost wild air about her. On their quiet drive to the beach, she was nearly perched at the edge of her seat, straining at the confines of the seatbelt. She practically jumped out of the truck when they pulled into the deserted parking lot at the pub. He had strayed north of her as they walked along the beach. He had been lost in his own thoughts when the wind blew against his back, making it nearly impossible to hear Kelsi call for him. He felt guilty when he turned and saw her crying and in distress. He couldn't spy any seals out in the water, but clearly, seeing the seals had upset Kelsi. He hoped the bath would help calm her fears.

He busied himself about the kitchen, and a kernel of fear and apprehension settled in his stomach. Ian tried to push it off, but he couldn't help but wonder if Kelsi would be leaving him this night and return to the sea.

Kelsi came down from the bath, looking dejected. It was evident that it was difficult for Kelsi to choose between Ian and her family. She drained the wine Ian had given her. Not one, but two, and then three glasses. The kernel of fear of Kelsi possibly leaving him grew in Ian's stomach. He looked and looked at her, not having words to say.

They both nibbled at the pizza, absorbed in their individual thoughts.

He kept glancing at her, watching her wallow in misery. She had pulled her legs to her and hugged them with her arms. She looked like she was far away and even a little frightened. Ian didn't know how to break her out of this trance-like behavior. It was almost as if she was in shock.

"Kelsi," he began, not knowing really what to say to her "Kelsi, what can I do to help?"

Her deep, black eyes that looked back at him were dull and edged with unformed tears.

"Nothing," she said in a strained whisper and paused before saying with finality, "Nothing."

Kelsi stood up and wobbled on her feet. "I think I want to go to bed," she told Ian.

"Sit down for another minute. Let me clean up, and I'll go to bed with you," Ian suggested.

Kelsi sat in a daze on the couch while Ian put away food and washed the dishes. When Ian returned to the living room, he pulled her to her feet, and she wobbled again. He helped her carefully up the stairs. Ian helped her dress in her night clothes, being careful in his touch. Kelsi slumped into bed, and Ian carefully pulled the sheets and covers to her chin.

"Are you coming to bed soon?" she asked quietly but plaintively.

"In a minute," Ian soothed.

Ian tucked Kelsi into bed and went back downstairs. The kernel of fear of Kelsi potentially leaving was blossoming into a case of bad heartburn. He was worried.

He rummaged in the cupboard for some antacids to chew. He sat on the couch and looked out at the watery Thorofare. The black, sparkling water didn't give him any answers. Suddenly, he closed his eyes, not wanting to see the water. It reminded him that Kelsi could be there and that she could go away.

When Ian went back upstairs, Kelsi was sleeping soundly. He gazed at her, with her hair splayed out over the pillows and the curves of her body underneath the sheets. His heart ached heavily with unanswered questions. What was that saying: If you love something, let it go, and if it returns, it is yours forever? Did he believe that?

He undressed and lay on the bed, not touching Kelsi this time. He folded his hands behind his head and stared up at the ceiling. Ian couldn't think. Eventually, he fell into a restless sleep.

2 4

KELSI

Kelsi was morose. Feeling the ocean's pull and seeing the seals bobbing in the swells profoundly affected her. She wasn't used to these human emotions. She had emotions as a seal, but they were trumped most of the time by the need to survive. Being a Selki, human emotions were bound to slip in on occasion. Now that she had been in human form for more than a few hours, the human emotions were pushed to the surface. The emotions welled inside Kelsi in a morass of complicated thoughts and feelings. Part of Kelsi wished for the simple emotions and needs of survival when she was a seal. She loved Ian. She loved her seal family. Kelsi was anxious about being a human and coping in the world of written language.

Kelsi curled up in a ball on the bed after Ian pulled the covers around her. She lay in the dark, her thoughts flitting hither and yon. Should she find a way to meet with the seals? Ian was supportive, but this, too, was complicated. Kelsi understood now that she was in the human world and that she could not come and go between seal and Selki self easily. She didn't know what to do.

Kelsi tossed and turned, pulling the sheets and blankets with her. Finally, she fell into a restless, dream-filled sleep.

Kelsi dreamed of swimming through the ocean, large strands of seaweed caressing her as she scooted along the bottom. She dreamed of bobbing on the surface, watching the sky, and lying in the sun, stretched long and curved in a banana shape.

Later, Kelsi dreamed of Ian. She dreamed of his laughter and the sparkle in his eyes. Kelsi dreamed of him touching her in every place on her human body. She moaned and grew wet, dreaming of making love with him.

The discordant sound of Ian's cell phone alarm jolted Kelsi from her dreams. Ian quickly turned off the alarm and got out of bed, yawning. He went into the bathroom while Kelsi lay in a dazed, sleepy state.

It wasn't long before Ian returned and dressed quickly and quietly. He gave Kelsi a dismissive kiss on the hair and left. She was puzzled and a little bothered that Ian was not touching her as usual. He must have thought that she was sleeping.

Kelsi lounged in bed, listening to the morning sounds. It struck her that she was alone in Ian's house – in a human's house- for the first time. It was an odd and interesting feeling. She got up and smoothed the sheets and covers, remembering how Ian had straightened the bed in the last few days. She went downstairs.

The neighborhood was quiet. Kelsi looked out of every window. One woman was walking a small dog. Kelsi drew back, not wanting the woman to see her; she only wanted to observe. A few streets over, she heard cars rumbling. She went to the kitchen to get some water.

Kelsi took the water and stared out the living room window at the Thorofare. It was low tide, and the water was shallow and muddy. Birds wheeled in the sky, and seagulls screeched. Another sound startled her from next door. The sound of metal moving. She ran to the window and peered out. Donna had opened the garage door and backed her car into the driveway. Brenna came racing down the steps with a backpack and a lunchbox. Once Donna had closed the garage door, they backed out of the driveway and went down the road.

The quiet settled around Kelsi. It was like being alone on an island, she thought, or when she was swimming alone at sea. She wasn't frightened or uncomfortable, just thoughtful. Ian had given her instructions on how to turn on the television. She followed his instructions to watch the programs he wanted her to watch. They were clearly for children. The colors on the screen were bright. There was a lot of movement and a lot of artwork. She focused on the words, trying to say them as Ian did. Kelsi watched until she was hungry, tired, and bored.

She went out to the kitchen to explore the refrigerator. She wasn't sure she wanted to work the stove, not yet. Not until Ian had coached her a little more. In the refrigerator was the leftover pizza. She pulled it out and found that it was amazingly good cold. As she ate, she wished for some of Beth's scallop chowder. It had been so delicious.

Kelsi looked around the kitchen. Beth's kitchen had been tidier than Ian's. She liked the bright, clean countertops and organized cupboards in Beth's kitchen. Ian's kitchen wasn't exactly dirty, but it could use some organizing and cleaning. Kelsi set about to pull everything from the cupboards. She used the soap by the sink and some water to clean inside the cupboards and put everything back neatly. With the food, she used the pictures on the cans and bottles to put things together that were alike or very similar. It felt good to look at the kitchen when she was done. She liked it much better this way.

With that task completed, Kelsi went back to the television. There was a cartoon on. The little animal gamboled across the screen didn't make sense to Kelsi. She switched channels. There were a lot of talking people that didn't make much sense. She found a channel that had some sparkling things on it – jewelry. It fascinated Kelsi, but after a few minutes, she became bored with the hawking of the television hosts. She turned off the television. She was getting hungry again and went back to the kitchen.

It took her a couple of tries, but Kelsi was able to use the can opener and open the can of tuna that Ian had purchased for her. Kelsi didn't remember the ingredients he had added, so instead, she picked out the tuna from the can with her fingers. She drank every drop of juice. Satiated, she contemplated what to do next. The tide was coming in. She wondered if she could sneak out, get into her pelt, and go for a swim. Kelsi went to the large picture window that looked out over the Thorofare. Another house was on the opposite side, where Brenna and Donna lived. This house had a large dog that was on the deck. He looked fierce. Kelsi couldn't go out as a seal with him on the deck. Disappointed, she went upstairs and pulled out the box with her sealskin.

Kelsi opened the box. There, her sealskin lay in all of its furry glory. Kelsi stroked it. It was a different experience to touch it as a human. It felt good. She imagined herself inside the skin. It definitely had its limitations compared to being a human. Kelsi closed the box and shoved it under the bed. She dressed, now thinking she could walk to the beach to see if the seals were there. It couldn't be too far. She and Ian had arrived in moments in the truck.

Kelsi got her blue coat from the front hallway closet and left. The sun was bright, the air was crisp, and the smell of the ocean was strong in the air. She became anxious to get to the beach as soon as possible. Kelsi turned the way Ian had turned his truck and used her senses to guide her to the sea. As she walked, it seemed much longer to the ocean than riding in the truck. After several blocks, she was beginning to get chilly. A few more blocks and she walked past the convenience store where Ian had purchased the hot chocolate for her. Her mouth watered for more, but she didn't have the plastic Ian used to get the hot chocolate. She didn't know how to use it either. She continued to walk. The smell of the sea was getting stronger. Kelsi quickened her pace.

A few more blocks. A few more steps, Kelsi chanted to herself. She walked across the wide street, not paying attention to the vehicles. She heard screeches and some horns and jumped. Someone was shouting at her. Kelsi didn't understand what they were saying. The sea breeze pulled the words away from her ears. Kelsi could see the wall that protected the sand and the ocean. Hurriedly, she walked up the steps and then stood, just looking at the breakers.

The tide was indeed high. It reached further toward the soft, deep sand bordering the dunes. Kelsi walked with difficulty, her feet and boots sinking into the sand. The boots had dried, but she didn't want to repeat yesterday's experience. She noted where the waves were and kept a distance from the breakers coming to the shore.

Kelsi scanned the ocean before her. She stood still, just looking. There was a dolphin playing just beyond the breakers in the open water. They loved to play. Kelsi knew that. She didn't see any seals. Kelsi knew if any were near the shore, they would likely be in the open area, away from houses. She walked north.

Kelsi strolled along the beach. It was much quieter today. The beach was devoid of humans, with only an occasional surf fisherman. The wind was gentle today and pushed Kelsi with soft, small gusts. It had rained during the night. Wispy clouds blew quickly across the sky, leaving a large swath of clear, cerulean blue. The wispy clouds foretold of a weather change. The crystal, clear, blue sky topped the Antwerp blue of the ocean. Gentle swells had replaced the angry waves of yesterday. The gentle breakers made their way to shore, glinting with green as they somersaulted to the beach. The waves showed an edge of lacy foam that caressed the sand. It was peaceful.

Kelsi began to realize how tired she was when she narrowly missed a tidal pool. She didn't want to ruin the boots again today. Kelsi needed to rest. She walked toward the dunes and sat on the thick, soft sand. Circling her knees with her arms and resting her head on her knees, Kelsi stared at the horizon where the sea and sky were one.

She daydreamed of the sea. Kelsi dreamed of swimming through the water and skimming along the bottom of the ocean. She dreamed of bobbing with only her head above water, watching the world.

Her mind switched, and Kelsi thought of Ian with his red, golden-brown curls and mottled brown eyes. His eyes! They were soulful and told her so much about his emotions. Kelsi thought of the light fur of red, golden-brown hair on his chest, legs, and arms. How many times had her hands danced along the top of these curls in the last few days? Kelsi thought of Ian's hands and how strong and sure they were. They were gentle, too. They touched her, and her body sang with pleasure. His lightest touch brought joy, comfort, and a sense of belonging. The last few days with Ian were like a blissful dream. Kelsi questioned whether she could continue as a human. She felt pulled between her two halves, her seal half and her human half. She wracked her brain for the stories from her gran and her mum of any Selkis who had chosen to stay on land – forever. Kelsi thought and thought. No story came to mind at first. Finally, Kelsi remembered the story of one seal woman who came to shore and stayed there. She chose to stay with her man – a fisherman, forever. Kelsi didn't remember how it turned out.

Kelsi shook herself out of her daydream. Time had passed quickly, or she thought so. In fact, she really didn't know how to tell time at all. She knew the sun had risen in the blue sky and started on its path to the west. It must be late afternoon. Kelsi knew it was time to walk home to Ian's house. She stood up and brushed the sand off the back of her coat and her legs.

With another long look out at the ocean, Kelsi sighed when she saw no seals and trudged down the beach, putting her head down in the wind.

2 5

IAN

*I*an was still worried about Kelsi's decision to stay or not when the alarm went off that morning. He had had a restless night, wondering, wondering, wondering if she would stay with him. He wasn't angry. He was just unsure and a little afraid that she would leave him. When the alarm went off, it was in near relief. He got out of bed as quietly as possible, showered, and dressed. He gave Kelsi a peck on the hair as a goodbye, not wanting to wake her.

Ian tiptoed downstairs, grabbed one of the bags of leftover pizza, and went off to work. Mike was waiting for him, acting like an old mother hen. Ian told him so. Mike gave him light tasks, and Ian went off to nail away at stud work. Easy work. Ian didn't care. He nailed the studs mindlessly. His hands knew how many nails for each stud. He wondered about Kelsi. He wondered what she was doing. He wondered if she was still at his house.

The day crawled. Ian worked through lunch so he could leave a little earlier than usual. Mike didn't squawk but gave him an odd look. Ian didn't care. He jumped in his truck at four in the afternoon and headed home. He just had a feeling.

When he got home, the front door was ajar. He went in, calling Kelsi's name. Silence was the only greeting. Ian went through the house, trying to quell the panic rising in his belly. Systematically, he looked in the backyard and in every room of the house, calling Kelsi's name. He pulled the box from under the bed with a courageous, deep breath. The pelt was still there. Ian breathed a brief sigh of relief. But where could Kelsi be?

He took the steps two at a time and went to Donna and Brenna's house next door. He pounded on the door. No answer. Ian looked up and down the street. Where could Kelsi have gone? He went out back and looked up and down the Thorofare. He didn't see anyone, and no one was on their pier in the neighborhood. He wondered if she had returned to the beach. Hell. That was it! She probably went to look for those seals. Ian jumped in his truck and drove to the beach, driving as slowly as possible through the streets, looking for Kelsi. He drove up and down, looking at the small, suburban homes that lined the inner streets of the island. The silent houses blinked at Ian in the late afternoon sunlight. No Kelsi.

He drove to the beach to the parking lot of the pub. Some cars were there. He didn't think she would be in the pub. She didn't have any money.

Ian started to walk up the beach. Automatically, he started to walk north on the beach. He didn't know why. The beach was deserted save for one surf fisherman and a few shorebirds. The air was definitely crisp, November air. It had a bite to it. He pulled his coat closer about him.

Where was she? His worry turned to anger. Ian clenched and unclenched his fists in frustration. He strained his eyes, looking up and down the beach. No Kelsi. He gazed out at the sea. Nothing. A lone tear leaked from the corner of his eye between the wind and his frustration. He wiped it away angrily.

Ian had just about given up that Kelsi was at the beach when he saw a slim figure off in the distance heading his way. He thought the person was wearing blue, but the sun's glare skewed his vision. He shouted Kelsi's name, but his words were torn away in the wind. Ian started to jog toward the figure.

"Kelsi?" he called out as he jogged. "Kelsi!"

The figure that was walking with its head down suddenly looked up. It was Kelsi. Ian caught up to her and took her in his arms. He was so angry with her yet so relieved to have found her. His heart and his brain were a muddle of emotions. After holding her for a few minutes, waiting for his heart to return to a natural rhythm, Ian took Kelsi by the arms and shook her.

"Kelsi! Why did you leave? Why did you leave without telling me? I was so scared!" Ian blurted to her.

Kelsi's eyes were wide in her pale face. She answered him, "Ian, how? I can't write your language yet, and I do not have a phone."

Ian heaved a sigh, thinking about what Kelsi said. "You're right," he admitted. "We'll have to figure out how to communicate when I'm at work."

Ian took Kelsi's hand. They walked back to his truck, not speaking. They drove home, not speaking. Ian knew Kelsi kept glancing at him, but he kept his eyes on the road.

"Ian?" Kelsi prodded. "Ian?"

He didn't speak until they got into the house. He got himself a beer and a glass of wine for Kelsi. He sat on the couch. Kelsi looked worried.

"I was terrified, Kelsi," Ian told her, "When I came home to find the door ajar and you not here."

"Ian, I just took a walk," Kelsi insisted. "That was all."

"But, last night, we talked about you heading back to the sea. I was worried you had changed your mind."

"I had, I have, a lot of thinking to do," Kelsi confessed to Ian. "I walked to the beach to look for the seals we saw yesterday. They were gone. I wish I could have talked to them. I think the pull of the sea and my sea life will always be a part of me. It has to be because I'm half seal! I know it's difficult for you to understand, but I've given up my life for you."

Ian looked at Kelsi thoughtfully. Slowly pondering on what she said, he nodded.

Kelsi continued. "I had to think more, Ian. As much as I feel the connection between us, I had to think about this life. It's hard for me! I don't know how to be human! I'm stumbling through to be with you. It's frightening and very confusing."

Ian nodded. He had a glimmer of understanding. It was frightening and confusing for him as well. He told Kelsi this.

"What are we going to do?" Kelsi asked him. "What should I do?"

"I think this is going to be an ongoing battle for you, Kelsi," Ian told her. "I'm as frustrated as you are in many ways."

"What are we going to do?" Kelsi repeated.

Ian took Kelsi's hand between his two before he suggested, "Relax and enjoy what we have."

"And you need to be my teacher, my teacher at how to be a human," Kelsi said, a suggestive glint in her eyes.

Catching her drift, Ian grinned but said, "I will be happy to continue with those lessons, Kelsi, but right now, I'm starving. I skipped lunch so that I could leave a little earlier. Let's see what we can cook up quickly for dinner."

Ian pulled Kelsi up and off the couch. They went out to the kitchen.

Ian stopped, "Hey," he said, "I didn't see it earlier, but it looks different in here. Cleaner and tidier. Did you do this?"

Kelsi was delighted that Ian noticed. "I really liked how your mom's kitchen looked," she told him, "So I worked at cleaning and re-arranging a little."

"It looks great, but you'll need to let me know where you put everything," Ian commented.

He opened the doors and drawers to see where Kelsi had put things. He was astonished at the order in the food cupboards.

"I thought you said you couldn't read," he said when he turned to Kelsi. "How did you do this?"

Kelsi looked at Ian and then looked in the cupboard. She was puzzled by his comment.

"No, I can't read," Kelsi reminded him, "but I can look at and match pictures." She was a trifle insulted.

"Fair enough," Ian said.

Ian took a jar of spaghetti sauce from the shelf and a box of pasta.

"Here, this is pretty easy to cook. I'll teach you how to make pasta and sauce," Ian told Kelsi.

He made a pasta dinner, showing her how to boil the water, put the pasta in the water, set the timer, drain the hot pasta, and pour the sauce on top. He loaded two bowls with the pasta and topped them with shredded parmesan cheese.

"This smells good," Kelsi told Ian. "I think I could do this, but the hot water is a little scary."

Ian nodded as he carried his bowl to the table. "You will need to be careful with that. I showed you on the box how long it takes to cook this pasta. They're all different."

"So, I need to learn to read," she said matter-of-factly.

He nodded. They ate their dinner and watched the dregs of the sunset through the window. An egret was wading in the water at the edge of Ian's property. Geese flew in a "V" shaped formation over the Thorofare, landing across from Ian's house. Kelsi's senses were alert to the birds. If she were in seal form, her whiskers would have twitched. She sat very, very, very still. Ian followed her gaze. He smiled when he saw the egret.

"Beautiful, aren't they?" he commented.

Kelsi's eyes were unfocused. "Yes, yes, they are," she agreed.

Curiosity overcame Ian, and he asked, "Did you ever eat anything like that?"

"Like that egret? No! It's much too big," Kelsi answered. "I didn't often eat birds. I don't like their feathers. In desperation, I might have to eat one," she told him, remembering the duck she had consumed the other day. Still, Kelsi continued, "Sometimes, they like to eat us, though."

"What?" Ian was shocked. "How can that be?"

Kelsi nodded quite seriously. "Baby seals. Sometimes, the gulls will attack a baby seal's afterbirth. I've been told that the gulls eat the baby seals' eyes far away from here, so they are defenseless. It's horrible."

Ian stared at Kelsi open-mouthed, but Kelsi continued talking easily as though she was talking about the weather.

"Could you help me with some of those books you borrowed from the library?" Kelsi asked Ian as she finished eating her pasta.

"Sure," Ian agreed. "Sure thing." He shook his head in amazement at their conversation.

"Let me clean up tonight," Kelsi suggested, "and you can relax."

Ian took his plate to the counter and pulled another beer from the refrigerator. He sat in the living room, staring at the Thorofare while Kelsi busied herself cleaning up the kitchen.

His emotions were ragged, and he felt as though his emotions had been tumbled like a mess of clothes in the dryer – all jumbled and tangled together. What had he gotten himself into with Kelsi? The realization that she gave up her seal life and chose to be with him astonished him. He thought about what she had given up to be with him. He thought about his fear and worry when he thought Kelsi was gone and the incredible relief of finding her pelt in its box under the bed.

This relationship wasn't easy. Ian felt he was a friend, lover, and parent all at the same time. All of this was wrapped up in discovering Kelsi and her astounding life as a seal. Ian felt he was caught up in a strange sort of fantasy film. He had gone from being a regular guy, doing his day-to-day thing, to living and loving a creature that, until now in his world, had only existed in books. His perspective had skewed off its norm, and he felt a little lost.

The evening had turned to velvety darkness over the Thorofare. The light was still on in the kitchen, and Kelsi sang very low in her beautiful alto voice. He shivered. Her voice was mesmerizing. Was it Selkis who lured fishermen and not the sirens of the sea? He would need to ask her.

Was he lost? Or had he found his port and anchor with Kelsi? He looked up to see her coming into the living room, her smile just for him.

He was beginning to think the latter.

2 6

KELSI

After cleaning up from dinner, Kelsi went to where Ian was settled on the couch in the living room.

"Did you watch any of the children's literacy shows on PBS?" Ian asked. When Kelsi nodded, he added, "Did you like them?"

She shrugged. "They were all right," Kelsi answered. "I didn't understand some of the ones that you called cartoons. Also, I didn't really find instructive stuff on the other channels."

"I'm not surprised at that," Ian said ruefully. "Give me a minute to read through the instructions here," he told Kelsi.

Kelsi sat with her hands folded, waiting as Ian read and nodded.

"Okay," he said, "we need to start with the absolute basics."

Ian went to the other bedroom and came downstairs with a stack of three-by-five-inch cards and a marker. He took a minute and wrote letters and some words. He went to the kitchen drawer to get some tape. He taped words around the kitchen and the living room, such as *lamp*, *table*, *sink*, and *refrigerator*. Soon, the house was festooned with labeled cards. He came back and sat on the couch. He told Kelsi about the alphabet and how it made up the written word. He recited the alphabet and showed her the cards he had written. He had her say them over and over again. Then he led her around the kitchen and living room and read the cards that went with each object. Ian showed Kelsi how the letters helped make up the words. He had her repeat them after he said them. He had Kelsi state what the things were on her own. Lastly, he took some paper and printed her name clearly in large letters. Ian handed Kelsi the pencil and told her to trace over his writing. She did so with a shaky hand. Then he had her write her name, Kelsi Muir, repeatedly.

"Does your name have a meaning?" Ian asked as Kelsi traced her name.

Kelsi paused with her writing. "Yes," she answered. "Kelsi is a version of the word Selki, without the 'e,'" she added. "Muir means 'of the sea.'"

Realization dawned on Ian. "Cool," he commented, "very cool. While I'm at work tomorrow, you'll need to read all these labels and practice writing your name."

Kelsi rolled her eyes at Ian.

"Hey! No eye rolls at the teacher," he admonished but gave Kelsi a quick kiss to soften the harsh tone in his voice. "And I think you've had enough for one evening. Let's go up to bed," he suggested.

They walked upstairs and got ready for bed. Ian spooned into Kelsi and took one of her breasts in his hand, massaging it gently.

"Is it worth it?" she asked him in a small voice.

"What?" he answered.

"Me! Am I worth all this trouble?" Kelsi asked vehemently. "For Sedna's sake! You are taking a lot of time to teach me how to be human!"

"Kelsi, Kelsi," Ian whispered, kissing her neck. "You're not too much trouble. We just need to do this one step at a time."

Ian gave a wicked laugh before he said, "Like this. First one breast massage and now the other."

He moved his hand to her other breast, massaged it, and played with her nipple. Kelsi couldn't do anything but react. She gasped involuntarily. Pleasure raced through her body.

"Oh, Ian!" Kelsi breathed in a soft rebuke. She knew he wanted to mate again. She could feel him grow hard. His rock-hard penis now poked at her bottom. Kelsi turned slightly and angled her body. Ian entered her, and she gave into the pleasure that he provided. This position reminded her of how seals mated. She quickly chased that thought out of her mind. She would tell him later.

"There is nothing, nothing more wonderful than mating with you," Kelsi said, sighing when they were finished.

"I'm glad you think so," Ian told her. "I feel the same way."

Their now liquid limbs were entwined. Ian kissed her shoulder, and he snuggled into her, holding her tightly. Kelsi lay quietly, listening as Ian's breath slowed to the relaxed rhythm of sleep. His arm, so tightly around her, relaxed a modicum. He reminded Kelsi of a river otter she met, lost on the ocean. It had a shell clutched tightly to its chest. Kelsi felt like that shell clutched tightly in Ian's arms. She also curled herself up like a shell and went to sleep.

TRUE TO HER WORD, when Ian left for work, Kelsi sat in front of the television to watch some of the children's educational shows. Ian had turned on the close captioning, so Kelsi tried to match the speech with the words. After an hour and a half, she was bored. She practiced writing her name, looking at the cards, and naming everything. The morning passed for Kelsi. She was feeling a little bored. Kelsi looked around. Yesterday, she straightened the kitchen. Today, she thought, she would tackle the dining and living rooms. Ian had pointed out the cleaning products under the kitchen sink, so she went to get cloths and polish, window cleaner, and paper towels. She worked content to see things getting into their places.

The doorbell rang.

Kelsi stopped, standing quite still. It took her a moment, but she remembered the sound from the other night when Donna and Brenna had stopped by. Maybe they were at the door. After a few moments of silence, there were a series of knocks at the door.

Kelsi put down her cleaning materials and went to the door. She opened it carefully to see who was there. It was Beth, Ian's mother! Startled, Kelsi opened the door further.

"Hello, Kelsi!" Beth greeted. "May I come in?"

Kelsi nodded and opened the door wider to let Beth enter the foyer.

"Of course!" Kelsi answered.

Beth came in. Her cheeks were pink under the freckles from the chilly weather, and her red hair pulled back in a ponytail, had a few wisps floating about her face from the breeze teasing them loose. Beth settled comfortably on the living room couch, taking off her coat and folding it over the couch's arm. She had a colorful canvas tote bag in one arm and put it beside her on the floor. Beth looked around, noticing how things were tidy and clean. She saw the cleaning products on the coffee table. She smiled approvingly. Kelsi sat at the other end of the couch and looked at Beth quizzically.

"I didn't have your phone number, so I thought I would just drop by," Beth began.

"Oh, I don't have a phone," Kelsi interrupted.

"Oh," Beth replied, "well, it's good I dropped by then. Have you been cleaning?"

"Just tidying up," Kelsi said. "I liked how your house was so organized and neat. I thought Ian's house should be the same."

Beth almost blushed. "Thank you, Kelsi. That's a lovely compliment, but compliments go to you for taking on Ian's house." She paused, "This house is sort of a behemoth."

Kelsi looked at her questioningly again.

"A behemoth, a monster of a house," Beth said. "Ian took on a lot of repairs when he bought it. His father and I were not sure it was a good idea."

"A be-behemoth?" Kelsi asked, "Sort of, like, umm, a kraken?"

"Well, I'm not sure what a Kraken is, but it sounds about right," Beth answered.

"A Kraken is a giant squid – a monster," Kelsi explained.

"I'm not sure my words are coming out correctly. Ian purchased this house, and it needs many, many repairs. It's a good location, I'll give you that. Not too many folks could get waterfront at the price that he did. After Superstorm Sandy, Brigantine was literally underwater. He must put in a bulkhead, which will cost a fortune!"

Beth shook her head as though she still couldn't believe that Ian had purchased the house. Kelsi took in the information, only understanding part of what Beth was saying. She nodded in agreement, hoping it was the appropriate human gesture. It seemed to be as Beth continued on.

"And the color!" Beth continued. "The turquoise is so dated. Ian's going to need to update that as well."

"The turquoise?" Kelsi asked, "I like it! It's the color of the southern seas."

"You're so poetic," Beth remarked, "and you are correct. It's very beachy."

Beth looked around at the little cards posted on every object and the adult literacy books on the coffee table.

"It looks like you're beginning your studies of learning to read," she commented.

"Yes," answered Kelsi. "We're going to work on it every night until the classes begin again in Atlantic City."

"Well, that's why I'm here," Beth told Kelsi brightly. She picked up the colorful canvas bag. "I tend to save some things," she confessed. "I hope to have grandchildren someday. I've been saving some of Ian's books from when he was a little boy. I thought they might help."

Beth pulled some books and a small box from the colorful tote bag.

"These were some of Ian's favorite books as a child," Beth told Kelsi, "And they're beginning readers, so they will help you learn the words. This," and she held up a copy of Dr. Seuss's *One Fish, Two Fish*, "is just silly, but you can learn words easily with the rhymes. Ian loved *Are You, My Mother*."

"Oh! And I found these," Beth said, giving the small box to Kelsi. "This is a card game to help you learn words."

Kelsi looked at the books. "Thank you."

There was a bit of awkward silence.

Finally, Beth asked, "Would you like to go to lunch?"

"Sure," Kelsi answered. "That would be nice."

"Well, get your coat, and we'll do that."

Kelsi went to get her coat. When she returned to Beth, she asked, "How will Ian know where we are? He was really, really upset yesterday when I took a walk to the beach. He came home and couldn't find me."

"Oh!" Beth replied, a little surprised. "We can leave him a note, I guess." She looked around for some paper, wrote the note, and put it on the kitchen counter. "All right, I think we're ready now. Do you have a key?"

Kelsi shook her head.

"Oh!" Beth replied, surprised again. "I actually have one. We can use mine."

She and Kelsi exited the house, and Beth locked the door.

"Why do you lock the door?" Kelsi asked her.

"To ensure no one goes inside," Beth commented, "You *must* have lived very primitively."

"Oh, I did," Kelsi replied.

Beth opened up the car doors. Kelsi got in and watched Beth pull the seat belt around her. Ian handed the seatbelt to her when she rode with him, so it was new for Kelsi to pull the seatbelt around herself. She did so and locked it into place.

"Should we go to Pirate's Swoop?" Beth asked Kelsi.

Kelsi nodded. "Ian took me there for breakfast. It was good."

Beth nodded and backed out of the driveway. She followed the same road Kelsi had walked to the beach the day before. It only took a few minutes to get to the restaurant.

Pirate's Swoop had only a few diners, as it was long after the lunch rush. The waitress seated them, handed them menus, took their drink orders, and walked away. Beth studied the menu.

"Everything is so good here," she commented as she read the menu. "It's so hard to choose."

Kelsi looked uncomfortable. She couldn't read any of the words on the menu, and Beth had not looked up. Kelsi squirmed a little uncomfortably in her seat. The waitress brought their drinks: water for Kelsi and hot tea for Beth. The waitress stood, waiting to take their order. Beth looked up. It was then that she realized that Kelsi could not have read the menu.

"Oh!" Beth exclaimed, and then she turned to the waitress. "We'll need a couple more minutes."

The waitress went away.

"I'm sorry, Kelsi. I forgot you couldn't read," Beth told her. "What have you and Ian done in the past?"

"Ian ordered for me," Kelsi told her.

"Tosh, you can order what you want," Beth said. It sounded as though she didn't like Ian ordering for Kelsi. "Let me read you some of the choices. I know you liked my scallop chowder. Their clam chowder is excellent here. What do you want, a sandwich, salad? A hamburger or seafood?"

"The clam chowder sounds good," Kelsi told her. "And I love fish."

"What about the fish and chips?" Beth suggested. "Have you had that before?" she asked.

Kelsi shook her head. She hadn't.

Beth explained, "It's cod. The fish is batter-dipped and fried. It comes with French fries."

"I love cod," Kelsi told her. "It's one of my favorite fishes."

"Done," Beth said triumphantly. She motioned for the waitress to come over.

"Two cups of clam chowder and two orders of fish and chips," she told the waitress.

The waitress left, and Kelsi and Beth sat. It was too quiet. Kelsi wasn't sure what to say, so she sipped at her water rather quickly. Beth sipped her tea and glanced out the window at the concrete wall protecting the beach and ocean.

"So, Kelsi, I was pretty busy cooking the other night when you and Ian came over. I can't remember asking you about your family," Beth commented.

"It's my mother and my sisters," Kelsi said. "We live on a remote island in Northern Canada."

"What do you do there?" Beth asked.

Kelsi looked at Beth with an odd look, "Live," she told Beth.

Beth glanced sharply at Kelsi's remark.

"I didn't mean to be rude," Kelsi said, a little worried that she may have offended Beth. "We lived on the island." She gave a little sardonic laugh and commented, "It was cold in the winter and warm in the summer. Nothing like the civilization here!" She considered the luxury of a real house with running water and central heat.

"What about your father?" Beth asked.

"I've never known my father," Kelsi answered truthfully.

Beth pressed, "But other than observing seals, what did you do?"

"We survived," Kelsi said. "Every day was a new day to get food and to be safe. We had a lot of fun, too. We loved to sing with each other, swam in the ocean, and we danced on the beach," she finished a little wistfully.

"It sounds idyllic," Beth said.

"In many ways, yes," Kelsi answered truthfully. "It was very peaceful. It wasn't quiet, though. The ocean is loud, and the seals are loud, too! They sing, growl, and bark. They're a noisy bunch."

"Well, that would be their way of talking to one another, right?" Beth questioned.

Kelsi nodded, eyes wide, wondering how Beth might know this. "Absolutely!"

The waitress brought them their cups of creamy chowder. Kelsi tasted it.

"This is good," she said to Beth, "but it's not as good as yours."

"Thank you, Kelsi. I promised you I would teach you how to make it, and I will," Beth replied.

They finished their chowder just as the waitress brought steaming baskets with the fish and the French fries. Kelsi watched as Beth picked up a French fry and then the fish. The fish was still piping hot, and Beth dropped it back into the basket that it was served in. She blew on her fingers.

"Careful," she warned, "it's very hot!"

Kelsi nibbled at the French fries. They were good. She watched and copied Beth, putting some ketchup on the side and dipping her fries into it. Kelsi liked this, too. When the fish was slightly cooler, she took a bite of it through its crunchy coating. Kelsi found that she liked this—the way humans cooked food! It was absolutely delicious.

When she paused from eating, Kelsi asked, "What was Ian like as a pup?"

Kelsi put her hand to her mouth, realizing her mistake in her words. But Beth didn't notice Kelsi's faux pas.

Beth got a dreamy look on her face. She wiped her fingers and mouth as she chuckled before answering, "A pup! Yes, that describes him. He was like a rough-and-tumble puppy. He loved being outside and would roll in the grass as if he was swimming. Meg used to get so upset with him when she was in her prissy stage. She complained bitterly that he smelled of the outside. Now, look at the two of them. She's the one who is outside all the time, and Ian works indoors. Go figure."

Kelsi could see him in her mind's eye, a little, curly, red-headed boy who loved to play. "Oh," Beth said, remembering, "we couldn't keep Ian out of the water. He loved to swim. He won many trophies. He begged to go to the beach as often as possible. He even liked to play in the rain." Beth smiled fondly with her memories.

Beth broke away from her daydreams and asked Kelsi, "Did you live on the island all your life? What was your childhood like?"

Kelsi could answer these questions honestly. "Yes, I have spent my life on the island. As a child, I lived outdoors. I love to swim. I love the beach.

I still do." She didn't elaborate and inform Beth that she didn't live in a house. She couldn't talk to Beth about being a Selki. Not yet, at least.

They finished their lunches. Beth told Kelsi that Meg wanted her to go on the trawler for a day and take her on a spa day. Kelsi didn't know what that was and said so. Beth told her details of facials, hairstyles, manicures, and pedicures. Kelsi was interested. She had noticed the pretty-colored nails on some women and was intrigued.

Kelsi thanked Beth for lunch. They returned to Ian's house. He was just pulling into the driveway when they got home. He looked surprised to see his mom and Kelsi together in his Mom's car.

"What's all this?" he asked after giving his mom a hug and Kelsi a kiss.

"I brought Kelsi some books," Beth answered her son, "and I took her to lunch. Don't be surprised if Meg calls. She wants Kelsi to go on the trawler and have a girls' spa day."

Ian nodded.

"Ian, open the door for Kelsi and let her inside to keep warm. I need to get home to cook your father and Meg some dinner," she said. "Goodbye, Kelsi. We'll do this again soon."

"Thank you, Beth," Kelsi said. "For everything."

Beth hugged Kelsi before saying, "I'll see you soon."

Kelsi went inside after receiving a small kiss on the temple from Ian. She was thoughtful as she hung her coat up in the hall closet. Beth was such a surprise to her. She liked her very much and hoped the feelings were returned. Beth seemed to appreciate that Kelsi liked her clean and tidy home. She was also very supportive of Kelsi learning to read. Beth was so kind she thought she could tell her she was a Selki.

Kelsi smiled inadvertently as she imagined Ian as a young pup, swimming joyfully on land and water. Beth's descriptions and memories were delightful. She laughed aloud, thinking about him as a young boy, and hugged herself in happiness.

2 7

IAN

Once Kelsi was inside, Ian closed the door and turned back to his mom to open the car door for her.

"Ian, I really like Kelsi," his mother began, "but there's something about her..." her voice trailed off.

"Mom," he told her firmly, "she's the *one*."

His mother's eyes had a worried look. "Are you sure, son?"

"I'm sure. I am very, very sure."

"But..." Beth trailed off. She took a breath. "It's your life and your choice. I just want you to be happy."

"I am happy, Mom. Kelsi's the best thing that has ever happened to me. It sounds so corny with the phrases of 'it was meant to be,' or 'love at first sight,' but in this case, it seems to be true."

Beth's eyes softened. "I understand," she told Ian, "More than you think. That's why your dad and I have been together so long. There's something..." and she trailed off again.

"Yeah," Ian stated, "something. Ain't love grand!?"

Ian gave his mom an impulsive kiss on the cheek. He grinned and shut the door for her.

Rolling down the window, Beth added, "Kelsi needs a key to your house and a phone."

Ian nodded thoughtfully in agreement. "You're right," he said.

"Didn't you know, son? Mothers always are!" Beth laughed, shut the window with a grin, and backed out of the driveway, waving as she drove away.

Kelsi was in the living room looking at the books Beth had brought. When Ian entered, she stood up and threw her arms around his neck.

"I missed you terribly today," Kelsi told him.

Ian kissed her and told her, "Lucky me." He looked at the coffee table and asked, "What's this?"

"Books from when you were a little boy," Kelsi replied. "Your Mom thought they might help me learn to read."

Ian sat down and picked up the books one by one. "I loved these books," he said, leafing through them. "I think they'll help. Let's read them together, and I can point out the words."

Ian handled the little books lovingly. Kelsi sat beside him on the couch as he read and pointed to the words. He read through each book twice and then had Kelsi try to read some of the words. He was impressed that she was a fast learner.

Ian's phone rang. It was Meg. She talked a bit to Ian and then asked to speak with Kelsi.

"Do you want to go on the trawler with Pops, Dad, and me?" Meg asked.

"On a boat?" Kelsi asked. "Riding on top of the water?"

"Yes, Kelsi!" Meg laughed. "The boat will be riding on top of the water. I'll need to pick you up very, very early. Is Thursday all right? The weather will be fabulous, and I hope we'll have a good run."

They arranged for Meg to pick up Kelsi at three-thirty in the morning. Ian rolled his eyes at this but agreed. He had grown up with his scallop fishing family and was no stranger to their hours.

"We'll have to get you some warm clothes tomorrow night," he told Kelsi. "It gets mighty cold with the wind and the water."

"I know, Ian," Kelsi assured him, "I just don't know what it's like without my warm pelt."

"I don't think it would go over too well if you turn back into your seal self for the trip," Ian teased. "Can you see your seal self, sitting up in the car?"

Kelsi laughed at this. "It would be interesting, but I think I've turned much too human to even want to attempt something like that." She turned to Ian and put her hand on his belt. "I'm finding life as a human very, very interesting. Besides, as a seal, I couldn't do this."

Kelsi unzipped Ian's zipper and reached in to pull out his penis. She lowered her head and started licking and sucking. Ian lay back on the couch, groaning.

"Oh, Kelsi," he murmured over and over.

Her mouth was warm and wet over his penis. It was one of the closest things he could imagine to heaven on earth. His nerve endings were on high alert as her tongue curled around his hard shaft. He clutched at her hair, tangling his fingers in her curls. She licked him up and down, teasing him with her tongue. Ian moaned again, and she took all of him in her mouth quickly and deeply.

He couldn't help himself. He erupted with a cry, and Kelsi rode the wave of pleasure with him. When he could breathe again, he looked down at Kelsi. Her eyes were shining bright. He caressed her chin and touched her hair.

"Thank you," he said.

Kelsi smiled at him.

"Do seals do that?" he asked, curious.

Kelsi chuckled. "No," she told him. "Absolutely not. The bulls pretty much take the seals when they want to. There isn't really anything consensual about it. I really like having the choice to mate. I like being able to make you aroused and to make you happy."

"Oh, Kelsi, you do," Ian said with his voice tinged with wonderment. "I don't understand it, but it's very true."

Kelsi lay her head on Ian's lap. He brought her hand up to his lips and kissed it.

That night, they lay in bed together. Kelsi was curled up against Ian. He had one arm behind his head and one around Kelsi. He wondered what his mom was sensing about Kelsi being a little different. It worried him a bit. Maybe he could ask Meg or at least keep an eye on Meg's reactions to Kelsi. He thought again of his grandfather's unreasonable attitude toward Kelsi. It didn't make sense. He hoped Kelsi being on the trawler wouldn't be too much of a problem for Pops. Meg surely asked him if

Kelsi could go on the trawler. Lord! He hoped so! He knew Meg could be impulsive. He wondered if he should call his dad and ask him. It was too late now. He would call tomorrow night.

To fight his constant thoughts, Ian drew Kelsi in closer and went to sleep.

KELSI

Wednesday passed like Monday and Tuesday for Kelsi. She spent the bulk of the morning watching the children's television programs and practicing the alphabet and the words that labeled nearly everything in the house. She looked at the books Beth had left her and tried to sound out some words and guess at others. She had made some progress.

Kelsi moved on to another part of the house to tidy and clean. She enjoyed the work and liked watching how everything looked brighter as she straightened and polished. She took pride in her efforts. After lunch, though, she was ready to go for a walk. She had talked with Ian about this. Since her handwriting skills were negligible, they had devised a system. She had picked up some razor clams and a moon snail shell on the beach on Monday and put them in a small, cut-glass bowl on the coffee table. She told Ian if she made an arrow with the razor clams and the arrow pointed at the moon snail shell, it meant she was at the beach. They had made a deal that he would come to pick her up if she left that signal and discussed the roads she would take to and from the beach.

Kelsi left the signal and went to get her coat. She also pulled out one of Ian's baseball caps. It was a fine day but a little windy. She had discovered that combing her hair could be painful if tangled. She would have to ask Meg what to do about this tomorrow. Kelsi set off for the beach, enjoying the fresh air and sunshine. The salty smell of the ocean pulled her as well. Kelsi relaxed the closer she came to the ocean. As she always did, when she went over the dune and saw the waves crashing on the shore, her heart leaped inside her in excitement. She still had a love affair with the ocean.

Automatically, she scanned the water, looking for seals. Nothing. No seals were bobbing beyond the breakers. Kelsi sighed, a little disappointed. She remembered that she and her family and seal community would haul out together in a spot. They would enjoy the sunshine and the heat from the sun-warmed beaches and rocks. Their chatter focused on the fish they had found or the pleasures of stretching out in that sunny location. She missed their chatter.

Her sisters coyly asked which bull she would want to mate with and teased her unmercifully. They were looking forward to mating and having their first pups. In that way, Kelsi felt different from her seal family.

But it gave her pause. Would she want to have a pup with Ian? What would it be like to have a human child to care for? Beth was certainly interested in having a grandchild. Kelsi remembered the interactions she had seen between mother and child at the stores and restaurants. She smiled to think of Ian as a father. He would be a good one. She was sure of it. Just the thought of carrying his child sent a flutter to her belly.

Kelsi walked and walked, looking for the seals and picking up a stray shell or two. She was fascinated with the moon snail shells and the lovely whorls of the whelk shell skeletons. She found she was filling up additional bowls and baskets for her beach-found treasures at Ian's house.

Kelsi would sit for a while, soaking in the sun. Today, more surf fishermen were at the shore because it was a warmer, sunnier day. She carefully walked around their poles. Most of them seemed to be in a meditative state, mesmerized by the sea. On occasion, one would get excited and pull in a striper, sea bass, or a blue fish. Some of them spoke other languages that she didn't understand.

Kelsi kept an eye on the sun. She knew where the sun should be, and when the sun hit its mark, she headed toward the agreed spot to meet Ian.

Kelsi had a jaunty step and jogged toward Ian. A huge smile lit her face when she saw him, and when Ian. When he saw her, he broke into a grin and held out his arms. She ran right into them, loving the feel of his arms around her in a huge hug. Squeezing him tight, she looked up into his smiling eyes. He gave her a kiss. And then another, and Kelsi relished the tingles that coursed through her body from his kiss. The kiss promised mating later.

They walked hand in hand toward the truck. Ian told her he had gone out at lunch and made her a key. They drove to the store to pick up some additional clothes for Kelsi to wear on the boat.

"They'll certainly have a slicker for you to wear," Ian told her, "if the weather turns foul or there's too much spray. I thought we could pick up some sneakers for you and some boots. I also thought you might like to layer some clothes. The weather looks good for tomorrow, so you should be good with a long-sleeved T-shirt and maybe a flannel shirt."

They located some sneakers for Kelsi on clearance from the summer. Ian took her to the men's section for the T-shirt and flannel shirt. Kelsi fingered the cloth. It was very soft. Some of the shirts were softer than others. She liked the colorful plaids with dark and light blues accented with a thin strip of red or yellow in the design.

Ian took Kelsi through the store's grocery section and put a few more things in the cart. He pointed out the words on the boxes and cans. It was later in the evening, and only a few children were in the store with their parents. They seemed tired and fussy. Kelsi observed how different parents monitored their children. Some of the children screaming for things set her teeth on edge. If they had been seal pups, they would have been slapped with a flipper. Kelsi noticed, too, the people with small babies in carriers. She thought of having a pup with Ian again. Briefly, she imagined them shopping together with a baby along. Ian didn't notice her bemusement. Before leaving the store, Ian suggested picking up chicken fingers and fries from the deli.

"It's not the healthiest meal," he told her, "but it's fast, and we can eat it in the car on the way home. I skipped lunch to get the key, so I'm starving."

The bucket of chicken smelled good to Kelsi, but she could distinctly tell that it was from a bird. She wrinkled her nose.

"What?" Ian asked. "You don't like chicken?"

"I'm not fond of bird," Kelsi said, "too many feathers." She made a face.

"What?" Ian asked, trying not to laugh but not succeeding.

Kelsi scowled at his very apparent amusement as he guffawed in the truck.

Ian wiped the tears streaming from his eyes from laughing so hard before he said, "Don't worry, Kelsi, humans don't eat chicken with the feathers still on them. I think you'll like this. Try it."

Gingerly, Kelsi took a large piece of crispy, brown, breaded chicken from the box. She sniffed it.

"It still smells like a bird," she commented as she nibbled a bit of the coating. A surprised look came upon her face as she tasted the crispy, savory coating and the warm, moist chicken. "But it tastes good!" she finished, surprise in her voice.

"Good," Ian said, taking a bit of his chicken finger and smothering another grin. He looked out his window to hide his amusement and started the truck.

They feasted on the chicken and fries on the way home in what Ian called a car picnic.

Ian had Kelsi try out her new key. They took their bags into the house with the remains of their dinner. Ian told Kelsi to get all of her clothes together for the next day, reminding her how early she would be getting up.

"Maybe, I should bathe this evening?" Kelsi asked Ian.

"Good idea," he said. "I'll finish putting this stuff away and be up to bed soon."

Kelsi ran the warm water and added bubble bath. She climbed in and washed. The smooth slipperiness reminded her of lovemaking with Ian. She couldn't help it. She started to touch herself to give herself pleasure when Ian walked in carrying a glass of wine for her and a beer for him. He put them on the edge of the sink and began to undress.

"What are you doing?" Kelsi asked.

"Joining you," Ian told her, his erection springing from the confines of his underwear.

Kelsi scooted up in the bathtub, making room for Ian. He joined her, carefully stepping into the hot water of the tub and sinking down with her. Ian thanked the previous owners silently for putting in a garden tub that would hold two people.

Ian stroked Kelsi's breasts and tweaked gently at her nipples, gently twisting them, not hurting but giving her great pleasure. Kelsi arched her back.

"Can we do this in the pond?" she asked before correcting herself. "Umm, tub?"

"We're certainly going to try," Ian told her, his voice gravelly with desire.

Their lovemaking was quick in the tub. Their bodies, slippery from the soapy bubble bath, glided over one another. Kelsi would have to tell Ian later that, for the most part, seals mate in the water. She didn't think it was as enjoyable as this, though.

When they had finished, Ian helped her out of the tub and dried her off gently. Drowsy, Kelsi pulled him toward the bed. They would only have a few hours of sleep until Meg picked her up in the morning.

Sleepily, she told him they had mated the way most seals mate. Ian was surprised and said so.

Kelsi laughed drowsily, her closing eyes winning the race to sleep. "I'm sure it's not as much fun," she mumbled, yawning. "I never tried it, mating with a seal, I mean." She yawned again and snuggled in closer to Ian. It was only moments until she fell asleep, tucked into Ian's arms.

Her sleeping time was brief. The alarm went off at three, jerking Kelsi awake with its electronic bells and buzzing. How she disliked the thing! Ian groaned beside her and slapped at the bedside table until he picked up the phone. He glared at his phone to turn off the alarm. Kelsi pulled herself from bed, dressed in her layers, and kept the rain boots with her as Ian woke up and downed a cup of coffee. He looked sexy in his sleep pants and T-shirt. When he yawned and stretched, she saw a line of his reddish, gold hair peek from where the sleep pants dipped. Inwardly, she groaned. There'd be no time for anything...*fun*.

At three-thirty, Meg promptly knocked on the door loudly. She hugged her brother and asked Kelsi if she was ready. Kelsi nodded and picked up her rain boots.

Ian gave her a hug and kiss and told her to have a good time. Meg led her to her little red car. Meg drove quite differently from Ian in his truck. She zoomed much faster in the little car. Kelsi loved it but grabbed hold of the handle above the window when Meg rounded a corner at a fast speed.

"It only seems faster on two wheels," she joked.

She saw Kelsi's blank face. "Oh, it's a joke," Meg explained. "We didn't go on two wheels. Are you hungry?"

Kelsi nodded.

"Well, I'm going to get coffee for Pops, Dad, and me. What do you want?"

"Hot chocolate, please," Kelsi answered.

"How about a few donuts, too?" Meg asked.

"I don't know what a donut is," Kelsi told Meg.

"Well, then, you're in for a treat. They are yummy, in small quantities," Meg told her.

Meg went to a drive-thru of a building and almost yelled at a tall, lighted sign with pictures of food and drink. To Kelsi's surprise, a voice talked back! The voice said to pull forward, and Meg did so. Meg handed the girl at the window some money. The girl handed a carrier with the hot drinks to Meg. Meg passed it over to Kelsi, asking her to put it on the floor between her feet. The girl handed Meg a small, flat box, too. Meg also handed this to Kelsi, asking her to keep it on her lap.

It only took a few more minutes to get to where the boat was. There was no traffic. They had to head off Brigantine Island and cross a bridge to what looked like a city. Meg told Kelsi it was called Atlantic City. But they didn't head for the tall buildings. They turned on a road that looked like it went toward Brigantine, even though Kelsi knew there was a bay. Turning down a road, Kelsi saw the docks with boats lined up. Other fishing boats and trawlers had lights on. Other people were getting out of their cars, too.

"C'mon," Meg motioned for Kelsi to hurry. "Pops and Dad will be a little pissed because we're running late. These treats should mollify them."

Meg raised the box of donuts in the air and gestured for Kelsi to carry the coffees and hot chocolate. Meg led her to a boat. Kelsi had seen boats like this from a seal's perspective. She knew they were dredging up things from the bottom and had heavy, metal nets that lifted from the deck and out toward the ocean with a long arm. Seals would stay far away from such boats. Sometimes, they followed the fishing boats in to grab extra fish that didn't make it into the net. Bluefish were not smart; a seal could usually get a nice meal by staying far behind the boat. Meg showed her how to climb on. Meg went first, handing the donuts to Ian's grandfather and then taking the coffee from Kelsi. Kelsi clambered aboard. Ian's grandfather grunted a greeting at her, clearly not liking her presence. By way of greeting, Ian's dad, John, gave her a hearty "Good morning!" They introduced Kelsi to Tim and Patrick, two other crew members on their boat.

Meg passed out the cups of coffee and opened up the box of donuts. She urged Kelsi to take one. Kelsi bit into the soft, squishy baked good. It was delicious but very, very sweet. The donut was almost too sweet with her hot chocolate. Meg had downed one donut quickly and went to get another. She offered another to Kelsi, who shook her head no.

Ian's grandfather and Meg had untied the boat from its mooring. While Meg picked up Kelsi, coffee, and donuts, John and Pops checked the boat. They were ready to go. John started the engine. It was unbelievably loud to Kelsi. Meg shouted and pointed over the noise for Kelsi to head to the boat's bow. Kelsi did get a better view and stayed out of the way.

John expertly guided the trawler from its mooring, out of the marina, through the bay, and out into the open sea. It was still very dark when they made it to the open sea. Kelsi looked up at the stars.

She hadn't been at sea at night for a long time. For one thing, it was much too dangerous, and she had had no desire to be snatched up by a shark. Last year, one of her friends dared her to go swimming in deep water at night. She had always been one that was up for a challenge. Kelsi had found the deep ocean at night very, very scary but very, very beautiful.

Like that night, the stars were heavily sprinkled across the night sky. They were mirrored in the ocean's black water. A bit of bioluminescent plankton swirled in the churning water of the trawler, chasing away the stars. Kelsi was enchanted.

Meg came up behind her. Kelsi had not heard her approach. Kelsi jumped visibly when she heard Meg ask, "Having fun?"

Kelsi nodded and yelled, "It's fantastic!" over the roar of the engine.

Meg told Kelsi they would be heading east for quite a while before beginning to trawl. She told Kelsi she had some chores to complete and that she should stay in the bow of the boat. Kelsi offered to help, but Meg shook her head.

"Enjoy the ride!" Meg told her and went back to her chores.

Kelsi did enjoy the ride. She looked over the open ocean, appreciating its vastness. It's something she had not seen since she became human. As they headed east, she could see the glimmer of dawn rising on the horizon. Kelsi felt like a seabird, especially on this trawler with its two large arms of steel holding the metal nets high up in the air at an angle, like a bird in flight. Kelsi hummed to herself in complete happiness.

Ian's grandfather came up to the bow of the boat as well. He startled Kelsi, and she jumped back from him. He stood there a long time, not saying a word. At that point, Kelsi thought of him as a shark, not circling but just waiting. She waited.

Finally, he said gruffly, "I know what you are, young lady. You need to get away from my grandson. It's not good for him to fall for someone the likes of you!"

Kelsi was taken by complete surprise. She gaped at him and couldn't begin to think of a retort.

"And you think you're so clever, with your name and all," he sneered. "I know all about your kind. The only good you'll do is bring us a good harvest today. If you want to help Ian and his family, sing."

He walked away from her. Kelsi stared at him. What did he mean? Sing? Would that help them harvest scallops? If it made him like her more, she would do it.

So, Kelsi sang. She sang of the scallops dancing in the deep. She sang of the scallops gathering to be brought up in the net. She sang to all the animals moving about in the watery cities below. She sang of fishermen working their catch.

While she sang, Kelsi was in a trance-like state. She didn't hear the rattles and movement of the metal nets going into the water and sinking to the bottom as they chugged along. In a while, they pulled up the nets, pregnant with scallops.

"Wow!" she heard Meg say.

Kelsi made her way carefully on the deck. The net spilled the scallops onto the deck. Meg, Tim, and Patrick worked a complicated series of ropes and a pulley system that daunted Kelsi. The large metal nets spilled hundreds, perhaps thousands, of scallops on the deck and a sundry of starfish and other sea creatures.

"Now you can help," Meg told Kelsi. "This is an unbelievable catch!"

Pops was standing a little way off. He nodded his thanks to Kelsi. Apparently, her singing drew the scallops into the net. Belatedly, Kelsi remembered the stories of Selkis bringing luck to the fishermen. If a fisherman had a Selki in his boat, his catch would multiply. Ron Dunaway knew she was a Selki! He knew the legends. How?

Meg handed Kelsi a pair of gloves. They sorted through the catch and tossed the sea stars and other fish back into the water. The scallops went into large orange buckets. The buckets were carried to an area where they could be shucked. Pops was already shucking. Meg showed Kelsi what to do. They shucked the scallops into other buckets and returned their shells to the sea like the sea stars and fish. Once free from the shells, the shucked scallops were washed off, put in an icy saltwater brine, and packed into white cheesecloth bags. The bags were put on ice in the hold of the boat. Kelsi helped out as she could, her mouthwatering at the raw seafood. As a seal, she crunched scallops, shells, and all. She found the human way of eating scallops, without the shell, more delicious and easier to eat. The nets were back in the water again. They dragged the nets for about an hour before hauling it again. When Meg had stepped away with a bag of cleaned scallops, Pops gave Kelsi the eye and nodded her toward the bow again.

"You know what to do," he told her.

Kelsi went back to the bow and started to sing again. She rested her arms on the rail and sang of the blue ocean meeting the blue sky. She sang of seagulls wheeling overhead. She sang until she was hoarse from singing. There was a melancholy sound to her singing now. She was mournful about the attitude of Ian's grandfather. She wondered how he guessed she was a Selki. And why did he disapprove of this? It didn't make any sense to her. His knowledge of what she was frightened her. They hauled up the nets again. Their catch was even larger this time.

"Holy cow!" Meg crowed. "I can't believe this! C'mon, Kelsi. Let's get shucking."

They worked to sort, shuck, clean, and pack the new catch of scallops. The day was long, but Kelsi didn't mind the work. In the late afternoon, they headed back to the marina. They had been far out to sea, out as far as the Hudson Canyon area in the Atlantic.

Meg brought her some food from below. They sat cross-legged on the deck to eat.

"I can't believe our haul today," Meg told Kelsi. "I haven't seen anything like it in years. Pops has talked about hauls like this in the past. I know we've been working as fishermen to conserve and properly care for the scallop beds to ensure a good harvest, but this is unbelievable." She paused. "I think I'm repeating myself. Sorry."

Kelsi was going to answer, but something distracted her. A way from the boat were several bobbing heads. Her eyes widened, and she wondered if she knew the seals. If only she were closer to communicate with them! But how silly would that be? It would only give fodder to Pop's fury, and Meg and the crew would probably think she had gone stark, raving mad! Meg saw where Kelsi's glance had gone. Her mouth dropped open once again.

"It's that what I think it is? Are they seals?" Meg asked in total wonderment.

"Yes," Kelsi confirmed, "they are seals. I was surprised to see them. I've been down to the beach nearly every day, but I haven't seen any."

"Oh, they're usually good at going to the refuges and away from humans," Meg said. "I'm not surprised you haven't seen any. They don't usually come ashore unless they're sick or hurt or something. We're lucky in Brigantine to have the Marine Mammal Rescue Center. They go all over the state to assist marine mammals in need."

"That's fantastic!" Kelsi told her.

They both watched the seals. Kelsi saw Pops watching them as well. He was careful but kept sliding glances her way and judging her reaction to the seals in the water. Kelsi tried to remain calm.

By the time they reached the marina, Kelsi was exhausted. She thanked John for taking her on the boat. He smiled and told her any time. Kelsi nodded at Pops and the crew and wearily climbed onto the wharf. Meg was still in a jaunty mood after the great catches they had made that day.

"I'm going to take Kelsi home while you guys load the fish for the wholesaler," she said to everyone.

"I know we're smelly, but do you want to grab a pizza and a beer or something?" Meg asked Kelsi.

Kelsi shook her head. "Another time, okay?" she asked Meg.

"Sure! No problem," Meg answered, "and Mom said you were up for a spa day sometime."

"Yes, yes, I am," Kelsi told Meg. "Let's do that soon! It sounds lovely. I need to do something with my hair," she complained. "It's all knotted from the wind today."

"I should have told you to braid it," Meg said.

"Braid?" Kelsi questioned.

"Oh, come on, Kelsi! You can't tell me you never braided your hair on that island of yours, can you?" Meg commented.

"Actually not," Kelsi told Meg honestly. "I've always had it hanging down. It seems to tangle more here. I don't know why."

"Probably the humidity," Meg said matter-of-factly, "It wreaks havoc on hair. The good news is that we'll have dewy, young skin for many years if we're diligent with the sunblock." She grinned at Kelsi.

Meg dropped Kelsi off at Ian's door. Meg came in to talk with Ian for only a couple of minutes.

"Kelsi is exhausted, Ian," Meg told him, "so take care of her. She'll probably want a bath. Just make sure she doesn't drown in it from exhaustion. Okay, bro?" Meg ended, giving her little brother a hug and a kiss on the cheek.

Ian gave a salute to Meg. "Got it, boss."

Meg laughed and lightly poked him in the stomach with her elbow as she left.

When Ian closed the door, he turned to take Kelsi in his arms and give her a hug and a gentle kiss.

"Tired, babe?" he asked her.

Shaking, Kelsi nodded in his chest but raised her face, revealing a quivering bottom lip, a frown, and tears clinging to her lashes.

"Oh, Ian," she told him, "Your grandfather knows I'm a Selki!"

2 9

IAN

Ian stared at Kelsi in amazement. *What the hell? Pops? How could that be possible? Kelsi surely was mistaken,* he thought. Ian wondered if he should tell his family Kelsi was a Selki. Now, it seemed, Pops knew already. But how? He wracked his brain for Kelsi's encounter with Pops at his parents' house. He couldn't think of anything she said or did that would cause Pops to know. How did he know? How could he know?

"What the hell?" Ian said. "How? Why would you say such a thing?"

He held Kelsi at arm's length and looked into her eyes.

"It's true," she said miserably, "he said he knew what I was. He said I was clever with my name. He wanted me to sing for the fish. He knew the legends of Selkis singing to bring fish to the fisherman for a good catch. He knew! He knew!"

Kelsi was crying now and nearly hysterical. Ian led her to the couch and sat and held her. He didn't understand. How could Pops know Kelsi was a Selki? What the hell was the stuff about her name? What did she mean by singing to the fish? He was totally confused. But, for now, he needed to take care of Kelsi. She was crying inconsolably.

"Breathe," Ian told Kelsi gently. "Breathe."

He stood, got Kelsi a glass of water, and returned it to her. He put his hand on her back and handed her the water with his other hand.

"Sip at this slowly and breathe," he told Kelsi.

It took her a while, but she eventually calmed down. She hiccupped a few times and took several deep breaths.

"Okay, Kelsi, when you can, tell me the whole story," Ian said, his tone weary and slightly distrustful.

Slowly, she told him everything, ending with, "He told me if I wanted to help you and your family, I should sing. He kept saying, 'sing, sing, sing,' so I sang." She shrugged.

"We need to get to the bottom of this. We're going to go and see him. I'm calling him right now," Ian said.

"Oh, please, not tonight," Kelsi requested. "I'm much too tired!"

"Okay, tomorrow night. Maybe we can pick up some take-out food and have dinner with him."

"All right," Kelsi agreed, exhausted both mentally and physically. She gave a rueful laugh as she sniffed. "I guess I really am turning human. To smell like fish is a trifle offensive to me. I'm going to go up and take a bath."

"And I'll call Pops," Ian told her.

Ian entered the bedroom where Kelsi was getting into comfy sweatpants and sweatshirt. He had an unhappy look on his face. Kelsi looked at him, concerned.

"He's not happy," Ian shared with Kelsi, "but I convinced him to talk to us. I'll pick you up tomorrow after work, and we'll head to his house after we pick up some dinner. Okay with you?"

Kelsi nodded, unsure of her speech.

"Come on," Ian told her, "I'm scrambling some eggs for us. You look like you could fall asleep standing up."

Kelsi gave him a wan smile. While they ate, Kelsi told Ian about her experiences on the trawler. Other than Pops' attitude, she had loved the day. She admitted she was a little afraid to get in the car with Meg. She told him about the sky and the stars that morning. She told him about the seals in the water with a wistful tone in her voice.

They were both tired after their extra early arousal that morning. Ian had not gone back to sleep for fear of sleeping through the alarm. Instead, he got to work early. They were making good progress on the house they were working on. He told Kelsi all about it. She looked at him admiringly as he described his carpentry.

"You're an artist," Kelsi told Ian.

"Oh, no," he replied, abashed.

"Yes," she insisted, "it's not easy to put a house together. You have so much passion when you talk about your work. You are an artist."

"Thank you," Ian said and changed the subject. "Why don't you go up to bed? I'll clean up."

He kissed her gently and turned her toward the stairs. Kelsi didn't protest.

It bothered Ian that he had a hard time believing Kelsi. Her story wavered between plausible in this odd relationship to unbelievable. Ian resented, a little bit, that Kelsi came between him and Pops. Pops was clearly upset in their conversation. Pops never liked talking on the phone and grumbled without giving Ian any insight. He sighed. He would need to wait until tomorrow night. Ian gave a last swipe to clean up the stove area.

~

THE NEXT DAY at work was long for Ian. Mike had come around and wanted to go out for a beer and catch up. Ian told him that he had to visit his grandfather. Mike was concerned, asking Ian if Pops was in poor health.

"No," Ian replied, "Pops is good. It's been a while since I've seen him, and we will have dinner together." He had not mentioned to Mike that Kelsi was in his life. He didn't know how to explain Kelsi to Mike. Ian had shared the story of Kelsi putting on a fur coat after she seduced him on the beach and was a little embarrassed by it. He didn't know if he could tell Mike it was a different girl or not. He and Kelsi had built up a small tower of lies about who she was and where she came from, and he stayed concerned that all the lies would crumble in a heap. Who would understand that Kelsi was a Selki? He had to stay with their ruse. He had told his mother that Kelsi was the *one*, but his beloved grandfather's doubts had him doubting. He wanted to put on a bright face for Kelsi, but inside, Ian was worried.

At the end of the day, Ian headed home. He had asked Kelsi not to go to the beach today. It was too bad she didn't know how to cook because she could have prepared something for them. She was tidying up, but he was doing the lion's share of work around the house as well as caring for her. He knew and understood that she was just learning, but again, that niggle of doubt crept in. Was this what he wanted? His Pygmalion? He wasn't at all sure.

He pulled into the driveway and went into the house. Kelsi was waiting in the living room, trying to read the books his mother had brought. She was doing fairly well, and he was impressed with her progress. He gave her a peck on the check. Kelsi looked up at him. He could tell by her confused expression that she caught something off about him.

"Ready to go?" he asked.

"Sure," Kelsi answered, and she got her coat.

Ian had called ahead and placed an order at a local Italian place. Kelsi waited in the car while Ian went in to pick up the food. He put the food in the back seat of the truck.

"How was your day?" Kelsi asked Ian.

"Okay," he replied.

Kelsi asked him several questions, trying to initiate a conversation, but Ian could only reply in monosyllables. When she eventually stopped talking, he was relieved.

They continued into Absecon, the same town where Ian's parents lived. His grandfather lived in a smaller home that looked older than Ian's, but it was in much better shape. Next door was a monstrosity of a home. It was a huge, one-story home that seemed to stretch on forever. Ian's grandfather's house looked like a shed in comparison. It was an older home, built in the nineteen twenties, Ian had told Kelsi. Pops had grown up in the house.

They pulled into the driveway. Ian took the food out of the back seat and opened Kelsi's door. He helped her out of the truck and walked up to his grandfather's front door with Kelsi trailing behind. After a couple of knocks, Pops answered the door. He invited them in, nodding curtly to Kelsi.

Kelsi and Pops silently sat in the living room while Ian went into the dining room with the food. He went into the kitchen, growing increasingly nervous with the silence coming from the living room. He was happy and fearful when he called out, "Dinner."

Pops and Kelsi rose to join him in the dining room. Ian had purchased a nice salad and ravioli with Italian sausages and meatballs. The ravioli was in layers with melted cheese. Kelsi had never eaten this before but enjoyed the rich taste when she took her first bite. The salad was also foreign to her, but she liked the crunch of the vegetables and the tang of the salad dressing. Tension thickened throughout the meal as the trio busied their mouths with food instead of conversation.

As soon as the last bite was eaten, Ian sat back and asked his grandfather, "Pops, what is your problem with Kelsi?"

His grandfather hesitated before he answered, "I know what she is."

Ian played dumb and asked, "What's that, Pops?"

Ian's grandfather looked at Ian and then at Kelsi. "Do you think I'm stupid?" he asked his grandson, highly offended.

"No, Pops," Ian answered gently, "I'm just trying to understand."

"Are you being stupid, son? Don't you know? Look at her name, Kelsi. It's an anagram for Selki."

Kelsi flushed at this. She had never told Ian of the anagram.

"A Selki?" Ian asked, sounding as if he didn't know what that was.

"Don't be daft, son," Ian's grandfather spat out at him. "She's a seal woman! I know!"

"How do you know, Pops?" Ian asked quietly.

"I can tell by the look of her. I can tell by her eyes!" Pops cried.

Both men looked at Kelsi. She looked down, blushing under the scrutiny.

"So, if she's a seal woman, what's the problem, Pops?" Ian pushed.

"Problem?" asked Pops. "I'll tell you what the problem is. The Selkis bring us fish on the boat, but other than that, they bring us heartache and trouble!" He turned to Kelsi and almost shouted, "You belong to the sea! You need to go back there! This is no place for you!"

"Pops, calm down!"

"I won't calm down, you young buck!" Pops snapped. "You have no idea what heartache a Selki can bring."

Kelsi looked up at Pops, and her eyes widened. "But, you know, don't you?" she asked, drawing a silent surprise from Pops. "I just realized you are likely of Selki blood. It's something about the eyes, isn't it? That's how you recognized that I was a Selki."

Pops deflated. "Yes," he finally admitted. "My ma was a Selki."

Ian sat in stunned silence for a few minutes before he spoke, "Why didn't you tell us before?"

"Would you have believed me, son?" Pops asked.

Ian thought for a moment. "Probably not," he answered.

"What happened?" Kelsi asked softly. "Did she go back to the sea?"

Pops looked down at his gnarled hands. "No," he said quietly, "no. She died. She died too young." They sat in silence for a few more moments before he burst out, "She shouldn't have left the sea! She would have survived if she had gone back, like in all the tales! I still have her pelt. It's in the closet. Ian, you used to fall asleep with it."

Memories washed over Ian. Was the fur hanging in the closet really his great-grandmother's seal pelt? He had always thought it was a coat. His heart rate quickened, and his emotions threatened to overrun him.

"What happened, Pops?" Ian asked gently.

"Your great-grandmother was a wonderful woman," Pops began. "She was devoted to my dad. They fell in love one night on the beach."

Kelsi looked at Ian, and Ian gazed in her direction.

"The story he told me is that he saw her dancing on the beach and couldn't help himself. He was from the old country Da was. He knew of the legends. He looked around and found her pelt and took it. She had to come home with him. He married her. But, not like the legends, they really loved one another. She didn't resent that he had her pelt, which always hung in the closet. One day, she became ill. She lost a child and got sick after that. She just seemed to fade away."

He stopped the story. Tears had filled his eyes. He looked at Ian. He looked at Kelsi.

"Don't you see?" he cried. "Don't you see? She would have lived if she had returned to the ocean and to her people! She could have visited. I still would have had a Ma! It was after World War 2," he told them. "She caught diphtheria from a returning nurse and never recovered."

"I'm so sorry," Kelsi said.

She put her hand on Pop's hand. He didn't pull away. He had kept this bottled up for so long.

Tears streamed down his face. "I couldn't go to her. They took me away. I was only five at the time. She was coughing and became weaker and weaker until she died. The human antibiotics didn't work on her. They kept her isolated, and she died alone. I tried to get her pelt to her, but no one would listen."

Tears continued to stream down Pop's face. "I've kept her pelt all these years," he told them. "It was the only thing I had left of hers."

Kelsi and Ian waited in stunned silence until Pops was calmer.

Kelsi, curious, had to ask, "Yesterday, you asked me to sing. You asked me to sing to the fish. Why?"

"Da was a fisherman, too. Ma liked to go with him. We all did. She would sing the most beautiful songs when we were on the boat. When she did, our nets would be full. After she died, Da took the boat far out into the ocean. The seals gathered around. He told them what had happened. He told them of his love for Ma. Since then, we've continued to have good harvests from the sea," Pops told them. "That's why our fishing business has been so successful."

"Then why resent me? Why are you so against Ian and I being together?" Kelsi asked softly.

Pops turned to Kelsi and looked her in the eye. "Because you belong in the sea!" he told her vehemently. "You're not human! You'll only bring heartbreak to my grandson!"

"I – I don't think so, Pops," Ian interrupted. "Things have changed since your mom died. There have been a lot of changes in medicine. In fact, what you told me is good. I'll need to get Kelsi to a doctor to get some immunizations."

Kelsi glanced at Ian sharply at this. Ian caught her glance.

"It will be to keep you safe and healthy in the human world, Kelsi," he told her.

"I still don't like it," Pops said. "I only see heartbreak."

"I'm not going to leave Ian!" Kelsi cried. "He's not keeping my pelt under duress. I'm not his slave! I want to be with him! I chose to stay on land!"

"Aye," Pops said. "I know. That's just like my Ma."

"I am not your Ma," Kelsi told him kindly but succinctly.

"Aye, I know," Pops said again. He looked much older now.

Kelsi looked pleadingly at Ian. He shrugged.

"Pops, there isn't any way to prove to you that we're going to be fine except for living each day together and doing well."

They stood up to go. Ian hugged his grandfather. He still was chilly toward Kelsi.

"I'm sorry," she said in a voice just above a whisper. "I'm so sorry."

Kelsi and Ian got into Ian's truck. They were silent for the ride back to the house. Finally, Kelsi broke the silence.

"I feel so badly for your grandfather, Ian. He's carried that burden with him since he's been five years old," she said.

"I know," Ian replied. "And it explains why the seal pelt has hung in the closet all these years. I can't help but wonder if my grandmother knew. I wonder, does my dad know he has seal blood in him?"

"And there's no surprise why we're attracted to one another," Kelsi told Ian. "You are part seal!"

"I can't believe it!" he said. He was overwhelmed with the revelation as well. "Thinking about it for even a little bit makes some things make sense."

Kelsi glanced at him with questions in her eyes. "Like what?" she asked.

"The swimming prowess," he told her, "Meg's affinity for fishing. Little things, I guess."

"Just another reason to be attracted to you more," Kelsi said to him with a smile.

She leaned against him as best she could, the seatbelt tethering her to the truck's passenger side. Kelsi tucked her feet beneath her and leaned over, her head barely touching Ian's shoulder. He reached over and patted her leg. Ian was still concerned about Pops and his feelings toward Kelsi, but knowing the true story gave Ian a sense of palpable relief.

IN BED THAT NIGHT, they snuggled close, holding one another.

"Do you think I should go back to the sea?" Kelsi asked Ian.

"No!" he cried. "No way! But what about you? What are you thinking?"

"Your grandfather gave me some things to think about. I didn't know or think about how human diseases could affect me. But I'm not worried," Kelsi said. "Really, I'm not."

Ian sighed in relief. "I was worried you might take his advice."

"And I was afraid you didn't want me around anymore."

"Never that," Ian whispered into her hair and repeated, "Never that, Kelsi."

They clung to each other silently and continued doing so until they both fell asleep.

30

KELSI

Kelsi awoke the next morning to find herself still entangled in Ian's limbs. Gently, she pulled herself from him. She went into the bathroom and looked out the window. It was still dark. The nights were getting longer and colder. She was glad to have somewhere warm and safe to live.

Kelsi looked at Ian for a long while before she went down the stairs. She sat in the living room and watched the light come, deep in thought. She definitely understood how Ian's great-grandmother had felt. Kelsi did not want to leave Ian. She wanted to spend every moment with him.

Kelsi was surprised when Ian bounded down the stairs loudly.

"Kelsi!" he cried. "Kelsi?"

Kelsi looked up from her spot.

"I'm here, Ian," Kelsi told him quietly.

He heard her voice and went toward her in the shadows. She held out her hand so that he could find her on the couch.

"Come back to bed for a few minutes, Kelsi," Ian pleaded. "You gave me a scare. Please," he begged.

She followed him up the stairs and crawled back into the warm bed. They spooned against one another. Kelsi was overcome with emotion. A tear slipped down her cheek. Ian held her tightly. And then she felt him grow hard against her. They turned to one another, not speaking but making love slowly and in silence like the gentle, rolling swells on the sea. They cherished each moment of their lovemaking. It was a comfort. More tears leaked from Kelsi's eyes. Ian couldn't see them, as it was still very dark. When they were done, he held her for a long, long time. He held her until the final moments, risking being late to work. A cold gray light filtered foggily through the window. Her emotions were singing. She turned carefully so that Ian would not know she was awake. She pretended to be asleep. She wiped her eyes more than once when he was in the shower. He came over to kiss her head when he left for work. The curtain of her hair hid her reddened eyes. Kelsi continued to pretend she was asleep by sighing and moving just a tiny bit when Ian kissed her. He pulled up the blankets, tucked her in, and left for the day.

Kelsi lay in bed, thinking about how she had given up her seal life to be with Ian. Was the sacrifice too great for Ian or for her? She didn't know. She missed many aspects of being a seal, especially now that she was learning more about human responsibilities. The many rules were hard to learn and remember. Kelsi sighed. She drifted off to sleep again for a short while.

When she woke up later that morning, she began what had become her ritual of watching the educational programming for children and going over the words and letters in the house. She continued to try to chunk words in the books and even looked at the cans and bottles in the cupboard and refrigerator. She tried to put the letters together and sound them out. Kelsi wasn't familiar with the names of most of the foods in Ian's pantry, so she guessed. She would have to ask him later if she pronounced them correctly.

Kelsi was restless. She did not feel like tidying up again today. The house wasn't too bad. She wanted to walk. After she had made some lunch, she headed toward the beach. This time, she left the signal of shells for Ian on the counter. They hadn't had time to pick up a phone for her. She didn't care because she didn't know how to use one.

Carefully, Kelsi locked the door with her new key. She put the key in the pocket of her coat. Her hair had been a tangled mess from the boat. Meg had promised to teach her to braid it. After a long session of pulling tangles and combing, Kelsi found a ribbon in the junk drawer in Ian's kitchen. She used it to tie her hair back as she had seen some girls on the television. It was out of her face and not tangling in the wind. It felt wonderful. She swished her long ponytail as she jauntily walked down the street toward the ocean.

Today was a gray day. Kelsi could feel the moisture building in the air. The clouds hung low. It was definitely getting colder. The damp wind seemed to go through her coat and clothes. Kelsi shivered if she stopped, but she was glad to keep walking.

As always, a great sense of relief washed over her when she saw the ocean. She thought she was silly, wondering if, deep down, she thought it might not be there. But there it was, in all its glorious, gray vastness. The breakers seemed quiet today, subdued by the heavy humidity. A bit of fog still hung over the ocean. She couldn't see very far out to sea.

Kelsi gazed, as she always did, scanning the horizon for seals. A dolphin or two were leaping and playing out there. She saw their slick bodies emerge from the water and somersault into the waves. She had not had much contact with dolphins. Some seals ate them. In her few encounters with them, she thought they joked too much. They always seemed to be laughing. They loved being dolphins. They had no desire to ever return to land as mammals. Their folklore said so. They gave up human ways to return to the sea. She admired that in many ways.

Kelsi thought she was different. As she walked up the beach, she remembered she had always felt different as a seal. Her family were Selkis, so it wasn't unusual for them to swim to a remote place, dance, and sing in the moonlight. Not all seals were Selkis, and the real, true seals with no Selki blood sometimes were jealous. They growled and snapped at the Selkis when they returned to seal form. Some shunned her family.

Kelsi was so caught up in her thoughts that she almost walked into a surf fisherman's line.

"Hey, there! Watch where you're going," a gruff voice called out.

Kelsi jolted out of her thoughts and saw the pole right in front of her. She stopped abruptly and turned to the gentleman nearby.

"Sorry," she said.

"Pay attention!" he snapped.

He was an older gentleman who reminded Kelsi of Ian's grandfather. She moved farther up the beach for her walk, where the sand was softer. It was out of the fishermen's way. Gulls wheeled overhead and screeched. Kelsi watched them soar in the cloudy sky. They almost disappeared into the foggy, low clouds.

Walking had made her quite warm. Kelsi unbuttoned the top part of her coat to let a little air cool her down. She went to her favorite dune to sit.

Kelsi marveled that Ian had Selki blood. It was no wonder why they were so attracted to one another. It was no wonder why they couldn't keep their hands to themselves. Ian was following the age-old need to mate – just not, thank Sedna, with every seal or Selki he met. She thought of Breách. She still didn't like him. But now, as her own passions grew for Ian, she could understand his blind need a tiny bit. She could now understand better Ian's blind need to mate with her.

Ian had talked to her about their relationship as 'meant to be' long before they knew he had Selki blood in him. She wondered about this. Is this true? There was a definite connection to him that she could not ignore.

Kelsi wondered about his great-grandmother. Like Kelsi, she had made the choice to be on land. Kelsi would like to know more about Selki, this woman. She wondered if Pops would share stories with her.

Kelsi stood up to make her trek back, noticing the day moving toward late afternoon. She made her way to their agreed meeting place, in the pub's parking lot. It was full of cars and trucks, but Ian's wasn't there. Kelsi waited a few minutes but didn't like the looks and comments of the men going in and out of the club while she stood there. They made her feel uncomfortable, like sharks swimming nearby.

She started toward home, looking up as she heard each passing car. None belonged to Ian. Dusk had gathered, and darkness was definitely on its way. When she got to their street, Kelsi was surprised that Ian's truck wasn't in the driveway.

She took the key from her pocket and fumbled with the lock. It took her a couple of tries, but she finally got the key in correctly and turned the lock. The house was dark. Kelsi turned on the lights. There was no evidence that Ian had been there. She wondered where he was. Kelsi wished she had a cell phone but also remembered that she didn't know how to use one. She sighed.

Kelsi sat down on the couch and leafed through the little books. She started when she heard a car on the street, hoping it would be Ian. She considered walking back toward the beach but was uncomfortable in the growing darkness.

There wasn't much of a sunset. The darkness gathered in a growing sea over the marsh. The gray clouds still hung low, but no rain yet.

Kelsi was beginning to get very worried about Ian. She had no way to contact him, his mom, dad, or Meg, and she wondered what to do. Kelsi began pacing, making a circle as she walked from the living room through the dining room, through the kitchen, and back to the living room. This wasn't getting her anywhere; it was just making her more anxious.

Kelsi heard the slam of a vehicle's door outside. It didn't sound like Ian's truck, but she still jumped up and ran to the door. She peered out. No truck. No car in the driveway. No Ian.

Kelsi listened; a garage door was going down. It must have been Donna and Brenna coming home. Kelsi paused. Donna and Brenna! Donna probably had Ian's cell phone number. Kelsi grabbed her coat and ran next door. She rang the bell and knocked quite loudly.

The outside light came on, and Kelsi saw Brenna's face peering from the living room window. Donna opened the door. Brenna's footsteps could be heard coming closer.

"Kelsi! This is a surprise. Is everything all right?" Donna asked.

"I don't know," Kelsi admitted. "Ian hasn't come home. I don't have a cell phone yet. Do you happen to have his number? Can you call him? Please?" Kelsi begged.

"Of course," Donna said. "Come in."

Donna ushered Kelsi into her house. It was sparingly furnished but lovely. Brenna gave her an impulsive hug, and Kelsi hugged her back.

"Hi," Brenna said shyly. "What's up?"

"I really don't know. That's why I'm here," Kelsi said.

Donna fished her cell phone from her purse and looked for Ian's number.

"Here it is," she said and pressed a button.

The moments seemed to be forever, but Ian answered.

"Ian?" Donna asked, "I have Kelsi here. She's pretty worried."

Donna listened to Ian and what he had to say.

Donna interrupted at one point to ask, "Do you want me to bring Kelsi there?"

Donna listened some more and finally hung up the phone, promising Ian he would bring Kelsi to him. He didn't ask to speak to Kelsi. Kelsi looked worriedly at Donna.

"He's fine," Donna assured Kelsi. "He's at the hospital. His grandfather had an episode and was rushed there by ambulance. The family is there. Ian asked me to take you over to the hospital. Apparently, his grandfather asked for you."

"What?" Kelsi was astounded. "Okay. I need to go next door, get my key, and lock the door."

"I'll go with you," Brenna volunteered, "while Mom gets the car out of the garage."

Donna nodded at this, distractedly put her phone back in her purse, and got her coat.

Brenna grabbed her coat and followed Kelsi out the door and up the steps of Ian's house.

"Don't forget to turn on some lights," Brenna suggested.

"You're right. Thanks, Brenna," Kelsi said, and she put on a light in the kitchen and one in the living room. She also turned on the light on the porch before she locked the door and pocketed the key. Donna had pulled the car out of the garage and was waiting.

"I don't really know anything, but the hospital is decent. If there are any severe issues, they would transfer Ian's grandfather to another hospital," Donna said.

Kelsi nodded. She didn't know what to think. She had never seen nor had ever been to a hospital. Ian had talked about it when his arm was burned, but what he told her had no meaning to Kelsi.

Donna drove carefully in the night. Kelsi felt safe in her car and didn't feel the need to hang on. From the back seat, Brenna leaned forward as much as she could in her seatbelt and patted Kelsi's shoulder.

"I'm sorry Ian's grandfather is sick," she said, "but I'm glad it's not Ian."

Kelsi nodded distractedly. Her mind whirled in thoughts. She couldn't help but think Pop's confession last night had somehow caused some of this.

Donna drove across the bridge on the highway and headed to where Kelsi had seen tall buildings in Atlantic City. She drove through the streets, carefully avoiding any pedestrians who seemed not to care and just stepped out into traffic. Donna huffed once but didn't say anything.

Donna pulled up to the curb outside the hospital. "Do you want us to go in with you?" she asked Kelsi.

Kelsi looked at her blankly and with a little panic on her face. She nodded. "Yes, please. I've never been in a hospital before."

Donna nodded once at Kelsi and pulled across the street to an adjacent parking lot. Darkness had fallen, and the rain had just begun. It was a cold, heavy rain. Kelsi shivered. Donna led the way through the hospital lobby and to the information desk.

"Ron Dunaway?" Donna asked the young lady behind the desk.

The young woman's forehead creased in concentration as she looked at the computer screen. "Do you mean Ronan Dunaway?" she asked Donna.

"Yes! That's it!" Kelsi blurted out. If only she had known his full name earlier. She would have known he had seal blood. At least, it would have been another piece to the puzzle. The name Ronan meant little seal. It explained a lot to her.

The young lady behind the desk gave them the room number. Donna, Brenna, and Kelsi walked through the rest of the lobby to the tower of elevators. The doors opened on one of the elevators, and Donna and Brenna stepped inside with Kelsi following with trepidation. This looked like a very small room to her.

"Let me guess," Donna said drily, "it's your first time in an elevator."

"Yes," Kelsi said in a jittery voice.

The elevator started rising, and Kelsi involuntarily cried out at the movement. She held out her hands to steady herself.

"Here!" Brenna said and took Kelsi's hand to rest on the wall. She took Kelsi's other hand. "I used to be scared to ride in elevators, too," she told Kelsi.

Kelsi looked at Brenna gratefully. The doors of the elevator opened, and Donna and Brenna stepped out. Brenna pulled Kelsi along. Donna led Kelsi and Brenna down the hallway.

John, Beth, Meg, and Ian were standing, looking somber, just inside one of the rooms. They looked up when Donna, Brenna, and Kelsi walked in. Kelsi automatically went to Ian, and he put his arm around her.

"Thank you," Ian told Donna. "I really appreciate you bringing Kelsi here."

Donna nodded. "Let me know if I can help in any way," she told Ian.

Brenna gave Kelsi a small wave. Kelsi gave her a small wave back. Kelsi was overwhelmed by the hospital's sights, sounds, and smells. She saw Pops in the bed, hooked up to all kinds of tubes and wires. It looked like Pops but a much smaller version of the man. He was very, very pale.

"What happened?" Kelsi asked quietly, noting there was a hush in the room.

"Not sure yet," John answered Kelsi. "We're waiting for tests to come back."

Meg, who had been sitting beside Pops and holding his hand, stood up to hug Kelsi.

"He asked for you," Meg said, "but he mixed up your name. I think he's having some confusion of some kind. That's pretty normal for someone his age, plus he may have had a small stroke."

"What did he say?" Kelsi asked, puzzled.

"Well, it wasn't very loud, but he said he needed to talk to that Selki Kelsi girl," Meg told her. She smiled at Kelsi with a watery smile, "See, he was mixing up your name and called you a Selki. I don't know what that is. I think he mixed up the letters in your name."

"Oh," Kelsi said quietly, looking up at Ian.

Ian squeezed her shoulder.

"Can he hear me?" Kelsi asked Meg.

Pops was lying so still and quiet in the bed.

"I always think people can hear you," Meg said. "They have him pretty drugged up right now. Go ahead, sit by him."

Ian released his arm from around Kelsi and nodded to her. Kelsi went to sit by Pops. She took his hand between her two. She concentrated. She pulled energy from the earth and the sea into her and sent it through her hands into Pops. It was the same when she healed Ian's burn. It was a gift Selkis had to help heal with the energy from the earth and the sea. She didn't know if Ian's family would understand, so she didn't tell them. She whispered a prayer to Sedna and continued to hold Pops' hand. Kelsi kept focusing on his healing. Eventually, Pops opened up his eyes. Slowly, he focused on Kelsi.

"Thank you, girl," he told her.

That was the best compliment he could have given her, calling her girl. Kelsi gave Pops a brilliant smile and kissed him on the forehead. He knew of the energy of Selkis, and he didn't question it.

Pops looked at his family standing around the end of the bed.

"What are you doing?" he croaked in a whisper. "I'm not dead. This isn't my wake."

"Oh! He'll be fine!" Meg said. "Already like his old self. The doctors and the nurses better watch out!" Her voice was a little sarcastic, but the tone held a multitude of relief.

"Oh, Pops!" Beth cried. "You gave us a scare."

Kelsi had stood up, squeezed Pops' hand, and pulled her hands away. Beth moved in, and she touched his white hair. She kissed him on the forehead as well.

"Stop your fussing, Beth," Pops grumbled. He was smiling and obviously enjoying the attention.

John patted his father's foot beneath the sheet gratefully. A nurse bustled in and asked them to leave for a few minutes.

"We're headed to get some coffee, Dad," John told his father. "We'll be back in a few minutes when they're through with whatever they need to do."

"Get on with you," Pops said.

Kelsi shook her hands to rid them of any negative energy before giving Pops a luminous smile

"You'll be all right," she stated rather than asking as they turned to leave the room.

"I will, girl," he returned and then, with a twinkle in his eye, called to her quietly, "Selki, Kelsi girl."

Kelsi grinned at Pops and ran back to kiss him on the cheek before heading out with the family.

31

IAN

A wave of guilt washed over Ian when he saw Kelsi walk through the hospital room door with Donna and Brenna. He dropped everything when he received the call that Pops had gone to the hospital. He had thought about Kelsi but didn't know how to reach her. They still had not purchased a cell phone for her. That was something he needed to rectify and soon. He was so glad she had gone to Donna and Brenna's house next door for help. He was grateful they were home, knowing their schedule was unbelievably busy. He was about to leave the hospital for home when Donna called. Pops had asked for Kelsi. They were all surprised, considering his gruff demeanor toward her.

When Kelsi came in, Ian looked carefully into her eyes. Kelsi didn't seem angry. He didn't expect her to be, but he wanted to be sure. He pulled her into a one-armed hug and kissed the top of her head. God, she smelled so good to him!

Ian had been surprised when Pops had asked for Kelsi. After last night, he wasn't sure if Pops ever wanted to see him or Kelsi again. It had been an emotionally charged evening. Ian wondered if Pops revealing the truth about his mother had been too much for him. He had been keeping so much inside of him for so many years. He wondered if the stress of forgiving his mother and himself caused Pops to pass out. They would have to see.

When the nurse came in to care for Pops, they all left the room. None of them had eaten dinner, so Ian had suggested the hospital café. Last year, Ian worked at one of the nearby buildings. He discovered that the hospital's café was a lovely little restaurant with homemade soups and sandwiches. It was Friday night, so that meant it was salmon burger day. His mouth watered at the thought. They had the best salmon he had ever tasted – as if it had been caught just hours earlier.

When they got into the elevator to go to the café, Kelsi clutched his hand. She looked up at him, and he understood. This was a new experience for her. She was always a surprise to him. He liked that about Kelsi. He hoped it would always be so.

They ordered their meals. Ian had suggested the seared salmon sandwich to Kelsi. Her eyes opened wide in delight when she bit into the large wedge of salmon on the Kaiser roll that was topped with bacon and a sundried tomato mayonnaise. His dad and Meg had ordered it as well. Ian was pleased that his family liked it.

Beth commented, "I hope Pops gets out of the hospital before Thanksgiving."

"I think he will," Meg said, "as long as nothing serious is wrong. He looked much better before we left. I just don't know why he collapsed on the boat."

"Well," John replied, "he is in his late seventies. He's been in such good health all this time. We never think of him possibly getting ill."

"So, what time do you want Thanksgiving dinner?" Beth asked her family to change the subject.

They shrugged in reply.

Kelsi asked, "What's Thanksgiving?"

"Oh, dear," Beth said, "that's right, you wouldn't know. It's an American holiday where we feast and feast. It's the third Thursday of November."

"Oh," Kelsi answered, not understanding.

"We do give thanks," Ian told her, "but many Americans like to have it as a day to gorge on good food."

"Can we bring anything?" Kelsi asked politely.

"Hmm," Beth mused, "do you two want to be in charge of drinks?"

"Sure," Ian replied. "That would be great."

"Then it's settled. I'm going to do the bulk of the meal. Meg will make a shrimp cocktail for everyone and scalloped oysters for a side dish. I thought I would make the pies on Tuesday so we can have them on Thursday. Does that sound good?"

Everyone nodded in response before finishing their meals.

"Now to check on Pops," John said.

They all trooped out of the café and headed back to Pops' room. He was sitting up in bed but looked pretty tired.

"You just missed the doc," he told them. "They're going to keep me overnight for a couple more tests, but they said I was dehydrated. Go figure!"

"I'm hoping that's all it is," Beth said. "Something easily fixed."

"Oh, I'm fine," Pops insisted. "You all go on home."

They all said their goodbyes to Pops. He was a little emotional. It seemed his revelation to Ian and Kelsi last night had released emotions that had been pent up for years.

"Thank you, girl," he said to Kelsi. He squeezed her hand before she left.

They went down the elevator and walked to their waiting cars in the parking lot. The rain had stopped and let a crisp, almost frosty, essence into the night air. Crisis averted; they hugged all around. Everyone was weary. Ian and Kelsi climbed into the truck.

"Kelsi, I'm so sorry," Ian told her.

"About what?" Kelsi asked him, truly puzzled.

"Tonight," Ian told her. "When I got the call about Pops, I dropped everything and wentto the hospital. I thought of you, but I didn't know how to reach you. By the way, we'll take care of you getting a phone first thing tomorrow." He returned to the subject at hand, "and I was going to head home when Donna called. Did she tell you?"

Kelsi nodded. "Ian, it's okay. No harm, no foul," she added, using an expression she had picked up from the television.

"You were smart to go to Donna and Brenna's house," Ian complimented.

Kelsi admitted, "Well, I was pretty worried about you. I waited at the beach for a while, but it was getting cold. And I wanted to get home before dark. I waited and waited, and then I heard Donna's garage door go up. I peeked out and thought they might be the ones to help."

They went to bed almost as soon as they got home. Kelsi fell asleep almost immediately. Ian lay awake again. He thought about his great-grandmother and great-grandfather. Did they have a relationship like he and Kelsi were having? Did they love and lust each other like they did? Now he wanted to know a lot more about his great grandparents. He and Pops would have to sit down for some long, long talks.

Ian thought about the seal pelt hanging in Pops' closet. It had been his favorite thing as a child. Funny that it had belonged to his grandmother, and she was a Selki, like Kelsi. That revelation was amazing to Ian. He put his hand on Kelsi's sleeping form. She stirred and moved closer to him.

Ian wondered about the pelt. Since he had Selki blood in him, could he put on the pelt and become a Selki, too? Was his blood too diluted? Did the pelt need to belong to the human it was matched with? What if there was magic still left in the pelt? Would he mutate like something from a monster movie? He would have to ask Kelsi or Pops.

His tired body didn't match his wild thoughts. He tossed and turned in bed. He was afraid of waking Kelsi, so he gingerly got out of bed and tiptoed down the stairs. He stared out at the inky black water of the Thorofare. What would it be like to be a wild creature out there? The thought was intriguing. He wondered what it was like swimming deep in the sea like a seal. He had always loved swimming and was very, very good at it. Now, he knew one of the possible reasons why he was such a good swimmer. Kelsi was lucky, he thought, with the option of two, distinct lives. He thought about her choice to stay with him – giving up her freedom, her family, and the life she knew. Someone told him that a seal's age was equivalent to seven years for every human year. That meant that Kelsi had been a seal for three years. She was twenty-one in human years. She had left her colony to escape mating. Interesting, since sex was their primary pastime. She was a virgin until she met him. He grinned at this. She was amazing in bed. Now aroused, he went back upstairs.

Kelsi was sound, sound asleep. He shook her shoulder. He kissed her hair, but she continued to sleep. Ian took her in his arms and finally settled into sleep, dreaming of swimming in the deep blue sea as a seal.

IAN TOOK Kelsi to the cell phone store the next morning after breakfast. He got the simplest phone they had and programmed numbers for her.

He taught her how to use it before they went to visit Pops. Kelsi tried to follow directions with the cell phone but became frustrated. Ian then became frustrated, sensing Kelsi's frustrations and emotions on the brink He was afraid she would cry. He didn't realize the depth and breadth of how overwhelmed she was and felt helpless. She burst into tears when they left the store, upsetting him more. Ian was flummoxed.

Kelsi dried her tears and thanked Ian for the phone.

"You'll need to practice calling people," Ian warned, "and get used to people calling you. I'll share your number with the family, Donna and Brenna."

"Brenna has a phone?" Kelsi asked, astounded.

"Of course," Ian told Kelsi, "all the kids have phones. That way, she can stay in contact with her mom if she is home alone or if she's somewhere with friends and needs Donna."

Kelsi thought about it for a few minutes before answering, "That makes sense. Maybe Brenna can help me."

Ian grinned. "She loves you, you know."

"And I feel the same about her. She's a wonderful pup," Kelsi agreed.

"Pup," Ian stated and started to laugh.

It wasn't long before they were both laughing, and Kelsi began to feel much better. By the time she reached the hospital, she was in a good mood. She was eager to see Pops and to see how he was doing.

Pops was in rare form and definitely feeling better. They were going to release him, and he was antsy. He had spent the morning waiting for the paperwork to go through. The nurse finally came in to remove his IV and give him directions about caring for himself at home.

"Will you be looking in on him?" the nurse pointedly asked Ian and Kelsi.

"For sure," Ian told the nurse, "and my mom and dad as well."

"All right then," she told Pops. "You'll be able to go."

"Finally!" Pops expostulated. He started for the door.

"Now, where do you think you're going?" the nurse said over her half-moon glasses. "You sit your bottom down until transport comes up with a wheelchair."

As the nurse told Ian to bring his truck around to the entrance, Pops grumbled and looked toward Kelsi. "They might help you in a hospital," he said, "but staying in one can make you *sick*."

Patting Pops' hand, Kelsi chuckled, thinking Pops would be just fine.

32

KELSI

*I*an dropped Kelsi and Pops at Pops' house. He left them to head to the grocery store to pick up dinner for them, a few quick meals for Pops, and some sundry items.

Pops and Kelsi sat in the living room. At first, their conversation was sparse and stilted, as they discussed the hospital and the weather.

Finally, Kelsi asked, "What was she like? Your mum?"

Immediately, Pop's eyes softened. "Beautiful." He sighed. "She had long, black, curling hair. She kept it up most times or in a braid, but I liked to touch it when she left it down. It was like silk. Her eyes were like yours, Kelsi-girl. They were big, dark, and beautiful." Pops gave Kelsi a warm smile.

Kelsi blushed.

After a comfortable silence, Pops said, "I think I want you to see her pelt."

He looked almost embarrassed at saying this. Kelsi knew this was very difficult for him. She followed him up the stairs to his bedroom, and he opened the closet and pushed back the clothes. His mother's pelt was hanging at the back of the closet. The gray fur shone richly in the afternoon sunlight that spilled into the room.

Kelsi pulled out the pelt and touched it with awe. Tears were in Pops' eyes, and he had to turn away for a moment. Kelsi lay the pelt on the bed and looked at it with reverence. Kelsi was sure it was still as beautiful as the day his mother had taken it off.

Kelsi wondered about the woman who had given up her seal life and hung her pelt in the closet. Had she done so of her own free will? Pops said so, but he remembered with the memories of a worshipful child about his mother. Kelsi wondered if she had had the urge to return to the sea or if she did so on occasion. She wished she could have met her.

Kelsi wondered about her own pelt. Her futures. What would her children think of the pelt? She knew, without a doubt, that she and Ian would have children together someday.

Hearing the slam of a car door out the bedroom window, Kelsi gently took the pelt and hung it up where she had found it. As soon as she closed the closet door, Pops' front door opened and closed.

"Thank you," Kelsi said. "Thank you for sharing the pelt with me. I wish I had had the chance to meet her."

Pops looked almost embarrassed, but he smiled an almost shy smile. He had been quiet while she examined the pelt. She knew he had watched her carefully.

"Where are you two?" Ian called.

"Coming right down," Pops answered. "Keep your hair on."

He turned to Kelsi and said with a grin, "If it were you, I would have said, keep your fur on!"

Pops cackled at his own joke. Kelsi broke into a grin and chuckled, too. She knew then that things were all right between them. She had grown fond of Pops. They went downstairs to see Ian.

Ian informed them, "Mom called. She's bringing dinner over here. So, I'll put the food I picked up in the refrigerator. Pops can eat it tomorrow."

"Beth likes to fuss," Pops said, "but she's a good woman."

They sat in the living room to wait for the rest of the family. Ian had fetched drinks for them.

When they were all seated, Pops turned to Kelsi and said, "I forgot to thank you."

"For what?" Kelsi asked.

"For helping to heal me."

"What?" Ian asked, unbelieving.

Pops turned to Ian. "Didn't you know, Ian? Selkis have some healing magic. Isn't that so, Kelsi-girl?"

Kelsi blushed at this and nodded.

"I don't understand," Ian said, "Please explain."

Kelsi explained that Selkis could pull healing energy from the earth and the sea.

"Remember the burn on your arm?" she asked Ian. "It healed overnight because I gave it some healing Selki energy."

Ian pondered this information. "I think I've heard of something like this. I think on land, it's called Reiki."

"I think," Pops said acerbically, "That it's known by many names in many cultures. Some people call it the 'laying on of hands.' I've heard some other expressions, too. Qigong and Pranic energy and more, but this old man can't think of them right now. Whatever it's called, it works. And I personally think it's called love." He teared up a little. And this little lady," he motioned to Kelsi, "was integral to extending my life."

"No," Kelsi said shyly, shaking her head.

"Yes!" Pops insisted. "Remember when you came in and took my hand, I wasn't doing too well. You held my hand and gave me some of your energy, and I was as right as rain."

Ian nodded thoughtfully, remembering.

They heard a car pull up with John, Beth, and Meg. They came in carrying two large casseroles and bags of things.

"What's all this?" Ian asked. "Do you need help carrying stuff in? I thought you were just bringing dinner."

"We are," Meg reminded Ian, "but you know Mom, Ian -- Pops will have food for a week."

"Hush, Meg. It's just a simple casserole and a few sides," Beth admonished.

Meg rolled her eyes at the rest of the family. Kelsi put her hand to her mouth to cover a giggle. Kelsi stood up to help. Beth, Meg, and Kelsi had dinner on the table in moments. There was a hot chicken salad, casserole, rolls, small potatoes, and green beans with butter and almonds. Beth had even brought paper plates and plastic ware to keep it easy for Pops.

"This is so good!" Kelsi complimented Beth, "You definitely need to show me how to cook this and more."

"Well..." Beth began, "I was thinking about that." She turned to her son, "Ian, could you drop Kelsi off this week when you go to work? We can work on the Thanksgiving meal and spend some time together. I can help her with her reading. You can pick her up on your way home. You're welcome to stay for dinner as well."

"Fine with me," Ian said. "Kelsi?"

Kelsi was put on the spot. "That sounds like fun," she said, "yes."

"Then it's all settled," Beth said smugly.

"It takes three days to prepare food for the feast?" Kelsi asked Beth.

"Oh, yes!" Beth answered. "You'll see."

On their way home that evening, Kelsi commented to Ian, "I love your family. They are a lot of fun."

"Glad you think so," Ian returned. "Sometimes, I find them overbearing."

"Does it really take three *days* to prepare the Thanksgiving feast?" Kelsi asked, incredulous.

"I guess so," Ian answered. "I wouldn't know. I just remember Mom working pretty hard that week. She's always had a wonderful meal. I think she wants to prepare a lot in advance so that she can relax a little that day. Meg, Dad, and I usually help her clean up while she puts her feet up in the afternoon. Dad, Pops, and I like to watch the football game. It's a good day."

"Oh, my!" Kelsi exclaimed. "It sounds like a lot of work for one day's feast!"

"You have no idea," Meg said acerbically, "but it's a nice day with family."

"Okay, I've been saying I want to learn to cook, so here's my chance!" Kelsi added enthusiastically.

MONDAY MORNING, Ian dropped Kelsi at his parents' house before heading to work. Mike had taken the week off to visit family in Pennsylvania, so Ian was in charge. He was a little nervous about the responsibilities.

Kelsi was nervous, too. Beth was in the kitchen, sipping coffee, when Kelsi arrived. She had cookbooks scattered on the kitchen island.

Ian gave her a quick kiss goodbye and told her to have fun. Kelsi gave him one longing glance but turned her attention to Beth.

"Let's hang up your coat and get you a drink," Beth told Kelsi. "And then, we'll make an action plan for the next couple of days."

Kelsi hung up her coat while Beth made Kelsi some hot chocolate. They sat together, sipping their hot drinks. Beth had a notepad and pen beside her.

"If we have the main dinner at three in the afternoon, everyone will want to skip lunch but then want snacks. I usually have homemade herbed cheese and a hot clam dip with crackers before the meal. For dinner, we'll have turkey, stuffing, gravy, my special mashed potatoes, mashed sweet potatoes, green bean casserole, rolls or cornbread, and pumpkin pie. Does that sound good?" she asked Kelsi.

Kelsi nodded. The foods Beth mentioned were foreign to her. She had tried cornbread when she first met Beth. The other things she had never heard of. Beth made several notes on her tablet and then went to the sink and removed two large trash bags from a box beneath the sink. Afterward, she motioned for Kelsi to follow her to the garage. Kelsi had not been inside the garage. She was surprised to see a second refrigerator and possibly a third.

Beth explained, "You'll see why I'm appreciative of your help in a minute."

Beth pulled a large Styrofoam cooler from the shelf. She opened the two trash bags, shook them out, nested them inside each other, and put them in the cooler. She pulled the edges around the cooler and put on the lid. Finishing this, Beth moved the cooler near the door to go into the house. She asked Kelsi to get a bag of ice from the freezer. Kelsi opened the door to the refrigerator first. Realizing her mistake, she opened the door to the next appliance. It was a freezer, and cold air spilled out to her. There were several packages of meats, ice cream, and frozen vegetables neatly on the shelves. On the bottom were a few bags of ice. Kelsi removed one and took it to Beth. Beth took the bag and dropped it on the garage floor. She picked it up and threw it down a few more times until all the ice was broken in the bag. Next, she took a pair of scissors from the shelves lining the garage, cut open the bag, and put the ice in the cooler lined with trash bags.

"Now the turkey," Beth told Kelsi. "I should have had John bring it in this morning, but I forgot. I can lift it if you can open the doors for me."

Beth opened the refrigerator door and took out an enormous, oval-shaped object. It looked quite heavy, and Kelsi attempted to help Beth.

"No, no," grunted Beth, "if you can just open the door to the kitchen."

Kelsi ran to do so. Beth hauled the turkey and heaved it into the kitchen sink.

"Whew! That was heavy!" she gasped.

"I'm sorry I couldn't help you," Kelsi told her.

"Unfortunately, it's a one-person job. I appreciate you opening the doors," Beth said to Kelsi.

She took scissors from a drawer and opened the plastic on the package. Kelsi was surprised to see the meaty carcass of a large bird inside.

"That's turkey?" Kelsi asked.

"Yes," Beth told her. "I'm going to brine it, and we'll roast it for Thanksgiving."

Kelsi looked skeptical.

"Really," Beth told Kelsi, "it's delicious."

"Now for the brine recipe," Beth said. She referred to a book on the kitchen island. "Kelsi," she instructed, "could you go to the spice cupboard and find the bay leaves? They're small leaves, about so," and she showed Kelsi the size using her thumb and forefinger. "Bay is spelled b-a-y," she told Kelsi distinctly.

Kelsi was proud of herself for finding the bay leaves. She handed them to Beth, who took out a couple and put them in a tall bowl.

"Now, I need cloves. C-l-o-v-e-s," she spelled aloud slowly, and she handed Kelsi the bay leaves to put back in the cupboard.

Kelsi looked for cloves and found them, taking them to Beth. While Kelsi fetched the herbs, Beth quartered an onion and an orange. She measured sugar and salt and put everything in the bowl.

"Would you please take this out to the garage and dump it in the cooler?" she instructed Kelsi next.

Beth followed her with two large jugs of water. Kelsi put the sugar, salt, spices, and vegetables in the cooler. Beth poured the water on top. She had brought a large wooden spoon and stirred and stirred. Kelsi watched with interest.

"I know it's a little chilly, but we'll only be a minute. Come out to the herb garden with me," Beth said.

They went out a door at the back of the garage that led to a patio. Kelsi saw pots with plants. Beth bent over and picked some of the greens. She handed one to Kelsi.

"Smell," she said.

Kelsi did so.

"That's rosemary, and this is thyme," Beth told her, handing her another herb with small, fragrant leaves.

Kelsi liked both scented plants. Herbs were a new experience for her. She gingerly touched the plants and held them to her nose, breathing deeply as they walked back to the garage. The plants in the ocean weren't anything like this. She loved swimming among the kelp fronds, but they reminded her of trees and not herbs. Kelsi was fascinated with the small, aromatic plants.

They went back inside the garage and put the herbs in the brine mixture. When they returned to the kitchen, Beth started to wash out the turkey on the inside. She asked Kelsi to open the door and the top of the cooler. Beth heaved the turkey out of the sink and set it in the cooler as gently as possible. Beth folded the plastic bags over the turkey. Then they got another bag of ice, put it on top of the turkey in the cooler, and closed the lid.

Beth returned to the kitchen with Kelsi following. They both washed their hands.

"Job number one, done!" Beth said, crossing it off her list with a flourish.

Next, she went to the pantry and looked inside.

"Oh, no!" Beth cried.

"What's wrong?" asked Kelsi, alarmed.

"I forgot to get disposable aluminum pans. Darn!" Beth said in exasperation.

She returned to the kitchen island, sat on the stool, and consulted her list. She looked at the clock. Beth looked at her list again.

"Well," Beth began, "let's make the herbed cheese spread and then go out for a bite of lunch when we pick up the aluminum pans. Does that sound good?"

Kelsi nodded. "That sounds fine."

Beth pulled a food processor out of the cupboard, chopped garlic from the refrigerator, and some herbs from the cupboard.

"Remember the rosemary?" Beth asked Kelsi.

Kelsi nodded.

"Can you bring me two or three more sprigs? And can you get more thyme? There's also a long, straight, hollow herb that smells like onions. Those are chives. You can bring a handful of them."

"Okay," Kelsi said. "I'll do my best."

She went out through the garage onto the deck to the pots of green. She looked at the various herbs and smelled them. She found the right one and picked two large sprigs. She smelled the herb, closing her eyes at the scent. It was sharp but lovely. Something about it reminded her of the sea. Kelsi picked more thyme and found the chives. She tore off several pieces, making a handful. She took the herbs back inside to Beth.

Beth put the rosemary, thyme, and chives in the food processor along with fresh parsley from the refrigerator, garlic, salt, pepper, and spices. She turned on the food processor, and its loud noise made Kelsi jump.

"It's not the quietest of kitchen appliances," said Beth loudly. "But it works well."

She handed Kelsi two packages of cream cheese and showed her how to open them. They put them in the food processor with the two Beth had opened. The processor whirled around and around, a little quieter with the addition of the cream cheese, until it turned a beautiful green color.

"Taste test!" Beth said, and she pulled two spoons from the drawer.

She filled the spoons with some of the spread and handed it to Kelsi. Kelsi tasted it. It was incredible! Kelsi loved the mix of herbs and spices, especially the bright, peppery finish.

"Yum!" she told Beth.

"It *is* good, isn't it," Beth replied rhetorically. "I think the secret is the addition of the white pepper and lots of it," she smiled in satisfaction.

Beth spooned the herbed dip into a variety of cut-glass bowls. She then showed Kelsi how to use the kitchen wrap, had her put it over the bowls, and asked her to bring them to the outside refrigerator.

"Lunch?" Beth asked.

Kelsi nodded.

"Let's get our coats," Beth said.

Beth backed the car out of the garage and headed down the road to a small shopping plaza. She asked Kelsi if sharing a large sandwich would be all right. Kelsi agreed. Beth led Kelsi inside a pizza shop where a large menu listed many items above the cash register. The air was redolent with garlic, oregano, and freshly baked dough.

"Trust me?" Beth asked.

"Of course," Kelsi answered.

Beth ordered.

When the sandwich came, Kelsi's eyes got huge. "Now I know why you wanted to share it!" she exclaimed.

They sat down at a booth. Beth opened the sandwich.

"It's an Italian-American grinder," Beth told Kelsi.

The roll was filled with meat, cheese, and vegetables. Kelsi bit into her half. It was salty and savory, and she loved it immediately.

"Yum," she said again to Beth. "This is great."

After lunch, Beth took Kelsi to the dollar store, where she picked up several disposable pans with lids for more dishes for the Thanksgiving meal. She also showed Kelsi a variety of workbooks. She had Kelsi choose a couple of beginning workbooks they could do together to assist her in her reading efforts. They drove back home.

Ian's truck was in the driveway.

"Where have you two renegades been?" he teased when they walked into the house. "I thought you were going to be cooking all day."

"Oh, you!" Beth scolded her son. "We have been cooking, but I had to get more disposable pans. I used the last ones for dinner at Pops' last night. And I took Kelsi to lunch at Bella Pizza for a grinder."

"Okay," Ian said.

"I didn't realize it was so late!" Kelsi exclaimed.

"As the old saying goes, 'time flies when you're having fun,'" Beth said.

"I did have a good time. Thank you," Kelsi told Beth.

"More tomorrow," Beth promised.

"So, how was it, really?" Ian asked Kelsi when they were in the truck. "Be honest," he said seriously.

"Fun!" Kelsi replied. "It's a lot of work preparing for this feast. Your mother is very organized."

"Yes, yes, she is," Ian agreed.

Twilight had come, and the streetlights were on. It was chilly. When they got home, the last few streaks of red and orange lit up the marsh behind the house. Ian showed Kelsi how to make macaroni and cheese from a box with hot dogs on the side. They sat in the living room and watched television while they ate. The television was beginning to make some sense to Kelsi. The heavy meal made her tired.

"How's work going?" she asked.

"Okay," Ian said. "I'm finding it a little challenging to be the boss since Mike's away. Everyone's in vacation mode. The client is coming on Wednesday to see how much work we've done, so we're pushing things."

"Oh," Kelsi replied, trying to sound as though she understood. "Your mom has a kind of busy cooking schedule for us. "We'll make pies tomorrow. She's planning on making mashed potatoes, sweet potatoes, and green bean casserole on Wednesday."

"Wow!" Ian said. "I don't think of her making all the stuff and how long it takes. I believe she's grateful for your help."

"As long as I'm a help and not a hindrance," Kelsi told Ian.

"How could you be a hindrance?" Ian asked her.

"How could I not? I know nothing about being a human. You and your family have been so very kind to me and teaching me. I keep thinking you'll say it's so not worth it."

"That's crazy," Ian said, shaking his head. "It's not a problem. I don't mind. I think Mom's enjoying it, too. Meg has never been the homemaker type. She's enjoying teaching you."

"If you're sure," Kelsi said, looking at him carefully.

"I'm sure," Ian assured her, looking her straight in the eye.

The next two days were a repeat pattern of Monday, just with different foods. Beth taught Kelsi how to make pie dough and pumpkin pie. Beth showed Kelsi how to peel potatoes and sweet potatoes and make casseroles. They put together green bean casserole with soup and nuts. The refrigerator in the garage was full to bursting. Beth worked with Kelsi on her reading, too. She was very patient. Kelsi thought she was making progress and could read the little books Beth had sent over earlier. She practiced with the workbooks they had picked up at the dollar store.

Ian was late on Wednesday. He arrived looking harried. He ran his fingers through his hair. Meg and John had just come home as well.

"What's wrong, son?" John asked.

"This house," Ian said. "The owner wants to spend Christmas in the house. I don't know how we will get it all done!"

"It will work out," Beth said soothingly to her son. "It always does."

"I had hoped to take Friday off," Ian said, "but now I can't. We've got to push forward. I'm offering overtime to anyone who wants to come in on Friday. Still, I'm not sure anyone will take me up on the offer."

"Speaking of Friday, do you want to come shopping with me on Black Friday, Kelsi?" Meg asked.

"What's Black Friday?" Kelsi queried.

Everyone jumped in, telling Kelsi about the stores, the sales, and the crowds.

"I – I don't think so," Kelsi told Meg. "I don't like crowds."

"Okay," Meg said. "We still need to get our spa day soon. Maybe next weekend?"

"Sure," Kelsi said, but she was distracted by Ian's distress.

The doorbell rang.

"I sent out for pizza," Beth told everyone. "Kelsi and I have cooked too much these last few days, and tomorrow's the big day."

John returned with a couple of pizza boxes. Meg pulled out paper plates.

"This was a good idea," John told her.

As they ate, Beth asked if Ian and Kelsi could pick up Pops on the way to Thanksgiving dinner.

"Sure," Ian answered. "What time?"

"Sometime between twelve and one," Beth told him.

Ian nodded.

Kelsi looked at Ian. He definitely wasn't himself. She was worried. After they finished their pizza, he nodded to Kelsi and motioned for them to go. She rose to get their coats.

"Thanks for dinner," he told his family, "but I'm beat."

"At least you'll have time to sleep in tomorrow," Meg said.

"Yup, that's a good thing," he returned to his sister.

It was one of those times when Kelsi wished she could drive. She mentioned it to Ian, who chuckled.

"One step at a time, okay, Kels?" he replied, shortening her name to a nickname.

"Okay," Kelsi agreed.

"What you don't realize is that we need to figure out a way for you to get some official papers – like a birth certificate. Seals don't have those. I haven't thought of a way to get it. If you get a Canadian one, you'll also need to get a Visa to have permission to stay in this country. We probably need to continue to go on the story that you lost everything on the trip here," Ian said wearily. "The problem is that the Canadian government doesn't have any record of you either. We'll have to figure something out."

"Oh," was the only answer Kelsi could give. She knew it wasn't an adequate one. "Thanks for thinking about it. Didn't your mom say everything always works out?"

Ian laughed with a touch of sarcasm, "Yup, Mom's the perpetual optimist. I usually am, too. I'm just exhausted today."

"Okay," Kelsi said, "so let's go home and relax."

Kelsi knew Ian was weary, and he was in an atrocious mood. Crabby. That was it. Just picking at little things with sharp, little pincers. She tried to be as nice as possible to him, to help him out, but it wasn't working. When he mentioned going to bed, she was relieved. It had been a very busy couple of days. Her days had been without solitude, and she missed her walks on the beach. As a seal, she had the freedom of solitude at any time she needed it.

And she needed some.

33
IAN

Ian had always thought about being the manager of his own construction company, but being thrust into Mike's shoes gave him a reality check. He was glad Mike trusted him with everything, but Ian had never realized how complicated everything was. Ian was sure there was a lot more to the job as well.

It was a holiday week, and no one wanted to come to work. The guys were calling out for vacation or sick time or not calling at all. Ian was trying to assign people to different jobs when he would have to switch things at the last minute. Each day was a new set of headaches. The worst part of being a manager was that he wasn't able to do much carpentry. Other things kept him from cutting, nailing, and putting things together and making them beautiful.

Ian was glad Kelsi was with his mom. It was one less thing to worry about. His mom had taken quite an interest in Kelsi and loved teaching her how to cook and read. She had indeed taken Kelsi under her wing.

Sometimes, Ian found it difficult to talk to Kelsi because she didn't have a background in the human world. He worried that their relationship was built on sex alone. It didn't seem to bother Kelsi, but he was the one working very hard to help make her more human. This stressful week, it all seemed very hard. He thought, a little wistfully, of months past when he could pick up a six-pack of beer and a sandwich and call it a day. Right now, he felt as though he was teaching Kelsi all the time. She was grateful, but Ian was exhausted.

Wednesday was extraordinarily stressful. The owners of the house they were working on came to Brigantine to check on the progress. They had made a detour in their holiday plans and wanted to see the status. They were summer people and hoped to make this their retirement home in the future. The wife was upset that the kitchen countertop was back ordered. The husband didn't like the tile just installed in the bathroom. They both expressed that they wanted to come to the house for Christmas in a month. Ian couldn't believe it. He stammered an answer and eventually said they would need to talk to Mike after the holiday. When they left, Ian went through the house, room by room, making lists of what needed to be completed. The daunting list gave him a headache. He knew he couldn't take Friday off as he had planned and begged some of the crew to come in and work for overtime pay. He wasn't sure if Mike would mind this, but he had to take the chance. He knew one of the guys would come in and was hoping for a couple more to come in and work as well.

Dinner was fine at his folks'. He wasn't feeling sociable, and by the time he and Kelsi had made it to his truck for the ride home, his mood was palpable. Kelsi's statement that she wished she could drive was the icing on the cake for Ian. He became anxious and short-tempered after explaining the legalities needed to make her a citizen without proper paperwork. He knew he shouldn't take it out on Kelsi but didn't know where to place the emotions.

After arriving home, Kelsi went to get him a cold beer when he sat on the couch. She was behaving like a little wifey! He wasn't sure he was ready for that either. It was a bad day.

"Sorry, Kels," Ian apologized. "I'm having a really, really bad day."

In a quiet voice, she answered, "That's okay."

Ian felt guilty now. He turned to Kelsi. "I think I just need to go to bed."

"Do you want company?" she asked him.

He paused to think about it. Finally, he answered, "Sure. That would be okay."

"I'll be up in a few minutes," Kelsi answered with dignity.

"All right, then," Ian answered, giving her a chaste kiss.

Ian went to bed. He wanted to wait up for Kelsi and wondered if he should apologize again. This relationship with Kelsi was like no other he had had with anyone else. He felt as though he was breaking new ground. Kelsi, being a Selki, just added more complications to it. He chalked up all of his negative moodiness to the bad spirit of the day. He was too tired to think anymore and fell asleep with the lights on.

34

KELSI

Kelsi looked out the window at the marsh and the wan moonlight. She thought briefly of walking to the beach but decided against it. Ian had told her of some of the personal dangers of being out alone at night, even though Brigantine was a relatively safe place. Maybe in the morning. If she went to bed soon, she could wake up early and take a walk to the beach. She knew Ian was tired and would likely sleep in.

Kelsi was satisfied with her decision and went up to bed. Ian was sound asleep. Kelsi prepared for bed and snuggled in next to him. He made a sound and reached out for her involuntarily in his sleep. She knew he wasn't angry. Kelsi knew she was getting the fallout after his horrible day. Kelsi was glad, in sleep, that Ian still needed to be near her. She smiled and drifted off.

The next morning, Kelsi rose early. Dawn had just arrived, and it proved to be a sunny but chilly autumn day. Kelsi dressed in her favorite teal sweater, black leggings, and boots. She put on a pair of mittens that Beth had purchased this week and pulled a hat over her hair. Beth had also taught Kelsi how to braid her hair, and Kelsi made a long side braid with her dark, glossy hair. She left the signal to Ian with shells that she was at the beach and left the house quietly.

Brigantine was peacefully quiet. It was a holiday, and Kelsi assumed that people were either asleep, like Ian, busy cooking, or away visiting. She only saw one car traveling down Ocean Avenue. The beach was deserted as well. The surf fishermen weren't there that morning. The beach was completely devoid of humans. Seagulls wheeled high in the air and dove in happy, joyful flights. A few were scrambling around for crabs and poking at the remains of shells.

Kelsi walked north in her usual fashion. She wasn't really thinking of anything, only enjoying the sunshine, the sound of the waves, and the feeling of solitude. Kelsi walked and walked and walked. She walked past the houses and the Pirate's Swoop restaurant. She walked until she was past the last street, 14th Street, in Brigantine. She was heading toward the state's natural area.

She had rounded the beach and saw a lump on the shore. She looked and looked, thinking at first that a human was lying there. Kelsi approached the lump carefully. It was a seal! She didn't know if it was alive or dead.

Kelsi walked up and looked at the seal. It was in bad shape, with its eyes and nose crusty with mucous. When it saw her, it started to snap weakly at her to get away. Kelsi did her best to talk to it in seal language. It lay its head back, not believing what it was hearing. Kelsi looked and looked at the seal.

"Brigid?" she questioned. Kelsi was sure she knew the seal.

She sat by the seal and lay her head down in the sand to look at it at eye level. It was Brigid!

Brigid wasn't a Selki, but Kelsi knew her from the community. She explained to Brigid who she was and that she was living here now. Brigid seemed too weak to do anything but listen. She looked so very sick.

Kelsi didn't know what to do. Brigid sneezed. The sneeze seemed to make her weaker, and her chest was heaving.

The weather was chilly. Kelsi stuffed her mittened hands in her pocket. She found the cell phone. She could call Ian! Kelsi pulled out the cell phone.

It took her a minute to remember how to dial Ian's phone. It rang and rang and rang. Another stilted voice came on, telling Kelsi to leave a message. She hung up. Kelsi waited a few minutes and tried calling again and again. Finally, Ian answered.

"Kelsi," Ian cried, "where are you?"

Kelsi explained about the very sick seal. She told Ian where she was on the beach. She asked him to please call the Marine Mammal Stranding Center. He promised he would and would be with her as soon as possible.

Kelsi lay closer to Brigid to give her some of her body heat. She put her hands on Brigid's back to send some of the healing energy through her. With Brigid's ragged breathing, Kelsi wasn't sure she was doing any good.

Ian was the first to arrive. Kelsi sat up at the sound of his approaching feet.

"Stay back," she told Ian. "She's very sick and very, very stressed. I know her, but she does not remember I am a Selki. Ian, I'm worried about her."

"Okay! Okay!" Ian replied. "The stranding center volunteers will be here soon."

Ian sat several feet away from Kelsi. When he heard voices, he ran to greet them. They arrived in a small group with a large crate and tools to help get the seal into the crate. Ian filled them in on the situation, telling them his friend was with the seal.

"What?" one of the volunteers cried. It was a man with small, round glasses. "She could be hurt! The seal could bite her!"

"I don't think so," Ian assured him. "She's very good with animals."

They were skeptical. When the volunteers approached Brigid and Kelsi, they motioned for Kelsi to move away.

"I'm trying to help," Kelsi said. "I'm giving her some energy."

"Reiki," Ian told them.

"She may be even too sick for something like that," one of the volunteers named Laura said. "I'm not sure this one will make it." She turned to Kelsi, stating sharply. "Lady, you need to move away from the seal! I need to examine her and get some antibiotics into her as soon as possible."

Kelsi moved slowly away and toward Ian with tears in her eyes. "She's sneezed several times," she told the volunteers. "She seems to be having trouble breathing."

The volunteers nodded. They went to work checking Brigid. They loaded her into the crate. Ian helped carry it to their waiting truck.

"Thanks, man," the volunteer, Dan, told him.

"What happens now?" Kelsi asked them.

"We'll take care of this little lady," Laura said. "I'm hoping some fluids, antibiotics, and stress-free rest will help cure her."

"What do you think is making her sick?" Kelsi asked her.

"My first guess would be Phocine distemper," Laura told Kelsi. "It's a seal virus. Dogs get a similar virus. It's spreading like crazy up and down the coast."

"Can you help?" Ian asked.

Tim, the guy in round glasses, and Laura both nodded. "We're the only facility in the state of New Jersey. We see them all."

"And we do our best," Laura said, "at saving every single patient."

"Thank you," Kelsi expressed in a heartfelt voice, "thank you. Usually, when a seal gets sick or hurt, there's no one to take care of them."

Tim and Laura nodded.

"We need to get back to the center and get her settled," Tim said. "And a few of us get to go home to a turkey dinner while the rest of us get to eat some crackers or something," he said with self-pity.

Kelsi watched them go with Brigid. She wondered if she could visit her. She hoped Brigid would get better. Ian turned to pull her into his arms.

"They're good. They're very, very good. The veterinarians, the technicians, and the volunteers will do their best to cure the seal," Ian told Kelsi.

"Brigid," Kelsi said automatically, "her name is Brigid."

Ian answered, "Brigid. They will do their best to help Brigid."

He tilted up Kelsi's chin. "C'mon now," he told Kelsi, "We're to pick up Pops. Let's go and have your very first Thanksgiving! I can't wait to see what you have learned to cook."

Kelsi gave Ian a gloomy smile. "I hope it tastes all right," she said doubtfully.

"It's going to be awesome," he said. "Let's go pick up Pops."

There was no time to think when they got to Ian's parents' house. Beth organized them all into action. She sat with a glass of wine when everything was in place while they watched sports. The turkey was cooking, and the side dishes were in the oven. Now, they needed to wait.

Kelsi was all right while they were busy, but worry overtook her when she had time to think.

"Ian, can you help me get a couple of things from the garage?" she asked.

When they entered the garage and closed the door, Kelsi threw herself into Ian's arms. "Do you think they'll let me visit Brigid?" she asked Ian.

"I'm not sure," Ian said. "And she's sick. I don't think they'll let you visit a sick animal. You might be able to see her through a camera, like on a television screen, but not actually visit her."

"Brigid is worried about the rest of the colony. This virus is spreading," Kelsi told Ian. "I'm so worried!"

Ian rubbed her back and held her. He could feel the tension in Kelsi's body like a taut string. Ian kissed her once. He kissed her again.

And then Kelsi kissed him with a passion he had not experienced from her. She was definitely giving herself to him more today than at any time before. He became caught up in the kiss.

And the garage door opened. It was Meg.

"Oops!" Meg said with a grin. "Sorry."

If Ian had had something to throw at Meg, he would have. She started to close the door.

"Now that you're here," Ian called after her, "help us!"

Meg came reluctantly into the garage. "Sorry," she whispered.

They brought in crudites, salad, and pie from the garage refrigerator, setting everything on the counter. Meanwhile, Beth had put out a spread of appetizers. Ian nabbed a couple of crackers loaded with clam dip and handed them to Kelsi. His Mom announced that the turkey was done. They removed it from the oven and let it rest for a bit. John came out to carve the bird while each took a side dish to the card table set up in the dining room for the extra dishes. Ian went to fetch drinks for everyone. They sat, and John brought in the platter of carved turkey. They gave thanks for good health, fortune, and friends old and new.

Kelsi wasn't sure she had ever seen so much food. Actually, she hadn't. She wanted to try a little bit of everything but wasn't sure she could eat it all. They ate, talked, and laughed until they were stuffed. They all voted to wait for dessert until much, much later. Ian, Meg, and Kelsi cleared and cleaned up.

"Really, Kelsi," Meg told her, "you cooked with Mom all week. You should sit down."

"I want to keep busy," Kelsi told her.

"Kelsi is pretty upset about the harbor seal she found this morning," Ian told Meg.

"I can understand that!" Meg said. "I'm so glad you found her. She could have died."

"She still might," Kelsi told Meg soberly. "She is very, very sick."

They relaxed and watched old movies. They ate dessert and laughed some more. Kelsi liked hearing stories of Ian's childhood. She wished she had some to share but shook her head when they asked her. Pops stood up for her and would quickly change the subject if too much attention was placed on Kelsi's family and their holiday celebrations.

It was Pops who saw Kelsi overwrought with worry over Brigid. He wasn't sure if words would help, so Pops took some action. He told his family he was tired and wanted to go home. The beauty of being nearly eighty, he said, is that most times, people listen and follow directions.

"And I have an early day tomorrow," Ian said.

"Me too," Meg grinned, "but with shopping!"

Everyone laughed. After Beth made everyone a to-go bag of leftovers and dessert, Ian and Kelsi left to take Pops home.

When they arrived, Kelsi had to get out of the back of the truck to get re-arranged to sit in the front. Pops waited on the sidewalk and hugged her.

"It will be all right, Kelsi-girl," he said.

"Thanks, Pops," Kelsi told him, hugging him back, blinking back tears.

Ian walked Pops inside and put his leftovers in the refrigerator. Kelsi waited in the truck. She thought about Brigid and their conversation. She said many in the colony were ill. Kelsi wondered if her family was sick or well.

Ian returned and got in the truck, breaking her train of thought. He looked at Kelsi.

"Are you all right?" he asked.

Kelsi nodded. "Just tired."

"I bet! You and Mom put together a fabulous dinner," he complimented Kelsi.

"Thank you," she replied, trying to smile despite the sadness she felt.

At home, they snuggled on the couch. Ian turned on the television, but Kelsi couldn't concentrate on the moving pictures and talking heads on the screen. She studied Ian's profile. Kelsi wanted him. She felt a bestial need to mate with him. She had inadvertently spoken her desire out loud.

Ian stopped and stared at Kelsi.

"I want you," she said. Kelsi turned off the television and pulled Ian off the couch. "Please," she begged.

In the bedroom, she took off her clothes and stood nude in front of him.

"Please," she said again. "Please, take me."

Ian scooped her up in his arms, his desire flaring from her words and her need. Kelsi helped Ian rid himself of his clothes while he kissed and nibbled. She took his hands and put them on her breasts. Ian complied, massaging them. She guided his penis inside of her. She didn't want foreplay. Not tonight. She needed to feel Ian completely inside of her.

Ian complied. He held up her legs, and she wrapped them around him. Ian pounded inside her, and she cried out in pleasure and passion. Kelsi screamed his name when he brought her to orgasm. He brought her to new heights as she rode the waves of pleasure over and over again. When they were finished, they were both panting from exertion.

Ian was about to roll off her, but Kelsi stopped him. "Just lie on top of me for a while, will you?" she asked.

Ian lay on Kelsi. He drank in her scent. She always had a salty tang about her that he loved. Ian buried his face in her hair and her neck. He kissed her lightly. Her nerve endings were on fire. She jumped. He kissed and licked at her. She almost begged for him to stop, but she couldn't. She wouldn't. It felt too good. When he took her nipples in his mouth, she jerked wildly beneath him. They both held on.

"Should I stop?" he teased her.

"No! No! No!" a ragged whisper came from Kelsi.

Ian moved slowly inside of her, and he became hard again. This time, their lovemaking was gentle. Kelsi was limp from her previous orgasms, but he brought her up again. She arched her back and held on to him. Kelsi didn't want to let Ian go. She wished he could stay inside of her forever.

When they were done, Kelsi nestled as close to Ian as possible. They both felt the magic of the evening and their lovemaking. Kelsi felt as though they had crawled inside of each other's skin.

The next morning, Kelsi woke up alone. She vaguely remembered a kiss and her murmuring goodbye to Ian.

She oriented herself to the darkness and the sounds around her. Kelsi remembered their previous night. She remembered Ian had to go to work. She remembered Brigid.

If Kelsi could find the colony, she could tell the sick ones to come to New Jersey. The Marine Mammal Stranding Center could help them wherever they beached in the state. Kelsi knew what she must do.

Kelsi went downstairs with her pelt in hand. Dawn was just breaking. She knew Donna and Brenna were gone for the holiday, and she was pretty sure the other neighbors were gone as well. Kelsi felt very alone in the neighborhood. It was high tide. It was now or never. She made a pattern with the shells on the kitchen counter. This time, she made a heart shape. She laid her clothes in a neat pile by the back door and stepped into her pelt.

Kelsi's pelt molded around her. She fell onto her stomach and her front flippers with a *whoomp*. It took her breath away for a minute. She had forgotten how difficult it was to maneuver on land like a seal. She had to get to the water as quickly as possible. She hoped that if someone had seen her, they thought a seal had beached by Ian's house and would be heading back to the Thorofare.

She slid into the water. Kelsi dove down as best she could, getting her body wet. She took a long, long look at Ian's house and swam up the channel.

Kelsi had forgotten all the little byways on the Thorofare since it had been nearly a month since she last entered the waters. She had to keep stopping, thinking, and sensing where the open ocean might be. Eventually, she made it. She swam north. Brigid had mentioned Paumanok or the Long Island area. It was a good, long swim.

Kelsi headed for deep water and swam and swam. She had forgotten the freedom of swimming in the ocean. Kelsi started to enjoy the swim while diving and twisting in the water. And then, she remembered her resolve, and Kelsi swam further. She ate when she could, swimming upside down, and scanning for food. She swam and rested, bobbing in the water. Once she rested for a few hours, she would torpedo herself through the water, seeking out the colony. She swam, using her senses to listen for other seals when she was underwater. Kelsi swam and rested, swam, and slept all that day. As she approached Paumanok, she swam closer to the shore, scanning the shoreline for seals.

Finally, she saw some. Kelsi swam closer to shore. Some of them growled and barked at her. She shouted weakly who she was and why she was here.

Kelsi found an empty spot on the beach. She hauled out and collapsed. She thought of Ian and felt a pain in her heart. Kelsi wondered how he was doing and what he was feeling. She knew she hurt Ian terribly and prayed he would forgive her for leaving. It didn't take long for her to fall asleep after her long, laborious swim.

35

IAN

Ian was exhausted but mellow after the previous night's lovemaking. He was working with Carlos in the house, trying to get ahead. Ian was laying a manufactured wood floor. The owners wanted hardwood, but Mike had thankfully talked them out of it as it would warp with the humidity. Ian worked steadily, thinking of Kelsi all throughout the day. He thought of calling her but decided against it. He wondered if she had gone to his parents that day. Ian was looking forward to getting home tonight.

Ian and Carlos knocked off at four-thirty, both anxious to get home to their families. Ian pulled into his house, noticing it was dark. He unlocked the front door.

"Kels?" he called. "Kelsi?"

Ian wondered if she had taken a walk to the beach. It was getting dark, so she should be home or nearly home. He almost jumped back into the truck but wondered if she had left her message with shells.

Her cell phone lay on the kitchen counter. Ian felt rocks in the pit of his stomach as he saw the heart shape made from the shells. He realized that Kelsi had left him a message. She was gone.

"No! No!" Ian cried.

He ran through the house, calling Kelsi's name in anguished cries. He looked everywhere for her. With trepidation, he headed toward their bedroom. He saw the box from under the bed. It was empty.

Ian sank cross-legged on the floor. He kept moaning, "No, no, no." Ian hugged himself and rocked and rocked. He wondered why. Why had she left? He thought of last night and the most amazing sex he'd ever had in his life.

Eventually, Ian got up and walked disconsolately through the house. He found the neat pile of Kelsi's clothes at the back door. He picked them up and breathed in her salty, sweet smell, which he loved so much. Tears brimmed in his eyes.

Ian didn't understand, and then he thought of Pops. He didn't stop to call, but he jumped in his truck and raced to Pops' house.

Pops had settled in for the evening. *Wheel of Fortune* was blaring. Pops was getting slightly hard of hearing. Ian knocked and knocked.

"Keep your hair on!" he heard Pops' gruff voice.

"Ian!" Pops exclaimed as he opened the door. He looked at Ian's distraught face. "What's wrong?" he asked as he ushered him through the door.

"She's gone," he told Pops miserably.

Pops sat heavily on his couch. He turned off the television.

"Tell me what happened," Pops said.

"I don't know!" Ian cried. "We've been fine! We've been wonderful! The only thing I can figure out is she was upset about seeing Brigid yesterday."

"But Brigid is being taken care of at the stranding center," Pops said. "I told her we could call after this holiday weekend and check on Brigid."

"Oh, Pops! What am I going to do? What am I going to do without her?" Ian cried. He put his head in his hands.

Pops leaned over. "Ian, son, Kelsi is a beautiful girl, but you keep forgetting she is really a seal! If you read the books on Selkis, they always return to the sea."

"But, she promised, Pops! She promised she would stay with me!"

"I know, son. But she's still an animal. She's still a seal. We don't know what instincts are driving her inside. We just don't know."

"But Pops! She was the one!" Ian felt desperate. "How can I find her?"

Pops shook his head. "Son, there's an old saying, if you love someone, let them go. If they come back to you, they're yours forever."

Ian clearly wasn't happy with this quote, even though he had thought about it. He took a deep breath.

"I need to go," Ian said. "I must go home just in case she comes back tonight."

"I understand, Ian," Pops told him. "I get it."

Ian stood up to leave and said wearily, "Thanks, Pops. Thanks for listening."

"Any time, son." His heart was breaking for his grandson.

Ian drove home and wondered where Kelsi was in the Atlantic. He wondered why she left. He turned on the light and left the back door open for her. But Ian didn't think she would come home. He was miserable. Ian slept restlessly, waking up every hour and reaching for Kelsi. When his hand touched the empty sheets where she should be, he remembered how much he loved and missed Kelsi. His heart ached. He felt sick.

Ian wasn't religious, but he prayed to whatever god was out there. He prayed to Sedna, the goddess Kelsi kept mentioning, to keep her safe and to bring her back to him.

36
KELSI

Kelsi slept fitfully on the cold, hard sand. She awoke to strange noises and her bones creaking. She thought of the soft bed where she curled up with Ian, safe and warm. Ian. Would he ever understand? Would he ever want to see her again?

As dawn broke, Kelsi went in search of sick seals. She found them. Many of the seals were very, very ill.

"If you can make it to New Jersey," she told them, "there's a place that can help you. Maybe you can go in a group. Spread the word."

Kelsi looked for her own sisters and her own colony to no avail. She asked each seal if they had seen or heard about her sisters and mother. No one had heard from them. She found a portion of her colony when she reached the most northern point of Paumanok. The Phocine distemper had made many of her people ill. Many had died. There was no word on her family. She heard that one of her sisters was ill with the virus, but everyone else was fine when they last saw them. Kelsi felt guilty for running away. She hoped and prayed to Sedna that they were safe somewhere. Breách was one of the seals that was very, very sick. She didn't think he could make the swim down the coast; he was that ill. He couldn't even speak to her. She told the colony about the center and how to get to New Jersey. Kelsi wasn't sure what to do now. Should she travel further north in search of her family or return home to Ian? Because the seals didn't know where her family was, Kelsi wondered if they had hauled out and transformed into their human selves. Could they be walking around somewhere as humans? She wondered about that and where they might be. She spent another night with the colony before she headed home.

The journey back to New Jersey took much longer than Kelsi expected. She stayed near the shore and hauled out frequently. She was exhausted. She was so tired...and felt stupid. Kelsi nearly got hit by a boat one time, and another time, she narrowly missed getting hurt by a shark. She needed to rest. She needed to breathe. She couldn't be getting sick. She couldn't. When she reached Sandy Hook, Kelsi didn't think she could swim another stroke. She let the waves help wash her into shore. Kelsi took her time to haul out. She rested there for three days, gathering her strength to reach home and Ian. Thinking of him pulled her onward.

Kelsi continued to swim south slowly. She started to recognize beaches. When she reached the northern end of Brigantine Island, Kelsi could go no farther. She hauled out again. This time, preparing herself not to see Ian ever again. Her chest was heavy. She was having trouble breathing. She knew she had caught the other seals' disease, the Phocine distemper.

3 7

IAN

*I*an was depressed. He couldn't eat, and he didn't shower. He sat in front of a dark, blank television or lay curled up on the bed. Pops had told his mom, dad, and Meg that Kelsi was gone. Ian called Mike and said he had the flu.

One day, two days, three days, four, Ian sat waiting. He went over every minute aspect of their relationship. By day three, Ian realized he had never told Kelsi he loved her. He was shocked. How could he not have told her? She was the one!

But Kelsi had not told him either—at least, he didn't think she had. In Gaelic, she called him beloved. She also said many other things in Gaelic, murmuring them to him in bed and while they made love.

A sharp, loud knock came at his door, but he didn't get up. He didn't want to get up to see who it was. He didn't care anymore.

Meg strode in. "Oh. My. God! It smells like a zoo in here! Ian!" she called. "Snap out of it, Ian! You're not doing anyone any good sitting here and stinking up the place."

Ian didn't move.

"Get upstairs and shower, or I'll drag you up there myself!"

Ian slowly got to his feet.

"Good," she said soothingly now. "You'll feel a lot better after a shower."

Meg pushed her brother to go up the stairs. He was in bad shape. She didn't understand Kelsi's actions either. Meg could only think that Kelsi couldn't write him a note because she didn't know how. But Meg wondered why Kelsi hadn't called. Something was wrong. Meg was concerned not only for her brother but for Kelsi, too.

Meg went to the kitchen to scramble some eggs for Ian. She thought she would make him cheesy eggs, one of their favorite comfort foods from childhood.

When she got to the kitchen, Meg noticed the shells in a heart shape on the counter. It had to be a message from Kelsi. That meant she still loved Ian! Now, the mystery deepened. But the shell heart told Meg that Ian shouldn't lose hope. You should never lose hope. She felt that in her bones, and she needed to tell her little brother, even if she had to bang it into his head.

Meg pulled out the frying pan and the ingredients for the eggs. She listened and heard the shower going. Good.

When Ian came downstairs, Meg had plated a heap of eggs rich in cheesy goodness. She also had a small plate for herself.

"Sit!" Meg ordered Ian.

He sat at the dining room table.

"Eat!" she ordered again.

Ian took a forkful of eggs. Even cheesy eggs didn't taste good to him. But they were warm and tasted better than anything else he had eaten in the last couple of days. Ian took another fork full of eggs. They slid down easily.

Meg smiled at him encouragingly. She ate some eggs, too.

When Ian had finished his eggs, Meg took her brother's hands in hers. "Look, Ian," she told him, "if Kelsi didn't love you, she wouldn't have left the heart of shells on your counter. Don't lose hope!"

Ian looked away. Meg squeezed his hands.

"Look at me!" Meg cried.

Ian turned to look at her.

"Don't lose hope!" she said loudly and distinctly. "Kelsi loves you. I know it!"

"I don't know anymore, Megs," he said raggedly. "I just don't know."

"I know," Meg whispered. "It's all going to work out."

She cleaned up and gave her brother a huge hug.

"Get some sleep," she told him. "I'll see you in the morning."

Hope and sleep. Those were two things Ian had been drained of. The heart of shells and stones gave him a modicum of hope. Ian stared out at the Thorofare. Where was she?

He got into his truck and drove to the beach. He went to the dune where he met Kelsi and stared at the roiling ocean. He couldn't see anything. No dolphins were leaping or seal heads bobbing now. He stared and stared, thinking about what Kelsi had said about the community of life in the ocean. Something out there knew where she was, only he did not. He strode back to his truck and went home, cursing his humanity.

3 8

KELSI

Kelsi dreamed of Ian. She knew he was close by. She rested more comfortably that night. The beach felt familiar. The stars were the stars of home. She slept better than she had in days. She counted the days she had been gone. It had been almost a week. She sighed. She hoped Ian still wanted her. She hoped he would forgive her. Kelsi hoped he still loved her. Even though he never said it, she knew.

She would swim down the Thorofare in the morning and be home.

Something woke Kelsi in the pearly dawn. The sun hadn't risen, but the stars were beginning to disappear from the sky. The horizon was starting to emerge from the water on the eastern horizon. Kelsi hauled herself into the water. She was tired and weak, but she had to get home.

She swam down the Thorofare. The tide was coming in, pushing her along as it moved toward the inland bays. She let it carry her as she moved along. Kelsi kept looking at the houses. She was getting closer and closer, and she knew it.

Every one of these homes had a dock. Ian's did not. She kept swimming until she saw that small turquoise house perched between two larger houses. Kelsi hauled herself onto the beach through the rough grass and up to the back door. She didn't have the strength to transform. She could barely breathe. She barked weakly, hoping Ian might look out. Her bark turned into a cough. She fell against the door with a thump. She pulled her hands and arms out of her flippers. She pulled back the seal head and let her hair stream down around her. She knocked, and she knocked, and she knocked until she couldn't knock anymore. Kelsi passed out, half in and half out of her seal body.

39

IAN

Something woke Ian. He started from a dream about Kelsi. What was it? He thought he heard something. It must be four or five in the morning. Perhaps the newspaper delivery had thrown a paper, hitting his property. It had happened before. Ian started to drift off to sleep again.

Meg had been right. He needed to get cleaned up. Ian needed good food. He had finally slept. But something kept pulling him out of his dreams. He thought he heard something again. It was a faint, faint knocking sound. He couldn't place it. His sleepy brain was working to figure it out. In his fog, he went through the litany of possibilities. He heard it again. Was it a knock? But it wasn't at the front door. Where was it from?

Slowly, Ian got out of bed. Could it be? Could it be that Kelsi had come back? Thinking of this, his brain went into overdrive, and his body followed. He ran to the back door and opened it. On the doorstep was Kelsi, half in and half out of her pelt.

"Oh, Kelsi!" he cried. He picked her up and cradled her gently in his arms. She lay limply against him. He kissed her head and her neck. Something was wrong! Her body was on fire. She had a fever.

Ian pulled his phone out of his pocket and called Pops.

"Pops! She's back! But she's sick! She's half in and half out of her sealskin! What do I do?" Ian cried into the phone.

"Calm down, son. See if you can take off her sealskin like you can a snowsuit. Take it slow. Don't hurt Kelsi. I'll be right there," Pops told him.

Ian half-carried, half-dragged Kelsi inside. He kept saying her name over and over again. If only she would open her eyes. He was so scared for her.

He pulled and tugged the sealskin, little by little, over her burning body. She was limp and couldn't help him, so his progress was tedious. Inch by inch, her beautiful skin emerged. He now had hope, as Meg had promised.

When Ian had gotten the sealskin completely off her body, he carried Kelsi's limp form to the bedroom and lay her on the bed. She was still burning with fever. And he couldn't wake her.

Pops knocked and came into the house.

"Up here," Ian called.

Pops came up the steps and saw Ian's pale face and Kelsi's paler one. Her breathing was labored.

"Call an ambulance, son," he advised.

Ian took out his cell and dialed 911.

40
KELSI

Kelsi heard Ian's voice. She was sure of it but wondered if it was a dream. Kelsi felt as though she was swimming in deep, deep water. The water was so deep she had to fight to get to the surface, but each push upward rendered her breathless until

she

could not

breathe.

She sank deeper and deeper. It was easier this way, she thought. Easier not to breathe, not to feel. She sank. Deeper and deeper, feeling the strands of something around her arms and on her legs. She thought she heard Ian's voice calling to her, "Kelsi! Kelsi! Don't give up hope!"

Coolness enveloped her, filling her nostrils and her brain and shooting through her veins, feeling oh so very exquisite. Now, she wasn't sinking in the water. Now, she was flying like a torpedo shot through the water. It felt like the flying that occurred when she rode in Ian's truck and Meg's little red car. It felt good to fly. She felt free.

In this darkened space, Kelsi slept very deeply. Voices woke her, familiar, loving voices and unfamiliar sounds. She could feel bright lights around her but couldn't open her eyes. She tried to move, but she couldn't. Something was restraining her. She felt something warm and wonderful course through her as she continued to hear noises. Blips, but not dolphin blips, jarred her from sleep.

Kelsi opened her eyes. Ian was there! Her Ian! He was looking at her with love and longing. Kelsi tried to smile.

"Ian!" she breathed.

Kelsi fell back to sleep, feeling safe knowing Ian was there.

41

IAN

"She's very, very ill," the doctor told Ian. "She has an infection and pneumonia. She's dehydrated as well. It's going to be a challenge to pull her through."

"But you will, won't you, doctor?" Meg pushed in next to Ian. "You will save her. I know I can count on you. I know there's hope."

"There's always hope," the doctor said, his dark eyes looking at Meg.

"I *knew* there was a reason I liked you," Meg told the physician. "Why don't we let Ian be with Kelsi?"

Meg, in her ever-pushy way, propelled the doctor from the room.

Ian had learned a lot in the last few hours. At first, the doctors didn't know what kind of infection Kelsi had. The tests came back inconclusive. They said it was a virus compounded by pneumonia and dehydration, but they didn't know what kind of virus it was. Pops saved the day. He remembered Kelsi saying the sick seal sneezed on her. She was likely around other sick seals when she was in the ocean. He explained to the doctor that she was near a seal with phocine distemper. Pops said it was contagious to dogs and had heard that humans could get a form of it. He suggested the doctor call the research center and find out. And he did.

But Kelsi looked so pale. Her breathing was unsteady. Ian was frightened for her, and so was Pops.

"Ian," Pops told him, "Kelsi used the Selki healing energy on me. You and I are part Selki. Why don't we try to give her some of that energy?"

Ian looked skeptical.

"Come on, son," Pops told him. "We need to try."

"How do we do it?" Ian asked.

"I don't know. When Kelsi did it, I think she just put her hands on me and thought positive thoughts of healing," Pops said. "That's the gist of it when I spoke about it with her."

"It's that easy?"

"I think so. I really don't know, but I believe that we have to try."

Ian held Kelsi's hand, and Pops held the other. They both closed their eyes and tried to pull the energy that Kelsi spoke about. They considered her healthy and well, as a human, not a seal. Her eyelids fluttered. Kelsi looked up at Ian and whispered his name. Ian didn't think he had heard anything so beautiful in his life.

Whether or not it was the right course of antibiotics and fluids or the healing energies from Pops and Ian, Kelsi's healthy, young body started to make a turnaround. Ian hoped that when Kelsi knew he was there for her, she would try to return to him. He had so much to say to her.

Kelsi became stronger little by little. When she could sit up and talk a little, the doctor came in to talk to them both.

"I have good and bad news," the doctor told them.

Both Ian and Kelsi looked at him questioningly.

"You'll be getting out of the hospital very soon, young lady," the doctor told Kelsi, "but you'll need to take it easy for a couple of weeks."

"No problem, Doc," Ian said to him. "My mom will wait on her hand and foot until she gets better."

Kelsi looked surprised at this...and grateful. The doctor nodded his approval. "The bad news?" she asked.

The doctor cleared his throat a couple of times. "I'm so sorry," he told Ian and Kelsi, having difficulty looking into their eyes, "but you lost the baby."

"The baby?" Ian gulped.

"You didn't know?" the doctor said.

"No!" Ian almost cried out. "You didn't know?" he asked Kelsi.

"No!" she said. "It's not possible."

"It is possible. I'm so sorry," Ian said.

"But, but, seals…" she started and then stopped. Taking Ian's hands into her, she looked at him helplessly.

"Can you give us a few moments alone, doctor?" Ian asked. "This is quite a shock to us."

As the doctor nodded and left, Ian took Kelsi in his arms the best he could between tubes and wires.

"Ian! I didn't know! It's not possible! When seals get pregnant, the egg stays in stasis until it's time to be pregnant. I shouldn't be pregnant for months now," Kelsi told him. "That was why I wasn't worried when we mated. I didn't think it was possible!"

"Well, I was just plain stupid," Ian said. "I'm so sorry, Kelsi. I'm so sorry."

The news of the pregnancy took them each a few minutes to digest. Ian sat and held Kelsi's hands.

John and Beth came through the door with Pops and Meg in tow.

"Why the sad faces?" Beth asked. "I thought you were doing much better, Kelsi? Ian?" She looked worried.

"It's okay. Everything will be fine," Ian said. "In fact, it will be wonderful. Now that you're here, I want to declare to Kelsi and everyone that I love her. I want to be with her every moment of my life."

"Ian," Meg asked excitedly, "is that a proposal?"

"It's not a very good one, but yes, it is." Ian turned to Kelsi and added, "Kelsi, I love you. Will you be my wife? Will you spend your life with me?"

Kelsi looked at Ian with deep love in her eyes.

"Oh, yes, Ian. I will. I love you so much," Kelsi told him.

"Huzzah!" Pops declared. "This calls for a celebration!"

"The celebration will have to be later, Pops, when Kelsi is out of the hospital," Beth said, then turned to Kelsi. "Honey, where were you?" she asked. "Where did you go?"

Kelsi took a deep breath, but Ian spoke first, "You need to sit down, Mom," he suggested. "You, too, Dad. And Meg." They all sat down. "We have quite a story for you. I'm not sure you'll believe it, but it's true. Right, Pops?"

Pops nodded. "Yup. Go on, boy. You and Kelsi can tell your part, and I'll tell mine. They should know."

"I don't understand," Meg interrupted. "Tell us what, Pops? How are you part of this?"

"Patience, Meg," Ian said. "I know you don't have much patience, but you'll need to listen. It started a long, long time ago with a man and a woman. My great-grandparents, in fact. A man and a Selki." With the questioning looks from his parents and Meg, Ian took a breath, smiled at the love that shone in Kelsi's eyes, and continued. "A Selki is a seal in the water and a human on land. This man and this Selki—They fell in love." Ian stopped and looked at Pops. "It's not like the legend with an unhappy ending. This one has a happy ending because many years later, it happened again—another man and Selki falling in love. That man is me, and the Selki is Kelsi. In some ways, they had no choice, just like Kelsi and I didn't have a choice. Blood calls to blood." After kissing Kelsi's hand tenderly, he added, "And I'm thinking we're going to live happily ever after."

The End

AUTHOR'S NOTE

Dear Reader,

I hope you enjoyed reading *Between Earth and Sea*. If you enjoyed this book, please leave a positive review at www.amazon.com or www.goodread s.com. Reviews are so very important. They help other readers find books to enjoy. Thank you in advance for taking the time to leave a review.

A portion of the proceeds from this book is donated to the Marine Mammal Stranding Center in Brigantine, NJ (mmsc.org).

Thank you for reading!

Sincerely,

Sharon Brubaker

ABOUT THE AUTHOR

Sharon, born in 1959, grew up in central Pennsylvania, surrounded by beautiful mountains. Writing has been a lifelong passion. For Sharon, writing is like breathing. She says she has more stories in her head to write down than lifetimes to live. Sharon is a national award-winning author, librarian, and the author of several educational publications. She is also an avid gardener and jewelry artist.

www.sharon-brubaker.com